I0637952

MAKING A LIVING

CAROLINE FRECHETTE

Renaissance

First edition.

Cover art and design by Caroline Frechette. Cover models: Annie Frechette, Frederic Desbiens and Felix-Antoine Thibault. Interior design by Caroline Frechette. Edited by Kyle Bentley, Evelyn Cimesa and L.P. Vallee.
Legal deposit, Library and Archives Canada, April 2016.
Paperback ISBN: 978-1-987963-08-3
Ebook ISBN 978-1-987963-09-0
Renaissance Press
http://renaissancebookpress.com
info@renaissancebookpress.com

For Joelle; this one's kind of yours, too.
Thanks for it, and so much more.

CHAPTER 1

When Nathan came to, the dead girl was crying.

He was relatively sure she wasn't supposed to do that. Come to think of it, he was almost sure he should have been dead, though he obviously wasn't. There was not much else he was sure about, but he did seem to have all of his parts, and he supposed if he were dead his head wouldn't hurt so much.

He looked around, trying to remember what happened. He was in an odd looking shack: walls of old tabletops and doors leaned awkwardly against one another, the holes left by the differences in their shapes plugged by a collection of smaller pieces of corrugated metals and plywood. There was a counter made from old plastic barrels; she was sitting on the other side of it, between him and the exit.

He tried to sit up, but his body felt like it was made of lead. He started to sigh but then remembered to keep quiet. The floor around him was littered with bits of broken objects and glass; the place had obviously been trashed.

It occurred to him then that the crying had stopped. He managed to turn his head towards the woman hiding behind the barrels, and saw that she was now peering at him curiously.

She was almost pretty from afar, if you ignored the milky, discolored eyes. Her hair was black, lightly curled, and pulled back in a ponytail that reached halfway down her back. She was wearing a lab coat that seemed like it had seen better decades. As she got closer, he could see that her skin was pale, almost gray. He wondered if she would kill him now.

"Are you all right?" she asked.

He blinked at her, and tried to move again, unsuccessfully. "I'm... heavy. Why am I heavy?"

"I drained some of your life force. Can you move?"

He knew he should probably be afraid, but he figured there was little point to it since he wasn't going anywhere fast. "No."

She stood and folded her arms, looking down at him with a thoughtful frown. "What were you doing here? Are you with the raiders?"

"No! I was just scavenging."

"Then why did I find you so close to my lab? All the new stuff is close to the entrance. Scavengers don't come this far in."

"I... heard the shooting. I didn't... I thought I could help. I wanted to check if you were dead. Well, you know. The real kind of dead."

She picked up the messenger bag he always carried, and started going through it quickly. He hoped it was a weapon she was after: she wouldn't find one.

She put the bag down, apparently satisfied with her search, and picked up his wrist, pinching it slightly while checking her smartwatch.

"What are you doing?"

"Checking your pulse. I'd like to do a full exam. But not here, the sun is about to set."

Nathan's chest constricted in alarm. "You're a doctor?"

She remained serious as she probed his neck. "Yes, I am. Where are you staying?"

"Why?"

"We can't stay here. You're alive. You'll attract ghouls."

Nathan tried to get up again, with no result. Somehow the thought of showing someone where he slept, especially a doctor, was much more frightening than the idea of lying helpless in a ghoul's den.

"Well... do you have power here?"

She blinked at him, confused. "Power?"

"You know... electricity. Is there an outlet?"

"No, there isn't. I had a generator, but the raiders took it."

"Oh. Well, I can probably manage anyway."

He tried to sit up again, but fell back down limply. She leaned over and picked him up. He tried to fight her off, with as much success as an umbrella against a typhoon.

"What are you doing? Put me down!"

"I'm taking you to your place. Or at least some place that's safer. So, where to?"

Nathan sighed. He had no idea where to go other than where he was currently staying, and he had no desire to have anyone else there, alive or dead. It wasn't that he particularly cared who walked in or out of his squat when he wasn't there, but he'd learned from experience that the worst things always happened when he was in close quarters with another person.

She started carrying him outside while he was thinking, and he protested. "No! Wait!"

"I told you, we can't stay here. The ghouls'll start coming out in just a moment."

"That's not it... my bag. I can't leave it behind!"

He found enough strength in his arm to move it weakly to the side, where his bag lay on the floor. She leaned over and picked it up, easily holding him in one arm, as if he weighed nothing.

'Got it. Now where are we going?'

Nathan breathed in deeply and tried desperately to think about a place other than his own. She stepped outside, and into the junkyard. She made her way through the piles of refuse that had been accumulating in the dump for decades. Her shack stood very deep in the yard, as far from the gates and the circulating trucks and raiders as she had managed to get. The smells of decomposition and rot were something that Nathan had always been used to for visiting the place so often; today, however, he could barely contain the breakfast that kept threatening to come back out the way it had come in.

She walked to the gate that marked the exit, staying away from the junk piles that were high enough to hide ghouls. She looked to make sure the street was empty before she crossed the gate. She stopped then, and looked down at him.

"Which way?"

"Put me down. I'm sure I can walk. You don't have to do this."

She rolled her white eyes at him. "Suit yourself."

She put him down on his feet abruptly, leaning him against the fence. His legs started shaking, his heart felt like it might explode, and sweat pearled on his forehead from the sheer effort of standing. He felt for the chain link fence and gripped it as hard as he could to remain upright. He only noticed he was panting when he spoke.

"... see? All... good."

She looked him up and down, and shrugged. "Fine. Don't say I didn't try to help. Stay here to die, if that's what you really want."

She shoved his bag in his stomach, and he caught it reflexively, letting go of the fence. He was winded, but for a few seconds, it did seem to him that he would be able to stand, even walk on his own, make it all the way home. He looked up at her then, and realized he had fallen to the ground without even noticing. His head was spinning, and when she leaned over him, he saw two of her dancing around one another.

"Changing your mind?"

He gritted his teeth. It seemed he had no choice at all. "All right. I'm staying on Bowater, out by the 59th district."

She picked him up again, throwing him over her shoulder like an old sack, and started to jog, while Nathan clutched his possessions weakly, fighting the urge to vomit as best he could.

The streets were empty, as they were most of the time in the unpatrolled part of the city that surrounded the richer, cleaner, and safer center. Called Three Walls after the state of its buildings, which were left to stand or fall on their own, the unpatrolled part of the city had few vehicles ever go through it, and none after sunset. The few shops and markets there were closed at least an hour before sunset, and everyone that had a door locked and bolted it at about the same time.

The light was almost gone from the sky when they reached the collapsing high rise where Nathan currently slept. He found he could turn, even lift his head at that point, which renewed his courage. He tried a different approach.

"Maybe you could drop me off here at the door, and when I feel better I could just go on up to my place..."

"Right. Which floor?"

He sighed. The dead girl seemed to have decided to take him all the way to his place, and it seemed that he could do nothing about it.

"It's pretty high up. The stairs are steep."

"Don't worry. I can't run out of breath."

He gave in. "Third floor," he muttered.

She found the door to the staircase, undid the complex mechanical latch, and shut it tightly behind her. As she started up the stairs at a more relaxed pace, Nathan could feel his nausea start to ebb, becoming more manageable.

There was a man on the floor in the hall of the third floor. The dead girl hesitated a while before stepping into the hall. However, as they made their way past the man, they could see he was simply asleep in a puddle of his own urine, and not a dead body ready to turn into a ghoul.

"Which door?" she whispered.

"319."

She stopped in front of the door and looked down at him, expectantly. "Keys?"

"It's open."

She could hardly hide her surprise; she was speechless for a few seconds. "... You leave your door unlocked? In Three Walls?"

He shrugged, unconcerned. "I lock it when I'm here. I leave nothing there that's even worth looking at."

She shook her head in apparent bewilderment, and went in. She took care to bolt the door behind her afterwards. "Aren't you afraid...?"

She started to speak, but fell silent as she turned to look at the apartment, her nose wrinkling in disgust. Nathan followed her gaze, and shuffled his feet. He had been uncomfortable at the thought of having someone in close quarters to him, but he'd never thought he would feel self-conscious about the way his place looked, because he had never really cared, as long as he was safe and hidden.

It had probably been a nice little place to live in, before the meteor. Now, decades of squatters had left it in a state that redefined squalor. The walls that were still standing were covered in graffiti, and stains of long-dried bodily fluids; the floor was littered with all sorts of garbage: discarded foods, soiled clothing, remnants of old picture frames, china, and other bits and pieces of unrecognizable origins. There was even furniture in various stages of decomposition, though all of it was damaged beyond use or reconstruction.

Some of the garbage had been arranged in designs, or even little sculptures, though most of it lay in haphazard piles. The windows hardly had any glass left on them; some were taped shut, others were stuffed with various fabrics, most were boarded up in some way or another. It was impossible to tell what the floor had been made of; the whole place smelled as if something had died there and had never been removed.

In the corner of what had once been the living room, some space had been cleared. There was a pile of blankets there that seemed to be slightly newer than the rest of the junk; a small heap of partially disassembled electronics lay next to it. She stared at it, taking it all in slowly.

"You... you live here?"

"I stay here. If I stay long enough, I might clear the garbage. But I don't often stay very long in the same place."

She stepped over the trash carefully, making for the pile of blankets. He gestured instead to the closest wall to them. "No," he said. "Not there; here."

She frowned at the direction he was moving towards. "Where?"

"The socket... the electric plug, in the wall. Take me to it.'

She shrugged, and carried him to the power outlet, lowering him to the floor. As she sat down next to him, he retrieved a paperclip from his pocket, and stuck it in the outlet, closing his eyes. She shouted out in surprise, moving to stop him, but it only took him a few seconds to recharge. Energy crackled out of the tiny holes and up his arm. He was filled with delicious fire, and felt powerful enough to lift a building. He sighed with intense satisfaction as he let go of it.

He stood and stretched, feeling refreshingly light and nimble after having felt so drained. His skin tingled with the residual electricity, and he smiled with relief before he turned towards her.

She was staring at him, in at least as much shock as she had been in when she first saw the squat. "What did you just do?"

He frowned at her, recoiling from her slightly. "I just... I recharged."

She started rifling through a bag that was hanging from her side; Nathan hadn't even noticed she had it. She produced a stethoscope, and pressed it against his chest, putting the other ends in her ears. "With a power outlet?"

"Well... yeah."

She leaned in close, her face an inch from his. She smelled strongly of chemicals, over the sickly sweet smell of rotting meat. "How?"

He shrugged, suddenly uncomfortable again. "I don't know. I just can."

She stared at him quietly, and at length, her milky white eyes didn't seem that unnatural anymore. "You're a Meteorian?"

Nathan had heard about meteorians while swimming the flux, and though he had thought this might apply to him, he'd never really had someone to talk to about it. Meteorians took their name from the meteor which had fallen on earth over forty years ago. Its radiation affected people for hundreds of miles around the impact site, causing the ghouls to rise and modifying some of them so that they developed strange abilities.

He still didn't really know what to say, so he shrugged and slipped away from her, heading for the pile of blankets. He plopped down on it, his back turned to her, and picked up the front half of an ancient radio. She watched him without following.

"... what else can you do?" she asked.

"I'm good with machines."

"How good?"

"I can fix them, make them work... I can talk to them."

She raised her eyebrows, and found an old wooden crate to sit on. "You're... a technopath? And you can manipulate energy?"

He finally turned to look at her, a bit apprehensive at her interest. He answered, warily. "So?"

"Well...!" She threw up her arms, gesturing at her surroundings. "Why do you live like this, then?"

"What do you mean?"

"You could have anything you want! Do you have any idea how rare what you can do is? How useful? I mean, I've never even heard of a living human, Meteorian or not, that's able to draw energy and convert it like that! Only ghouls can do that!"

He shrugged, uncomfortable again, avoiding her strange, unliving eyes. "I have everything I need."

8

She looked around, looking particularly long at the piles of refuse, the stains on the wall, and the pile of blankets he slept in, which appeared to have been partially eaten by rats or mold.

"I can see that," she said sarcastically.

He shrugged, this time with a little smile. "I do have everything I need. I have a warm place to sleep in, that I can lock from the inside; I can have food whenever I like, fresh prepared and everything. What more could I want?"

She looked down at the splintery wooden crate she was sitting on, then back up at him. "How about a bed?"

"What would I do with one of those? They're heavy, and they don't travel well. Anyways," he said, getting up, frustrated, "how is it any of your business?"

She sighed. "I don't suppose that it is. At any rate, I still want to examine you, make sure you're all right."

"I keep telling you I'm fine! Leave me alone already!"

She sighed, then shook her head and stood, grabbing her bag. "Fine. I'll go."

He thought she looked slightly hurt, but he wasn't used to being around other people, so he couldn't be sure. "You're... leaving?"

She raised an eyebrow at him. "Isn't that what you want?"

"Well... I mean... I didn't mean... I didn't want to be mean. I just don't like being poked." She didn't answer, simply standing there, as if she expected him to go on. He shifted uneasily, avoiding her stare. "That shack, in the dump... that was your home, wasn't it?"

"In a manner of speaking."

"Then... will you go back there?"

She shook her head, stuffing her hands in the pockets of her lab coat. "The raiders completely trashed it. Besides, they might be back. There were still things to burn, and they do love a party."

"So... you don't have anywhere to go?"

"Not in the strictest sense, no."

"Well, then..." He clicked his tongue, looking around nervously, hesitating. He didn't really want to say what he would say next; then again, he really didn't want not to say it, either. "... you can stay here, I suppose."

She blinked at him. "You're offering me to stay with you?"

"Yeah. As long as you agree not to poke me."

"Aren't you afraid of me?"

He frowned at her. "Should I be?"

"... you have noticed that I'm dead, haven't you?"

"So? The living have been consistently scarier to me than the dead."

Her mouth hung open as she stared at him. He scratched his head, then turned to his electronics again. She walked slowly to him, watching him while he retrieved a bottle from his bag and popped a pill in his mouth.

"I've been dead for a long time," she said at last. "I haven't really met a living person who wasn't afraid of me since I died."

Nathan shrugged, and started removing disassembling the radio. "Doesn't surprise me, really. That's the way people are. They don't really talk to each other, either, you know."

She had a smile. "I seem to recall something like that from when I was alive... tell me, what's your name?"

"Huh?" Nathan looked up, taken aback. "Oh. Right. Um, I'm... Nathan. What's yours?"

"Annie."

He looked up at her and saw that she was smiling broadly. He cleared his throat nervously, turning back to his electronics. "Sorry. I just, uh, I don't meet people much."

"So I gather."

She sat back down on her crate, near his makeshift bed, watching him quietly for a little while. "What are you doing now?"

"Um, building something."

"What?"

"I don't know. I haven't decided yet."

10

"Oh."

She leaned her head in her hands, watching him. Feeling observed, he stopped, and twiddled his screwdriver in his hands, staring at his unfinished creation. He finally looked up at her, timidly. "So... how come you can talk?"

"What do you mean?"

"You're not like the other ghouls. But you are one, yes?"

"Yes... I suppose I am. I was part of an experiment. It's a bit... complicated."

Nathan swallowed, and wiped his suddenly sweaty palms on his pants. "An experiment?"

"It was one of the first experiments to try to achieve eternal life with the meteorite."

"Eternal life?"

"Yes."

"With the meteorite?"

'Yes.'

"How?"

"Well... the radiation created the ghouls. Right?"

"Right," Nathan said carefully.

"The ghouls... well, we... can keep our bodies from decomposing by stealing the life force of living human beings. So, in theory, if ghouls had any minds of their own, they could remain animated and intact pretty much forever. The idea was to try to give that ability to a living human, in a living body, with a working brain."

She had a bitter smile, and hugged herself, leaning forward a bit. "At least, they got the working brain part right for me. But I'm still dead."

Nathan had a sympathetic frown. "So... you were a test subject?"

"Not... exactly. I was a scientist. I didn't realize that being a test subject was part of the deal."

"I'm sorry. Being a test subject is..." He shook his head, unable to make himself finish his sentence.

She raised an eyebrow at him, "You were a test subject too?"

Nathan put down the radio, and picked up a set of wheels he had removed from a small remote control car, not answering. He thought about the objects he had seen in her shack; the burners, the broken bottles, the metal clips...

"You were still doing experiments, though, in your shack."

"Yes. I'm... I'm trying to get back to... to normal." She looked at her hands, flexing her fingers slowly.

"You mean... alive?"

She answered very quietly, not looking at him. "... alive... yes."

"Is that possible?"

She stood suddenly, turning her back to him. She walked to the other side of the room, inspecting a pile of trash that had a bit less rot than the others. He looked at her for a long time; she was quiet, and did not move a single muscle.

He tried getting back to his construction, but found he didn't have the heart for it anymore. After a while, he popped another pill in his mouth, took Oliver out of his messenger bag, and got ready for a night of swimming.

CHAPTER 2

Anyone who could use a computer could surf, which was almost exactly using the internet had been before the meteor's advent; few people could actually swim it like Nathan.

He had never needed a keyboard or a screen. All he had to do was touch any jack on the computer, and there he was. It wasn't like leaving your body behind so your mind could go somewhere; rather, it was like opening a floodgate in his mind to a new and different sense which became a complement to the rest. He could still feel the warmth of the jack's metal against his skin, hear the computer's faint hum, and see the swarm of colors on the screen.

The conscious process of swimming, called associating, was like focusing your thoughts into what it was you wished to do, or know, and sending them out to resonate with the pertinent information. Depending on your skill, it could prove a lot more efficient than traditional surfing, or a lot less.

Most swimmers closed their eyes because they could not reconcile their senses with associating; it was too much like seeing, or listening. However, Nathan had been swimming so often and for so long that the sensation was just a natural part of how he perceived the world; he felt no more need to close his eyes when he did it than he did, for example, when he was listening to music. Besides, he liked to be as aware of his surroundings as he possibly could, even while swimming.

It was easy to concentrate on the overwhelming sense that was associating, and he was able to ignore Annie's proximity for most of the night as he swam. He was usually able to go on for even longer, paying little attention the hunger and other bodily aches that eventually nagged at him, but her mere presence in his squat somehow made him even more aware of these discomforts.

As the part of his brain that was associating flitted through the information it was receiving, he became aware that the light filtering through the dirty windows was brighter, and that Annie was moving about.

He let go of Oliver, putting the little computer on the ground before him, and sat up to look at Annie. She was apparently in the process of pushing most of the trash in one corner of the room. His eyes hurt as he watched her stiff movements, and he suddenly realized that his entire body was heavy with sleep. Hastily, he reached in his bag and took out the pills he had taken the night before. His hands shook as he struggled with the childproof bottle, and he sighed with relief when he finally got it open. The two he swallowed had some difficulty going down his dry throat.

She was watching him curiously when he looked at her again. He lowered his eyes, unsure of what to say. He had never gotten used to the company of others, living or not, and although he was vaguely aware that interaction was normally expected, he wasn't sure of the form it ought to take. Fortunately, his bladder was full enough to distract him, and he got up to go relieve himself in a corner of the squat. When he was done, he noticed that she was watching him with something like horror in her expression.

He avoided her eyes, confused, and hurried to sit back down in his blankets. He noticed with immense relief that Oliver was still lying right in front of him, open and working. He gingerly picked a dried instant noodle from the keyboard, and looked at the screen.

"What's your battery status, Oliver?"

"Less than twenty percent," replied the little computer, in its habitual haughty and annoyed tone. "You should recharge me.

You know how hard it is for me to boot up when I haven't shut down properly."

Nathan nodded, and pulled the power cord out of his bag. There was little to no power to be found in Three Walls, as most people there were simply vagrants and squatters, who could do little better than to scrounge what they needed from the nearby dumps. Nathan, however, had discovered long ago that as long as he could find a physical link to any source of power, he could reactivate long forgotten connections, and he never chose a squat where he couldn't do this. He plugged Oliver in his outlet, and turned to look at Annie.

She was sitting on her crate again, and her curious look had turned into a thoughtful frown. "That seems to be quite a personality," she said.

Nathan blinked, momentarily confused. "Huh?"

Annie gestured at the small computer with her chin, folding her arms. Nathan followed her gaze and looked at Oliver. "Oh. Yes. Oliver. He's got a mind of his own."

"And you did this? Gave him a personality, I mean?"

"It was an accident, really. I was linked with him one day, and I really wished I could talk to him, you know, like you talk to a person... and it happened."

This time she raised both her eyebrows. "Just like that?"

"I'm not really sure how. It took so much out of me, it knocked me right out. I don't know that I could do it again if I wanted."

She nodded once, visibly impressed. "I bet. I've only ever heard of one or two meteorians able to do that kind of thing, and to make it permanent... I've never even heard of that."

He shrugged, not answering. She sat back on the crate she had used as a chair the previous night, her arms folded over her chest. "And what have you been doing all night? Swimming? I know you weren't asleep."

Nathan thought he detected some trace of disapproval in her tone, but he wasn't sure why. "Oh. Yeah, I was swimming."

15

"Did you find what you were looking for?"

He glanced at Oliver again, running his fingertips across the keyboard longingly. He would spend his entire life swimming; transfer his whole consciousness to the flux if he could.

"Not exactly. I need more details. I'm finding too many things; I need your help to narrow it down."

"Oh?" She picked a green, sticky crumb off her lab coat and made a face at it. His stomach growled, so he leaned over to a pile of junk next to him and peered at the open can of beans he had left there. The fork was still in it; he was sure it hadn't been there more than two days. He picked it up, sniffed it, and started eating it. It tasted all right, but when he looked up, she was looking at him with an expression of disgust, and he continued to speak as much to divert her attention as anything else.

"Yeah, I need to know more about the project, the products that were used, and the type of radiation..."

He looked at her expectantly, as though awaiting her answer, and she blinked. "About what project?"

"The experiment you were in. You know, the one that made you... what you are. I need to know more if I'm going to find if there's a way to reverse it."

She stared at him, her mouth hanging open. With her pale, clammy skin, and her white eyes, Nathan thought she looked very much like a dead fish. He looked intently at the contents of the can he was eating, and shifted in the awkward silence, until she finally spoke.

"You... you mean you've been swimming all night to find a solution to my... problem?"

He nodded, but stayed quiet, her expression telling him she needed a bit more time to work this out in her mind. Finally, she frowned at him.

"You... you want to help me?"

"Well... yeah."

She stared at him in amazed silence for a little while longer, and shook her head dazedly. "Why?"

The question took him by surprise; he hadn't given it much thought, beyond the desire to help.

"I don't know," he said truthfully. "I mean, it's not fair you went through having experiments done on you that changed you forever, and if I can help make it right... besides, I don't have anything better to do."

"You don't have anything better to do," she repeated slowly. "Just like that?"

Nathan put down the now empty can and hugged his knees loosely, leaning his back against the wall. He shrugged, looking up at the ceiling. A thick black sludge was slowly beginning to infiltrate the space around the hole where a lamp must have hung, once long ago.

"It's not that I'm bored. I always find stuff to do. "I just want to help. I've never done anything that was... important. To someone, I mean."

She stared at him again, her eyes screwed up in an odd expression that his limited understanding of other people could not begin to decipher. He felt uncomfortable under her scrutiny, and shifted before reaching for the partially disassembled clock radio he had been working on the night before. She gave herself a shake, and her eyes suddenly narrowed in a suspicious look that was much more familiar to Nathan.

"What do you want from me?"

He sighed, and put down the clock radio, frustrated, and shot her an annoyed glance. "Look, if you don't want me to help..."

"No, no, I really do!"

He heard the barely restrained eagerness in her voice, and he fell quiet, turning to look at her again. She seemed to collect her thoughts, and hesitated before she spoke again. "It's... I've been searching for a long time, and you're very talented... I don't want to get my hopes up if..."

She licked her lips nervously. He said nothing, waiting for the end of the sentence. Finally, her white eyes focused on him again with as intense an expression as they could convey, and her voice was almost a whisper as she spoke. "... it would help if I knew what was in it for you."

Nathan looked at Oliver, and back at Annie. He tried to search his thoughts. This was a relatively new and surprisingly difficult activity for him. He'd spent most of his life devising new ways of running away from his thoughts; now that he turned and tried to look at them, he found that he wasn't quite sure where he'd left them. He didn't want to have to talk about experiments. Fortunately, there was another reason why he wanted to do this.

"Oliver... he's pretty much the only friend I ever had. Well, almost. There was someone else, when I was little. You remind me of her. She was nice to me too. Just like you. I want to do something nice too."

She looked puzzled. "You think... I'm nice to you?"

She repeated his words again, as though she couldn't quite grasp their meaning. Her expression was odd, much more complex than any Nathan had seen before; it seemed like an odd mix of pain and pity.

"You hardly know me. And... I'm dead. What makes you think I'm nice?"

He looked at her, a little bewildered. He had thought it was perfectly plain. "Well... you didn't kill me."

She seemed almost offended for a few seconds, and then heaved a deep sigh. "I only drained you because I needed the energy to heal myself. I'm not like... the other ghouls."

He frowned at her; he hadn't thought that at all. It was obvious to him that she was very different than any other ghoul; he didn't see how anyone would be unable to see that. Ghouls were savage creatures, who retained no trace of their former humanity, and did nothing else than drain the life force of every creature they encountered, usually killing them in the process. They seldom had the mental capacity to operate a doorknob, let alone speak.

"I know that. But I also know that it ain't just ghouls that kill."

It was her turn to frown in careful consideration. "So, to you, being nice is not killing people?"

"It's a good start," he said. "I also mean, you could have left me there to die. I'm pretty sure that's what anyone else would have done."

She seemed to think about this for a little while, and nodded. "I suppose you have a point there. But I was the one who hurt you, after all."

He shrugged. "So? Most people who hurt others worry about what's in their pockets that they can grab, not what's going to happen to them."

She rubbed her neck pensively, and became quiet. He watched her for a little while, and found himself a bit spooked. Her eyes were open, and she was leaning her head in her hands, her elbows propped on her knees. She had a perfect stillness that could never have been possible for a living body. She looked unnervingly like a petrified corpse, and not like something that could suddenly regain the ability of speech and movement.

He picked up the clock radio again, and started fiddling with it absent-mindedly. He found it hard to engross himself in his work with someone else in the room, quiet and still as she may be. He realized he had connected the wrong wire three times before she spoke again.

"All right." She sounded like she was coming to a conclusion after difficult deliberation. "I'll tell you about the project so that you can help me. But since you're helping me get my life back, I want to help you get yours."

He put down the radio and frowned, puzzled. "Mine? Mine what?"

"Your life."

"But... I'm not dead."

She raised her eyebrows and shook her head, an amused expression on her face. "You might as well be, living like this. I can show you a much better life. One a technopath of your talent should already have."

He raised an eyebrow, but after careful consideration could not find anything wrong with the proposition. "Fine. It's a deal."

She smiled, appearing genuinely happy. The expression was, on her features, even more disquieting than her impossible stillness had been.

She reached for her bag. "Good! Then I'll need you to strip."

"Do what now?"

She laughed at his horrified expression, and pulled her stethoscope out of the bag. "Well, if I'm going to give you a better life, I'll first need to make you healthy."

He rolled his eyes in exasperation. "I'm not sick."

She glanced at the can of food he had been eating from, the soiled walls, and the odorous filth that littered most of the floor. "Don't be so sure. Besides, if you're not sick, what are those pills you've been taking?"

"They're just stims. They keep me awake."

"How long have you been awake?"

"What does that have to do with anything?"

"You need regular and consistent sleep to be healthy."

"I feel fine!"

"You're not."

"Look, if you're going to be a pain in the ass, the deal's off!"

She snorted, and stuffed her stethoscope back in her bag. "Fine. Can I at least clean this place up a bit?"

He frowned suspiciously and looked around the room. "Are you gonna take my stuff?"

"Nothing important. I'll just clean out the trash. Though eventually we will have to replace your blankets and clothes, when I can manage the credits."

He blinked, and looked down at himself. He was wearing jeans he had just recently found in the dumpster, with hardly a hole in them, and just a few oil stains. He also had on a coat was only frayed at the elbows, although it was hard to see what the original color of it might have been. The two shirts he had layered underneath were mostly intact; he didn't take the coat off too often, so the shirts didn't get exposed to that much damage.

"What for? These don't even have holes in them!"

She wrinkled her nose at him, her face contorting with disgust. "They smell. Horribly. Like someone died in them. And never left. I mean, I'm actually dead, what's your excuse?"

He blinked again, and frowned, offended. "Hey. I know I've smelled people way worse than me."

She rolled her eyes and raised her hands, palms towards Nathan. "Fine! Fine. I won't touch any of your stuff. But I want you to look something up on the flux."

"What?"

"They're called human parasites. I want you to find out what they are and how you get them. Agreed?"

"Why? What will I find?"

"Just look it up. Carefully. I might ask you questions after I've cleaned, if I don't think you've looked it up properly."

He frowned, unsure. There was something in her tone that made him want to refuse, but at the same time, he had never been able to leave a question unanswered.

He grunted. "Fine."

She smiled, visibly satisfied, and pulled up her sleeves as she stood. "Excellent. Let's both get to work."

She stood to start cleaning the main room. He waited a few moments before reaching for Oliver; for some reason, he did not want to look too eager to find out about the parasites.

21

It wasn't very long before Nathan found what he was looking for, and he was not prepared for it. His free hand kept finding new spots to scratch that he had never known to itch before. He took advantage of the moments when Annie was out of earshot to finally let out a few words of disgust. He had seen what happened when people didn't become ghouls when they died, but he had never imagined that all these creepy crawlers could start eating at a body while it was still alive.

He had moved on from skin parasites to their intestinal counterparts when she came out of the small corner room that had once been a bathroom, her hands covered in muck and an expression of horror on her face.

"I can't do this."

He let go of the jack, disconnecting his mind from the flux. "Do what?"

"I can't keep cleaning with what you have. I mean, rags can only go so far. I need some actual detergent."

"Detergent?"

He had heard the word before. He frowned, trying to remember where. "Well... you could probably find some in the market."

"Good."

She went to her bag, and looked at her hands, wiping them on a piece of cloth before picking it up. She rifled through it and pulled out a softened, frayed plastic chip card. She pressed a finger to one of the squares windows, and made a face at the amount that lit up. Nathan watched her.

"What is it?"

She slumped down on the crate disconsolately, the hands holding the card hanging between her knees. She had kept most of what could pass for furniture, but the floor was now free of most of its earlier clutter. Unfortunately, it also revealed places where parts of it had rotten almost all the way through, and pools of slime in various shades of green and black now replaced the litter.

"Well, I would need at least three kinds of industrial detergents, not to mention some decent cleaning tools. But I doubt I could afford even one bottle of the cheapest."

"Oh, is it just credits you need?" He reached into his own bag, producing three different chip cards, all of which looked brand new. "I should have more than enough."

She frowned at him and stood, reaching for his cards. There was one from Hong Kong International Holdings, another from USCO Group, and a third one from a small institution she didn't recognize. They all looked genuine.

"Are these real?"

"Sure! It's way too much trouble to get fake ones."

"Too much trouble?" She shook her head, bewildered. She couldn't imagine any forgery being more difficult than actually having and maintaining an account with some of these institutions. "You mean you actually have an account with HK International?"

"More or less. The cards are real, and linked to a real account, but it's not my name on the account."

"How do you go around the background and credit checks for these? I've been struggling for years just to keep the one I already had from when I was alive!"

He shrugged. "I just ask the computer tellers to give me one. Computers like me."

She stared at him, and then at the cards. "Why do you have three?"

"I usually have more. I rotate institutions, and I only take a little at a time. But I always try to keep one from a major institution; it's easier to get into Inner Circle if you need to."

She nodded, looking a bit dazed. "How much have you got on these?"

"A few hundred on each card."

She stared at him again, and then shook her head. She handed him back his cards, and picked up her bag, pull out a hat, and a pair of sunglasses, which she put on. It was a good disguise;

you would have had to look pretty hard to spot the difference in skin tone and texture which unmistakably marked her as dead, but since she didn't have the sluggish demeanor of regular ghouls, it was unlikely anyone would look twice.

She smiled at him. "Ready?"

He nodded and stood, picking up Oliver to slide him in his messenger bag. She watched him, and asked her question as they were headed down the stairs.

"All your accounts are illegal?"

He shrugged, and looked outside carefully as they reached the bottom of the stairs, before hopping out onto the street.

"Well, yeah. I don't have a birth certificate."

"And you've never gotten caught?"

"Almost, once."

The streets were packed. It was mid-afternoon, the busiest time of day, and everyone was headed to or from the market. Ghouls were rarely active in the daytime, and raiders were equally scarce before nightfall. Nathan, avoided everyone indiscriminately, moving almost unconsciously to remain at the farthest possible distance to all of them.

"It was a few years back, when I first found out about money. I got an account with Starr Planetary, loaded it up with as much as I could think of, and just spent whatever I wanted. One day, I came back to my squat, and there were five Starr security vans there, tearing up the place looking for me. It's a big part of why I always carry Oliver with me."

Annie shook her head and let out a low whistle. "I see. You're lucky you weren't there when they showed up. Those private security companies are ruthless; they have no one to answer to but the corporations."

"Tell me about it. It's why I don't take too much too often, or stay too long in the same place."

She nodded her approval. "Have you ever thought of working for one of them? I mean, a technopath like yourself could get a terrific position anywhere."

He looked away. "No."

"Why not? I mean, you could make a lot of money, and they're always looking for more technopaths."

"I don't want to do that. Okay?"

She frowned, but did not press the issue. They were quiet as they reached the limit between Three Walls and Outer Circle. The open market stood on that limit, a vast area of stalls, caravans, becoming an assortment of actual stores as it reached Outer Circle.

Arriving from Three Walls, the first vendors there were the inhabitants of the squats and shacks, showing on makeshift tables made from old doors and plywood the junk they had scrounged from the dumps and abandoned buildings. Nathan rarely ever stopped at these tables; they almost never had electronics, and what they did have, he could scrounge himself.

Beyond those was the odd zone that had all the food vendors, from fried rat to canned beans, with everything in between. Nathan stopped at a caravan that reeked of boiling oil and purchased a couple of burritos. He offered one to Annie, but she only shook her head slightly.

"Let's get to the chemist's as soon as possible," she said. "I don't want to stay out here any longer than I have to."

He nodded and unwrapped his burrito hastily, and was about to bite into it when he suddenly stopped himself, frowning down at it. "Will this make me sick?"

She had an amused smile. "Probably not. It's the least offensive thing I've seen you ingest since we've met."

He shrugged, satisfied, and shoved half of it into his mouth as he begun to walk.

He hadn't quite finished his second burrito when they reached the shops. These weren't stalls or even caravans anymore; they were proper stores, with steel shutters which, while covered in graffiti, were otherwise unbroken. The majority of the shops this close to Three Walls were chemists; most of the Three Walls residents could not afford the clean food or new clothes that most companies sold, and had no power to work electronics. As a result, the only supplies that were marketed to them were medicinal or recreational drugs, the supplies to make them, as well as alcohol.

Annie ignored the first few stores they passed, and headed straight for one of the largest, a few streets into Outer Circle. Nathan finished eating as he watched her select her wares quickly and efficiently. She had obviously been here before, and she very definitely knew what she wanted. He let her go to the back counter alone, and listened in fascination as she ordered a dozen chemical components that came in various liquid, powder and pill shapes, and seemed to have names that were in a foreign language.

He noticed three men at one end of the store, looking at her and speaking among themselves. He didn't have time to worry too much about them; by the time he was finished paying for Annie's purchases, they were gone.

As they walked out of the store, Nathan peered at the two very full bags that Annie was now carrying.

"So... is all that for making detergent?"

"I also picked up a few things to make you some... medication."

"Medication? What for? You haven't even examined me yet!"

She grinned at him broadly. "I like that word, 'yet'. It implies that soon you'll let me do it."

Nathan snorted and looked away. They were crossing a street that would bring them back to the area where the food vendors cried out their wares.

It was a measure of how distracted he was that he didn't hear the running footsteps; thinking back on it later, he knew that he would have never been this careless if he had been alone.

Someone slammed into him heavily, knocking the wind out of him and making him fall. He felt something pull at him as he fell, and he had been on the ground for a few seconds when he realized that his messenger bag was gone. He felt his heart jump in his throat, and tried to ignore his dizziness as he stood up. He heard Annie groan, and was vaguely aware of her sitting up next to him as he begun to run after the men who had made off with their bags. She shouted for him to come back, but he ignored her. She couldn't understand: they had Oliver.

CHAPTER 3

He had already reached the worst part of Three Walls by the time he was forced to stop to think about what he was doing. He saw the men duck into a building, and leaned his hands on his knees, wheezing for breath. It had been a very long time since he'd had to run this fast. Maybe Annie had a point when she said he wasn't completely healthy.

She was just catching up to him, running quietly and breathlessly, if a little awkwardly, her movements, as always, oddly stiff. She looked angry when she reached him, and he felt a little infuriated that she didn't need to catch her breath.

"What were you thinking?" Her voice was a hoarse whisper. "Don't you know how dangerous it is to be here?"

He looked around. She was right: raiders and gangs thrived here. Not many people would cross this part of town alone, not even in broad daylight. His voice sounded plaintive when he answered.

"They have Oliver!"

"It's just a computer! Surely, with your talent..."

"He's not just a computer! He's my friend!"

He felt tears stinging his eyes, and breathed deeply through his nose to calm himself. Annie sighed.

"This is a really terrible idea. Do you realize that?"

"Well, you don't have to come, but I have to get him back!"

Nathan started stomping in the direction of the dilapidated warehouse in which the thieves had vanished. He had reached the door when he realized that he had been too angry to formulate a plan, and felt absurdly relieved to find that Annie had followed him.

The building must have been a warehouse, long ago; Nathan could still see the remnants of large machinery he couldn't identify, that had obviously been dismantled and stripped of most of their pieces. Now, however, it seemed the gang of raiders had been established there for a while.

There were makeshift beds strewn about in a corner, and the remains of a campfire in the middle of the room. About twenty men sat on old crates and containers that had been fashioned into tables and chairs. They looked alert and nervous when they saw Nathan and Annie at the door, but most of them relaxed when they took a closer look at the pair.

One of them, who seemed to be older and healthier than most, stood from his crate and walked towards them casually, an easy, yet somehow cold smile on his face. Two others stood to walk besides the man, and Nathan recognized one of them as the one who had taken Oliver. He could see his and Annie's bags on the floor, right beside the crates on which the men had been sitting. It was the first man who spoke, stopping within arm's reach of them.

"What have we here? We're not used to getting delivery."

There was a quiet, short laughter among the other men. Annie stepped inside then, positioning herself between Nathan and the approaching men. Nathan swallowed nervously, though his throat felt parched. Now that he was here, he had no idea what to do. He only knew that if he turned and ran, he would surely be killed, or worse. The man who had been talking seemed relaxed, but the other two had pistols clutched in their hands, pointed at him and Annie and looking more than ready to fire. Annie's tone was surprisingly confident when she spoke.

"We've come for the bags your men stole. We have possessions in there that are sentimental, and would be of no use to you."

The casual man laughed heartily, but the young man closest to his right side frowned, staring at Annie a bit suspiciously.

"Careful, Joe. This one looks weird."

The casual man shrugged and drew his pistol, the smile still on his face. "So what?"

Annie raised her hands and glanced at Nathan, visibly annoyed. He stared at her, and at the men. He felt frozen to the spot, and utterly useless. She must have seen it, because she sighed and looked back at the men.

"Look. We'll just go away. We'll forget about our bags, and you can forget you ever saw us."

"Doesn't work that way, little lady. See, you've invaded our territory, and we can't just let that go."

She looked up at them again, and took off her sunglasses, glaring with her dead eyes at the casual man whose friendly expression seemed to melt away. He produced a gun from the inside of his jacket, his eyes widening with fear. The young man to his right started to say something, but the two shots that resounded from the casual man's gun drowned out his words.

Annie was perfectly still. At first, Nathan thought the shots hadn't connected, because there was no blood, but he saw the holes, which went through her chest and belly. At that moment, she moved, much faster than Nathan had thought her capable of. She grabbed the casual man by the throat, hoisting him up until his feet were well off the ground. The man gave a strangled scream before a sickening gurgle was all that could escape from his throat, and his body started convulsing. None of his men made a move to help him.

Everything seemed unnervingly still as the man's body gave its last few twitches, and Annie tossed him on the floor unceremoniously, turning her attention to the young man who had been wary of her at first.

"He should have listened to you."

"What... are you?"

"More trouble than I'm worth. Your guns are useless against me. But luckily, all I want is those bags over there, and then I'll walk away and we'll never see each other again."

The young man seemed to consider this carefully. The others still had their guns pointed at Annie, but their attention was for the young man, who would apparently decide what was to happen next.

He turned his head back a bit, keeping his eyes on Annie. "Ralph, get their bags."

"But..."

"Now!"

He turned his head to bark the order at his man, breaking eye contact. Nathan was dimly aware of a short, bald man handing him a few bags reluctantly, before Annie took his arm to drag him gently out of the building. She leaned close to him, muttering.

"Follow me. Don't run."

Nathan nodded, and followed her dazedly. He stared at his feet most of the way back and only thought of opening his bag to check that Oliver was really there when they were climbing the stairs to his squat. Nothing was missing.

He watched her as she let him into his squat and closed the door after them. He went to sit on his pile of blankets, leaving Annie's bags on the floor in the middle of the main room, and hugged his own bag to his chest tightly. She remained quiet until he was comfortable, then went to sit on her crate.

"Did you... did you kill that man?"

She didn't look at him when she answered, inspecting the bullet holes in her clothes. The flesh under it seemed to have mended itself without a trace of ever having been broken.

"Yes, I did."

They were silent for a little while, until she was done making sure that her skin had repaired itself correctly. Then, she looked up at him. He had been sitting on his blankets, holding Oliver in his hands, staring at the little computer.

"I didn't have any other choice, Nathan. We might have handled the situation differently when we were still outside, but things could only go a certain way once we walked in."

He nodded a bit, and thought of the horrible gurgle that the man had made as he died. He winced, and Annie frowned at him.

"Nathan."

He finally looked up at her, his brow furrowed in an expression of worry. He remained silent, so she went on.

"Going in there was insanely reckless, and stupid. We're lucky to have escaped with our lives."

He sighed in annoyance. "I understand that. It's just... well, I've always been careful to avoid those situations. I don't understand how I didn't see them coming."

She nodded, relaxing a bit. "Just be careful, next time."

He grunted his agreement. She didn't say anything more, and he put Oliver on the floor, plugging it in so that the battery could finish charging. She watched him for a while longer, then reached down to grab her satchel.

"Well, now that we're all relaxed and in one piece, how about that medical exam?"

He glared at her, almost as annoyed at himself for being tempted by the offer as he was at her persistence. "Still going on about that?"

"Of course! I haven't gotten my way yet."

He sighed. He wanted to protest, but he found he didn't have the strength. "Will it hurt?"

"Not one bit."

"How long will it take?"

"Maybe an hour?"

He sighed again and closed his eyes. He felt slightly indebted to her for having saved his life and Oliver's; maybe that was why he wanted to say yes. It wasn't the parasites. Surely he felt too healthy to have those things growing inside him.

Feeling suddenly queasy, he heard himself answer her without having really formulated the thought. "Fine. What do I need to do?"

She had a satisfied smile and pulled a stethoscope out of her bag, standing. "Remove all your clothes, and come and sit here," she answered, pointing at her crate.

He hesitated, and thought about protesting again. But he had expected this, and his qualms about removing his clothes in front of Annie were dwarfed by the worry he felt about the state of his innards, and by the weakness left by the day's earlier adrenaline rush. He stood slowly, and began removing the many layers which covered his body.

The skin under it was surprisingly soft and delicate; he wasn't in the habit of bathing or changing, so his naked skin was something he had only seen rarely. His arms and chest were exceptionally white, especially when compared to his hands, which were brown with years of dirt. The multiple scars he could see on his chest and arms were also paler and puffier than the ones on his hands, which had long ago faded to pale marks hidden under the layers of dirt, hardly visible at all.

He looked up from his examination to locate the crate on which he was supposed to go sit, and felt, once again, very self-conscious when he noticed that she was staring at him with an odd expression. He frowned, and resisted the urge to throw his clothes back on.

"What?" he snapped, in a voice more abrupt than he had intended. She didn't seem to care or notice.

"What happened to you?"

He blinked, and looked down at himself. It hadn't occurred to him that his scars might be something to be discussed. "What, those? They're pretty old."

She shook her head, and he saw her eyes move along his body, tracing the pattern of lines and bumps which marred his skin.

"Still... I know life can be rough in Three Walls, but those... they can't all have happened at once."

"Well... it's complicated." He sat down and she started looking him over.

33

"How so?"

"It's sort of a long story."

"We have ample time."

He sighed. She pressed the stethoscope to his back. "Well?"

"Well, it starts where I grew up," he said.

"What do you mean?"

"I grew up in a lab."

She pulled the stethoscope from her ears and stared at him, frowning. "A lab? Where?"

He shrugged. "I escaped years ago. I don't know who owned it. I never really looked for it, or tried to go back, to tell you the truth. It was far from here."

"Why were you there? How did you get there?"

He frowned at her, feeling increasingly uncomfortable. She was showing genuine, almost passionate interest for the subject; sitting naked in front of her, he missed her detached coolness dearly.

"I don't know. I don't remember not having been there."

"How did you get out?"

"Actually, it was kind of simple. They had computerized locks on all the doors. I figured out I could talk to them, and I got all of them to open for me."

"What were they testing?"

"I don't know exactly what they wanted. I just know that what they did to me was painful, and the rest of the time I was stuck in a room with practically nothing in it."

"How old were you when you escaped?"

"I'm not sure. It was a few years ago, I think."

"How old are you now?"

"I don't know."

"And you really don't know what they were trying to do?"

"Not really. Can we get on with this?"

She blinked. She had just been standing in front of him, her exam interrupted, for a couple of minutes now. She quickly got back to listening to his heart. She was as quiet as she was

34

thorough as she finished examining him, poking, prodding and looking at every scar, blemish and orifice on his body, listening to various places with her stethoscope, drawing his blood, having him breathe in, out, cough, stand up, sit down... he was beginning to think she was making him do some of those things simply to have a laugh at his expense, when she finally pulled the stethoscope out of her ears.

"Are you eating enough?"

He blinked at her. "Well, I eat when I get hungry..."

"You're too skinny."

She turned from him, putting her instruments back in her bag. He frowned at her. "Are... we done?"

"Yes, you can put your clothes back on. I'll need some other samples, but you can give me those later."

Nathan hopped down from the crate gratefully, pulling his clothes back on. He chewed a bit on his lip as he looked up at her.

"So, do I have those... bugs in me?"

She blinked in confusion, and, after a short pause, laughed. "I'll see. That's what I need the other samples for. But, I'll admit you are healthier than I thought you would be. You don't have to worry too much about the parasites. If you have them, I'll be able to make you medication."

He nodded. He felt embarrassed and stupid, even worse because he couldn't understand why. She started pulling out the equipment she had bought earlier and setting it up. He watched her for a little while, and finally reached for Oliver. Too many thoughts were happening to him lately; the overwhelming presence of the flux seemed the only thing that would keep them at bay.

The night was well advanced by the time Nathan noticed he was running out of stims. He could stay awake with little to no problem during the day, when it was bright outside, but nighttime invariably brought with it grogginess and heavy eyelids. He had to consume significantly more of the little pink pills during that time to avoid sleep, and the terrors and nightmares with which it came. He had meant to pick up more after visiting the chemist with Annie; now, he would have to go back.

He took the last pill, sighing. He didn't like much having to leave his squat. While it was true that there was no place in Three Walls that was truly safe, anywhere was better than the open streets, the first place where ghouls and raiders looked for their prey.

He stood to go to a window, peering outside through a crack in the cardboard that replaced the long-gone glass, and tried to guess what time it was. The sky was still dark, but there were less stars, and a dim blue glow in the east. It would probably be dawn soon. He would still have to wait a few hours before being able to go to the market. He sighed again, and turned his attention to what Annie was doing.

She had set up what was starting to look like a veritable laboratory on the remains of the old couch. There was a microscope and several beakers. Some were set over burners, in which different colored liquids were bubbling and evaporating slowly, releasing an acrid smell in the air. She was sitting beside the makeshift table, engrossed in stuffing small capsules with a light blue powder. He watched her for a little while; she seemed very concentrated. She spoke without looking up.

"Done swimming?"

"For now."

"Are you going to sleep?"

He shrugged, moving to get a closer look at what she was doing. "Nah. I took some stims. I'll have to go and get some more, though. I'm out."

"Nathan, why don't you want to sleep? You must be tired."

He backed away slightly, folding his arms over his chest. "I don't feel like it."

"Hmmm."

She pursed her lips and watched him silently for what seemed like a very long time. She remained quiet sufficiently long to allow his discomfort to peak, and then turned abruptly back to her work.

"I'm sure there's more to it than that. But I suppose you'll need more time to think on it. In the meantime, you needn't go to the market for your drugs. I'm making you some stims right now."

"You are?"

His interest renewed, he drifted close to her to again inspect what she was doing. He spotted a Petri dish containing a dozen of the filled capsules.

"Those it?"

"Yes. They're different. It's a special formula that'll be better for your health. Why don't you try one?"

"Okay."

He picked one up and looked at it. It was yellow and blue, and much larger than the pills he was accustomed to; he hoped it would be as potent. He went to get some water from the rain collector on the windowsill to wash it down with. It went down easier than he expected.

"So what have you been learning on the flux?"

He shrugged, returning to her improvised lab. "I've been looking up the science on ghouls."

"Found anything interesting?"

"Not much, actually. Lots of different people say lots of different things. There's also a lot of people out there who worship the ghouls. It's weird."

She clicked her tongue in annoyance, her eyes still on her work.

"Yes, I heard about those. It's human nature, I suppose. They used to believe that the world was going to end in all sorts of silly ways, when I was a girl. So what do these people believe about the ghouls?"

37

"That they're here to bring the world back to its natural state. That they're created by God to punish us for bad stuff we did, or something. They say we have too much technology, and drugs, and that the meteorians are evil."

She turned to look at him. "I hope you know that all of this is rubbish?"

"Yeah... the problem is, every time I think I found something good, it turns out to be more propaganda and nonsense. I'm not sure where to look anymore."

"Well, you've just been looking for information on ghouls, right?"

"Yeah?"

She finished the last capsule, and started gathering them in a small plastic bottle. "Well, the research we were doing back at the company revealed a link between the radiation from the meteorite, and the ghouls."

He frowned at her. "Well... yeah. Everybody knows the meteor caused the ghouls."

"Yes, but what we were trying to know is how and why. For example, why did the same radiation also cause meteorians to happen?"

She waited a while for comprehension to dawn on his face. His brow furrowed, and his eyes widened in horror. "Do you mean... that there is a link between meteorians and ghouls?"

She nodded slowly. "Almost certainly. My research demonstrated that all meteorians will turn into ghouls upon their death."

Nathan felt his heart sink as he slowly turned to walk back to his pile of blankets. It was something to know you had a chance of turning into a monster when you died, but to be completely certain...

He remained silent as he pulled Oliver on his lap, letting his fingers drift to the jack, connecting his mind to the flux.

The few hours he spent swimming were definitely less than productive. The subconscious mind was a powerful force in this activity where it was one's thoughts which called forth the information needed: all his fear of turning into a monster could summon was more religious propaganda naming meteorians as witches, monsters, demons, or even the antichrist, whatever that meant.

When he realized he had called forth the same religious databank for the third time, Nathan finally let go of the jack with a sigh. His stomach was growling, and his head spun; for some reason, his body felt heavy and his eyes stung. He didn't usually feel this sleepy this soon after taking stims, and he wondered if Annie's modified formula was strong enough for him. He stood shakily. His legs wobbled under him, and he walked unsteadily toward where Annie was sitting on her crate, writing some notes. She looked up at him, her face expressionless.

"Are you all right?"

"I don't know. I feel funny."

He sat down heavily on the ground in front of her, swaying slightly. She put her pen and paper away, her attention fully turned to him.

"Funny how?"

"I feel woozy. I don't think your pills are working properly."

"I think they are. But your body is so badly in need of sleep that they're acting hours ahead of schedule."

Nathan felt blood draining from his face, and his heart start to pound. He was starting to find it difficult to breathe. "What? What do you mean?"

"Well, I made your stims in a special way."

"What special way?"

The spinning was getting worse; his mouth felt dry and pasty. She smiled at him. "They'll do everything stims do, for a few hours. But when the effects of the stims wear off, the other effects kick in."

"The other effects?"

Nathan felt fainter by the second; his palms were sweaty, his hands trembled. He tried to clamp them down on his knees to stop the shaking, but he found that he didn't have the strength.

"It is also a sedative."

Nathan's heart was trying to pound itself out of his chest. He wondered how he could feel so agitated and sleepy at the same time. His eyes felt wide enough to fall out of their sockets, and his breath was so shallow he could barely speak.

"A sedative? You mean it's gonna make me sleep?"

"Yes. Only for a few hours. Your body desperately needs it."

"You... you didn't tell me! You fed me this drug, and you didn't tell me!" He panted; his voice felt shrill in his ears, and his whole body shook with rage. "You poisoned me!"

He stood, shakily, and started to stagger toward the door. He simply had to get away; soon, he would be lying on the ground, helpless. If anyone was there with him, who knew what would happen?

"Nathan..."

He turned to look at her, and fell with the motion. She was walking towards him, and he tried to crawl away, screaming.

"Get away! You poisoned me! I trusted you, and you poisoned me!"

Her confused expression barely registered. He felt hot tears escaping from his eyes, and his voice was starting to become strangled as his throat clenched with fear. He let out a desperate moan and let his head drop to the floor as sobs started to shake his body. Annie knelt about a foot from him. Her voice was soft and soothing.

"Nathan... it's only sleep."

"It's... not."

He gulped for air, hiccupping between words. He raised his head to look at her, this time the fear and pain so naked on his face she flinched.

"You're helpless and... they can t-take you, and... and you w-wake up somewhere else and you're t-tied to a chair and th-they hurt you!"

He tried to lift his head, but found that he no longer had the strength. He let out a strangled moan again. Sleep was coming fast, and there was nothing he could do about it.

Annie's face was suddenly above his, smiling reassuringly, her black hair falling over her shoulder, almost touching his nose.

"Don't worry, Nathan. Nothing can happen as long as I'm here, watching over you. And I will be."

She touched his forehead gently, caressing his hair. He tried to speak, but his mouth wouldn't work; he could only moan weakly, his chest still quivering with sobs he barely had the strength to utter, until he finally no longer could keep his eyes open.

CHAPTER 4

None of his usual nightmares came to Nathan as he slept, so confusion and disorientation replaced the habitual terror he felt when he woke up. He had the unfamiliar feeling of something touching his hair. He blinked rapidly to get his eyes into focus, and saw Annie's face frowning down at him. He gasped, and recoiled from her instinctively. His movements were sluggish and unsteady, but he could feel the sensation returning to his limbs, slowly but surely. She let him go, remaining where she had been sitting next to his pile of blankets, where she had evidently brought him to sleep.

"How do you feel?"

He thought about it, but couldn't find anything wrong with himself physically. "Betrayed! How could you do this to me?"

"Oh, come on, Nathan. It's just a bit of sleep. What's the harm?"

"You drugged me! You made me helpless, and vulnerable, and... and..." He trailed off, unable to find the words to express himself exactly.

"Nothing happened."

"But it could have!"

He was shouting now, gesturing frantically, his face red with anger. She frowned, and raised her hands peaceably, remaining where she was.

"Nathan, calm down. You're fine."

"That's not the point!" His voice broke on the second word, becoming shrill; that hadn't happened to him in a few years. He finally managed to stand, the adrenaline dispelling the last effects of the drug. He had reached the opposite corner of the room, and stood with his back turned to her, his arms folded tightly against his chest. He turned his head to speak to her, without really looking at her. "You lied to me! I trusted you, and you did something bad to me! You're just like them!"

He felt tears sting his eyes, and he wiped them away angrily. Her voice was still annoyingly soft, and vaguely patronizing. "Them? Them who?"

He shook his head, crouching on the floor, hugging his knees. More tears came, but this time he let them roll down on his cheeks unhindered. His throat was tight. He had been such a fool; he knew he shouldn't trust people. Why had he thought he could trust her?

He started when he felt something on his shoulder, and saw that it was her hand; she was crouching beside him. Even through his clothes, her fingers felt cold, and stiff; yet there was something oddly comforting about the touch. He wiped his nose and eyes clumsily with the back of his hands. He hadn't cried since he was a very small child, and he didn't remember it made his face so wet.

"I'm sorry, Nathan." Her voice was still soft, but it was no longer condescending. "You're right. I acted just like I did when I was a researcher. And I'm sorry."

Nathan rubbed the tears out of his eyes and saw that she was looking at him very seriously, full of concern. He had the familiar feeling that something was expected of him, though as usual, he wasn't sure what. At any rate, whatever it was, he didn't feel like giving it. He wiped his nose again, looking away from her. She took his chin between her fingers, gently turning his face towards hers. Her hand had an odd, sickly-sweet scent, like something that is just beginning to rot.

"Please, Nathan. I just fell into old habits. I didn't consider your feelings. I don't want to have lost your trust. Won't you forgive me?"

Nathan felt his body shake as the last of his anger left him. He wondered for a moment if he was still feeling the drug's effects. He hugged his knees tighter, trying to control it, but a sob burst out of his lips, and the floodgates were open. She watched him quietly for a second or two, and then gingerly wrapped her arms around him, pulling him close. He let himself be held, unsure how to respond. It was only when he felt her pull away that he finally grabbed her sleeve, holding it tightly to stop her; when he felt her embracing him again, he buried his face in her shoulder and let the tears flow freely.

He wasn't sure how long it was that he cried in her arms; it seemed at once to last a lifetime and only a few seconds. When he finally let go of her, his nose was simultaneously plugged and runny, his eyes were sore, and his whole face felt puffy and wet. He had left a wet patch on her shoulder about the size of his face, but she didn't seem to mind.

She stood as soon as his breathing was more regular, and went to the spot where the bags still lay, half full of the earlier day's shopping. She retrieved a roll of paper towels she had bought for cleaning, and a small measuring cup. She walked back towards him, and handed him the towels; she waited patiently for his shaking hands to take them before walking to the window. She filled the measuring cup with water from the rain harvester, and walked back to Nathan as he was just finishing wiping his face with the quilted paper. She sat next to him quietly, waiting for him to be done before she handed him the cup.

"Here, drink this. It'll help with the headache."

He nodded, and the motion made him realize that it wasn't just his eyes that felt swollen; his entire head felt like it had grown three sizes inside a helmet that was already too small. He took the water, and it felt wonderful going down, refreshing and cool, calming his raw throat.

He drained the measuring cup in just a few sips, and let out a long, deep sigh. His breathing was more regular now, and he felt his body starting to slowly return to normal. He looked at

Annie. She was sitting next to him, leaning her back against the wall, and she was smiling softly.

"Are you feeling better?" He nodded again, putting the measuring cup down on the floor in front of him. She was still smiling at him. "You must be hungry."

His stomach growled with the first thought of food. He was starving, hungrier than he could remember being since the first weeks he'd been on his own after running away from the lab. He nodded slowly.

"I am... really, really hungry."

"All right. Come on. Let's go get you something to eat."

She stood, extending a hand to help him up. He took it, and his head spun a little as she pulled him to his feet, but he recognized that it was the reassuring weakness of hunger, rather than the terrifying loss of control from the drug.

As usual, he made sure to put Oliver in his bag before he went. It felt better to have the little computer with him; he would just have to be careful, this time.

He followed behind her quietly as they made their way to the market. It was late afternoon, and some of the vendors were already packing up for the day. Annie stopped when they got close to the part of the market where the food vendors had concentrated.

"Why don't you go get something to eat? I'll wait for you over there."

She pointed her thumb at a section of the street which was now empty, where a couple of merchants had been. Nathan nodded and made his way to his favorite truck, where he ordered two burritos. He thought he might eat more, but he'd taken the habit of only buying what he was certain he could eat. In the days before Oliver, food had been a much rarer commodity.

He went back to the spot Annie had pointed out. There were a few concrete blocks standing haphazardly on what remained of the sidewalk. Annie was sitting on one of them, looking down the street at something Nathan couldn't see. He came to a stop a few feet from the blocks, following her gaze. There was nothing very interesting there: abandoned buildings, ancient stores in which little remained, broken-down cars which lingered on what was left of the pavement, their doors ajar, and their windows smashed and vandalized.

"What are you looking at?"

She shrugged, redirecting her attention towards him, smiling. "Nothing much. I was just wondering... I think I used to go to school not too far from here."

Nathan frowned, climbing up on another block and pulling the wax paper from the top of his burrito. "School?"

"Right. You wouldn't know what that is, I suppose. It's something that hasn't been around for a long time."

"What is it?"

"Just a place where people went to learn. The years after the meteor came, when we were all trying to figure out what to do with the ghouls, it pretty much stopped. I think they still have them in other parts of the world, though."

Nathan hurriedly swallowed the bite he was chewing so he could speak. "I'm fine. Did you say you were around when the meteor came?"

"I was."

"But... wasn't that a long time ago?"

"About forty years. I was a little girl when it came."

"You don't look forty years old."

She chuckled, shaking her head. "Of course not. I was in my twenties when I died. I couldn't really keep aging after that."

Nathan finished his first burrito in silence; Annie appeared to be lost in her thoughts again. He was halfway through his second burrito when he asked his next question. "So, were things really different before the meteor?"

"Radically! Everything is different."

"Like what?"

46

"Well, the cities weren't like that. You would walk practically anywhere without being afraid, and there weren't parts that were practically abandoned, either."

"So everything changed just because of the meteor?"

"Well, mainly, it was the ghouls."

Nathan frowned and answered, speaking slowly, his mouth full.

"They're just ghouls, though. I mean, sure they can be a bit scary, but they're slow, and definitely stupid. It's the raiders that are dangerous."

"Well, it didn't seem that way back then. We didn't know what the ghouls were, or why they were here. All we knew was that the people who had died in the crash were coming back to life, and that they were killing us. There was a lot of panic."

"So, the ghouls made the cities like this? Or was it the meteor?"

"People did. I know ghouls don't seem so scary now, because people know what to do with their dead and because the police, or hitters, as you probably know them, spend their whole time finding and eliminating ghouls. But back then, there were swarms of them. We weren't sure how to kill them, and people who were killed by them often became ghouls themselves, so we were overtaken. It was weeks before the ghoul problem was under control, and by then, everything was different."

"It must have been pretty scary."

She nodded. "It was terrifying. I was just a little girl, after all, and I didn't understand what was happening. We were lucky enough to be just outside the area touched by the explosion, but it was also one of the places where the ghouls first appeared. My family was caught completely unaware."

"You seem to have made it okay."

She smiled a bit; it was an odd smile, that didn't look exactly happy. Nathan couldn't see her eyes under the sunglasses; her face was turned towards the sky.

"My father was a very capable man," she said. "He was a geneticist. A scientist. He made sure I was all right. My mother wasn't so lucky."

She fell quiet. Nathan wasn't quite sure what to say, so he stuffed the entire remainder of his second burrito into his mouth and began to try and chew.

After a while, she turned her head towards him. He still couldn't see her eyes, but her eyebrows were forming that inquisitive expression he had seen on her face so often.

"What about your parents, Nathan? Do you know what happened to them?"

He shrugged with his right shoulder, crumpling the wax paper and tossing it on the ground. "I don't know. I never really gave it much thought. I mean, I've been swimming the flux long enough to know where babies come from, but most of my life I wasn't even aware there was such a thing, let alone that I should have them."

Her eyebrows dropped down to touch the top rim of her glasses, and she pursed her lips in the manner she had of doing when she was considering something. Nathan found himself thinking how incredible it was that someone's face could convey so much of what was going on in their minds.

After a few moments, she simply shrugged. "I would say I'm sorry, but I don't suppose you miss them much, do you?"

Nathan didn't feel like he could answer that question either, so he didn't say anything. She frowned at the ground unhappily, and didn't look up when she asked her next question.

"Did you have anyone at all to take care of you in that place? You mentioned a friend, earlier."

He nodded. "Laura. I remember her from when I was little. She used to spend a bit of time with me, bring me food that was a bit better than what I usually got... she even gave me a bear, once, but the others took it away when she left."

Annie frowned at him, but didn't answer, apparently lost in thought. They remained in silence for a long time; the sky was starting to turn orange by the time Annie hopped down from her concrete block, looking up at Nathan. "Well, the sun is setting. We should go."

He nodded, and climbed down from his seat. He adjusted his bag, and bumped into her when he started to walk, because she had apparently stopped. He frowned up at her, mouth open to say something, when he noticed what she had noticed. A van was making its way slowly up the street toward them, dodging the potholes and debris.

He felt his chest tighten when he recognized the logo on its hood. He took an involuntary step backwards, pressing himself against the cement block he had been sitting on. Annie turned and frowned at him. She seemed about to ask a question, but changed her mind at the last minute and grabbed his hand firmly.

"Come on. We have to get out of here. But no running unless you have to, all right?"

He nodded. His body felt numb, and he was grateful when she pulled him along and his legs miraculously worked; he was almost sure he couldn't have moved on his own. He glanced over his shoulder at the van. There was no mistaking that logo, though he had never thought he would see it again. How had they found him? Annie pulled him into an alley between buildings, and looked at him again.

"Are you all right?"

He wanted to nod, but he couldn't. He swallowed, and glanced back at the van. "Why is Genome here?"

"You know them?"

"I grew up seeing that logo everywhere. It wasn't hard to find out who they were after."

The van was still moving, but this time more slowly. Annie pulled him back into hiding, and looked around herself for a possible escape. "All right. We can talk about that when we're somewhere safer. Now follow me, and keep quiet."

She pulled him along and went down the end of the alley, and around the building. Nathan gave a panicked look over his shoulder. "What are you doing? We're headed back towards them!"

"It's no use trying to outrun them on foot. I'm going to try to circle behind them. Maybe we haven't been noticed yet."

She stopped abruptly when they reached the end of the building, and he bumped into her again. She glanced down the alley to make sure the van wasn't there, and moved on to the back of the next building, pulling Nathan along. They passed four buildings this way before they reached a fence, and had no choice but to either go back where they came from or towards the street.

Annie apparently decided on the street, taking care that Nathan stayed behind her. When they reached it, she gestured for him to stay where he was, and carefully peered around the edge. She seemed to relax after a few seconds, and leaned over for a better look. After a few more moments, she sighed gratefully, turning to Nathan. "I can't see them. I think they're gone."

His legs shook with relief, and he put a hand over his heart. He'd seldom felt it beat that hard before. "Why were they here?"

She shrugged, leaning out of the alley to peer down the street again. "Who knows? Maybe it's just a coincidence. Maybe they're just carrying something somewhere." She gave the darkening sky a worried look. "We shouldn't stay here too long. Let's go."

She headed into the street, staying close to the buildings. Nathan hugged his bag to himself and followed her, glancing around himself nervously. There suddenly seemed to be a lot more places where danger could hide than there were just a few moments ago. Annie walked rapidly and purposefully, and he had to skip ahead a few times to keep up with her.

They had barely walked a block when he heard an unfamiliar crunching sound behind him. He started and turned to see the van pulling out of an alley, a mere twenty yards behind him. He gasped, and reached out in front of him, grabbing and pulling on the back of Annie's lab coat. She stopped and turned.

"What?" She frowned when she saw the van, but hesitated only a moment. She turned the other way, shouting at Nathan. "Run!"

This time, his legs worked to perfection, even better. Fear gave him strength and speed he had no idea he had; he easily ran past Annie, and kept going. The fear was so overwhelming that he barely felt the ache in his lungs, and he had run three full blocks and turned off in an alley before he realized that he was alone. He came to an abrupt stop, panting, and looked around frantically.

"Annie?"

The street was empty. He jogged back the way he came, tracing his steps. He left the alley and nearly jumped back in when he saw the van, right down the street, nearly at the same place he had left it. Before he turned back to run the other way, he noticed that the van was parked. Next to it, three men were holding poles, at the end of which were ropes.

Two of the ropes were wrapped around Annie's neck, another one around her right wrist. She was desperately trying to fight back with her free hand, but the poles were long enough to keep the men well out of her reach. They were pushing her through the double doors at the back of the van.

Nathan felt his heart pound so hard it seemed to be filling up his throat, threatening to burst out of his ears. He took a brave step towards the van, trying to bring up the courage to go help her, to fight off these men. His mind seemed to be at war with itself. It only lasted a brief moment; as they managed to get Annie in the van, one of the men noticed him. Nathan didn't stay to see what happened next. He turned, ran, and didn't look back.

CHAPTER 5

Nathan nearly collapsed when he finally came to a stop. He fell to his knees, his lungs raw, his head spinning. He didn't know how long he'd been running, or even exactly where he was; he had just kept going until he felt his body about to give in, with no other thought on his mind but getting away.

He tried to catch his breath and sat on his heels, looking at his surroundings. He had leapt into a small building, and knelt in what had once been its lobby. The desk in there was almost intact, and not much of the objects seemed to be missing; there were papers and pens, an old phone broken up in several pieces, even potted plants that had died and rotted a long time ago.

Nathan tried to stand and felt that his legs wouldn't quite support him just yet. He looked outside through the building's broken glass door. The sun had set; it was almost completely dark. He had to find a safe place to spend the night right away. He briefly thought of trying to find his squat, but he realized he would not be returning to there. It was too late in the evening, anyway, but more importantly, maybe the men from the lab knew where he was staying. He would just have to find a new squat. But he couldn't stay here, either. This place was too exposed; there was nothing to protect him from the many dangers of a night in Three Walls.

Grunting with the effort, he hoisted himself up and walked further into the building. If he could find a place to hide in and barricade on the second floor, he might live through the next few hours.

He had to step over a small pile of broken furniture which partially blocked the door to get further into the building. The next room was much larger, and much more chaotic. Papers of all sizes and colors carpeted the floor, like there had been an explosion at the center of the room and the pages were its debris. There were desks and chairs piled up over all doors, as if someone had tried to barricade all the exits. A pair of legs protruded from the pile of chairs and desks.

Nathan held his breath, and grew very still. He hadn't smelled a dead body coming in, which meant it was either very old, or very new. If it was old, there was nothing to worry about. If it was new...

He pressed his back against the wall, staying as far away from the body as possible, moving into the room as quietly as he could, his eyes locked on it. When he was far enough into the room that he could see around the barricade, he breathed a sigh of relief. The body was mostly bones, wearing the remnants of a suit that was now tatters. He wiped sweat off his brow; his whole body trembled, and he felt like he was going to collapse again.

He reached into his bag automatically, and searched for a few seconds before remembering that he didn't have any stims left. He let out a strangled moan and sank to the floor, grasping his head in his hands. How was he going to make it through the night without stims? He felt the panic start to cover his body with cold sweat. He closed his eyes and tried to concentrate to keep his breathing under control. He couldn't afford to panic; not here, not now. There was barely enough light left to see by. He had to move before it was completely gone.

He got back to his feet shakily, and climbed over the second barricade, trying to avoid the body. The door on the other side led to a flight of stairs. He walked in carefully, looking up to make sure nothing moved before heading to the second floor.

The chaos was far lesser there. The stairs led to an empty hallway, on which opened several doors. They weren't apartments; the doors had too many signs and lettering on them, and they were too far apart. He tried the first one; it was locked. He moved on quickly to another one. This one was slightly ajar, and led to a relatively undisturbed room. Several chairs were lined up against the wall, around a squat plastic table which was littered with old magazines. Nathan walked in, and closed the door behind him, locking it before making his way to the door next to the desk.

This one led to a small hallway, in which there were a few open rooms and one closed door at the end. Nathan looked carefully at the first open room; each seemed to be the same. Its central feature was an elaborate chair placed under an overhead lamp, and a table on which were laid out several instruments.

He took a few hesitant steps towards the chair, staring at it. It looked more comfortable than the ones in his memory, and it didn't have any restraints; still, he wondered what kind of place he'd wandered into. He gave himself a shake, and went on.

He was careful to look in each room to make sure they were empty; they were all the same as the first one. Finally, he reached the door at the end of the hall. He hoped it would be what he needed.

It was a small office, decidedly designed more for function than comfort. Filers and shelves lined every wall. The desk's surface was littered with papers, and an ancient computer lay on it. He closed and locked the door behind him, then pushed the desk against it. It was heavy and hard to move; it would make the perfect barricade. Safe at last, he let himself drop to the floor, exhausted.

Annie was gone. The sudden, intrusive thought knocked the wind out of him as surely as a blow to the stomach would have. He sat gasping and staring at nothing until the small office was completely dark, and then finally stood to go pull down the blinds. He went back to sit in the middle of the room, and pulled Oliver out of his bag, flipping him open. He just had to talk to someone. As he waited for the small computer to boot, he wondered how long it had been since he'd had an actual conversation with Oliver. It seemed to be a long time ago.

"Oliver? Are you online?"

"I seem to be functioning properly. Though if you are planning to connect to the flux, I would recommend plugging me in, or you'll just forget again."

"Oliver, I don't know what to do! Some men came in a van and took Annie away! They're from the lab! What should I do?"

"It all depends on what your possible courses of action are, and on your intended result."

Nathan sighed. He hadn't really expected Oliver to have an answer, but talking to him in his moments of great anxiety had always alleviated Nathan's fear. Right now, though, it made him feel strangely empty; all he could think about was how much he missed the way Annie's expressions added to the meaning of her words. He closed his eyes and tried to think.

What were they doing here? He'd never even seen anything, let alone a van, with that symbol since he ran away from the lab all these years ago. On top of everything, it seemed Annie knew them too. Were they the same people who had done this to her? And if so, was it her or him they were after? They had captured her. He'd never heard of anyone wanting to capture a ghoul; the hitters were usually the ones who went after them, and they were out to destroy them.

He looked down at Oliver's screen again. There was nothing he could do about it right at that moment, and without stims, he didn't know if he could concentrate enough to do anything coherent.

He kept associating with Genome as he swam, no matter how hard he tried to avoid, so he just followed the information where it led him. From the little he could gather, they seemed to be conducting research on ghouls and meteorians, though Nathan could not find any information originating from the company itself. Like many major corporations, their information was held on private networks, with their own satellites, with no connections available from the flux, a security measure that had become popular as the number of people able to swim the flux increased.

He felt his eyes blink and his head nodding; the day's emotions were starting to take their toll. He rubbed his eyes, letting go of the jack, trying to wake himself up. He stood up, pushing aside his blankets, and walked to the window. He took some water from the rain collector, and splashed it on his face. It didn't have the desired effect; the water was so lukewarm it didn't even feel wet. He turned to look at the couch where Annie had organized her little laboratory. The crate she used as a chair was pulled up close; her stethoscope was coiled on top of it, precisely in the place she should have been sitting.

He sighed forlornly and turned back to where he had left Oliver. He started and took a step backwards. There were men there, three of them, with poles in their hands, at the end of which were ropes. He was sure they hadn't been there before; he had a certain memory of locking the door, but then he wasn't sure anymore it was the right door he had locked. He turned to look at the entrance, and instead of it, found himself staring at the street where they had been, the van parked there, much larger than he remembered. By the time he had realized what it was, the men had the ropes wrapped around his neck and arms, and they were dragging him towards the van. He barely had time to start fighting back before he was pushed in.

Once he was inside the van, it wasn't a van anymore; it was the lab. He was back in that small, bare room with the monitors, the machines, and the chair. The men were pushing him towards the chair, and then they were pushing him in, fastening the restraints. This time he fought with everything he had. He wouldn't be in there again. He screamed, bit, kicked, and struggled. All of a sudden, he found that his limbs were free, and he was lying on the floor of a dark, unfamiliar little room; he was alone. He groaned as he sat up, rubbing his head.

He hated the way sleep always snuck up on him when he least expected it.

He stretched, stood, and went to look out the window. The sky was still dark; he couldn't have been asleep long. He glanced down at Oliver to see the time, but the little screen was dark. Oliver had been right; Nathan had forgotten to plug him in.

He looked around carefully until he located the power outlet in the corner of the wall. He crawled to it, trailing Oliver's power cord behind him. Concentrating, he closed his eyes and stuck his paperclip inside the small opening. It was nothing to get energy from a place he'd already managed to connect, but it was getting the energy there in the first place that was the tricky part. He'd found that in Three Walls, the further he went from Outer Circle, the smaller his chances were to actually connect it. After all, there needed to still be a physical path to get the energy from its source to where he was.

He was lucky this time. He had thought his chances were practically non-existent, but he could feel the energy pulsing faintly, somewhere far away. It took some doing, and the route he found for the energy was almost twice as long as it could have been, but at long last, he could feel the familiar tingle of the electricity rushing up his arm. When he plugged in Oliver's power cord, the little computer lit up and whirred back into life. Nathan sighed and leaned his head against the wall, folding his arms on top of his knees.

Annie. He had only known her for a few days. It was strange that the perspective of never seeing her again should cause at least as much discomfort as the fear he had of the lab, but there it was. He decided that as soon as Oliver had charged up sufficiently, he would go back on the flux and find the closest address for Genome. He supposed the very least he could do was access their data banks and find out what had happened to Annie, if he could. Then he would know if there was something he could do, and what. But he had to do something. If he didn't, then it was true, and Annie was gone.

There were three addresses registered to Starr Planetary Genome labs within a hundred kilometers from Nathan's current position. The first address was a section of a massive skyscraper in the heart of Inner Circle; the second was in the Outer Circle's warehouse district. The third one was the lab from his childhood, far outside of town, near the crater; Nathan recognized it from the satellite pictures.

He was already weighing his options as he disconnected from the flux. The lab near the crater was out of the question. Nothing could make him risk going back there. The office building also seemed risky. He would stand out like the sun in a clear sky in Inner Circle; as any Three Waller would. He wouldn't even be able to get to the building without being stopped by private security officers, or worse, hitters mistaking him for a ghoul, as was known to happen. The warehouse seemed to be the best choice.

He peered at the window. Feeble light was starting to filter through the shades; at long last, the sun was up.

He took his time putting away Oliver. Now that it was time to go, he found he was in no great hurry. He wasn't really even sure what he was going to do when he got to the warehouse. But the feeling of doing something was comforting, and it managed to dim the pain of Annie's sudden absence just enough to keep him moving.

Once he'd placed Oliver and his wire in his bag, he went to press his ear against the door. When he heard nothing but silence on the other side, he pulled the desk away, and opened the door slowly and carefully, making sure nothing would jump out at him from the hall. When he was satisfied, he started toward the exit, glancing again into each potential hiding place to make sure they were empty.

Everything seemed undisturbed, even when he got to the room with all the chairs and magazines. He crossed the room, and unlocked the door that would lead him to the outside hall.

He was about to step through when he heard a low, guttural gurgle coming from it. He turned towards the sound.

Less than ten yards from Nathan, right between him and the stairs, stood a ghoul. It was male, and wearing tattered rags that must have already been in poor state when it died. It was missing its right forearm, and part of its jaw; the whole right side of its face had rotted away from its skull. It was already shuffling in Nathan's direction by the time he noticed it.

Nathan jumped back in the room, pulling the door shut behind him. At least, there was only one. He looked around himself hurriedly. There was nothing there that'd make any sort of useful weapon. He ran back to check the small rooms in the hall. He had no more luck there; all the instruments were tiny, nothing that could destroy a ghoul's brain, which was the only way to dispose of one.

He ran back to the chair-magazine room. He could hear the distinctive sound of the ghoul's scraping fingers on the other side of the door; he couldn't stay here long. Ghouls seldom left when they had noticed prey, and they had a way of attracting others to them. More would come if he stayed.

He drew a deep breath. There was only one; if he thought it through and timed it right, he should be able to get out. The door did open on the inside; he might be able to use that to his advantage.

He picked up a chair, pressed himself against the wall on the hinged side of the door, put his hand on the lock and prayed there still was only one. He unlocked the door, and pulled it open as wide as he could, squeezing himself behind it.

He held his breath as he heard the ghoul shuffling in slowly. When it was through the door, he gathered his courage and charged at it with the chair, screaming. Caught by surprise, the ghoul stumbled and fell backwards. Nathan tossed the chair at the fallen ghoul and ran out the door, pulling it shut behind him. He could not lock the door without a key from the other side, but with any luck, he'd be well out of the building by the time the thing could figure out how to use the doorknob.

He took a quick look around to make sure there were no others; he seemed be alone. Still, he was careful going down the stairs, and especially making his way through the large barricaded room; but he encountered no other moving thing until he was outside.

The sun was still low over the horizon, but it was there. The streets were quiet, and apparently peaceful; it was that perfect time of the day when the night dwellers had gone back to their lairs, and the day people had not yet started to come out. He looked both ways when he reached the middle of the street, trying to orient himself, and headed north at a brisk pace.

His steps slowed as soon as he felt there was enough distance between him and the trapped ghoul. Now that he was no longer running from it, he was remembering what he was running to, and he felt less hurried with every step.

He went through the market to reach Outer Wall. Some of the itinerant vendors were just setting up shop. The food section was still empty, save for one barrow on which a man had placed some freshly brewed coffee, next to a fire he had apparently built in a large tin garbage can. There were also a few cookies covered in wrinkled old plastic wrap.

Nathan stopped to buy a cup of coffee and two oatmeal cookies. The cookies were so dry he felt like he was chewing sand; he ate the first one because he was hungry, but threw the other away. He stopped at another stall to buy two cans of beans from an old toothless woman, just in case he got stuck in another tight spot; they made as good weapons as they did meals. Nathan managed to find two cans that only had a few small dents. Afterwards, he headed to the chemist's to pick up a few more stims before heading off into Outer Circle.

He didn't visit Outer Circle too often, even if it had far less patrols than Inner Circle did. Although Nathan had nothing to fear from authorities, he had never been able to bring himself to feel even mildly sympathetic to anyone in uniform who had questions to ask.

The part of Outer Circle which was adjacent to the market was usually busy, but this early in the morning, it was nearly deserted. Nathan had walked through two blocks before he ran into another person, a man unlocking his store for the day. Out of habit, he crossed the street to avoid him, and turned off onto Highland boulevard, which circled almost all the way around the city through Outer Circle. If he followed it, it would eventually take him to the warehouse district.

He was almost finished with his coffee when the stores and apartment buildings started giving way to the warehouses. The sun had hardly climbed at all; it had taken him far less time than he had thought it would to get here. He stopped on the sidewalk to get his bearings while he drained the last few drops from the paper cup.

He gave a start when he heard the now too familiar crunching sound of tires on the pavement, and he turned to see where it was coming from. Just a few yards away, a large black van was making its way slowly down the middle of the street, moving slowly towards him.

Nathan froze for a moment. Had someone known he was coming after all? But as soon as the van came closer, he saw that it bore no logo, and he noticed the telltale barbed wire coiled around the front bumper. These were simply hitters.

Called that way after their strategy of choice which consisted of ramming ghouls with their trucks before finishing them off, hitters were the ghoul hunting patrols that went around every area of the city destroying as many ghouls as they could. This truck was probably simply the night shift returning from a night hunt with a truck full of terminated ghouls for the incinerator.

They didn't seem to notice him as they drove past. Still, he remained motionless until they were well out of sight, and heaved a deep sigh of relief when the van was gone. He dropped his now empty paper cup to the ground, looked around to make sure there were no more surprises, and headed towards his destination.

The Genome warehouse was just a few blocks off Highland. It was smaller than the satellite pictures had made it seem. In fact, it was so remarkably unremarkable in every point that Nathan felt vaguely disappointed. It was just a cement building, square and gray, exactly the same as most of the others around it, identified only by the neon Plexiglas logo on the top western corner.

Nathan stopped about fifty yards from it, walking around the block so he could get a good look at the building without getting too close. The front wall had a standard glass main entrance door, but the sides were windowless and bare, save for two loading docks which seemed impractical as an entry point. The eastern wall, however, had a single, electronically locked back door, and faced a narrow alley, fenced off by a mere chain link fence, shadowed by the closeness of its rear neighbor.

Nathan stood on the sidewalk, about seventy-five yards from the warehouse. He hadn't really been sure that he would do anything at all once he had gotten here. Now that he had, he was sure he would not turn back until he had the information he needed. He rummaged through his bag to find the stims he had just bought, and swallowed one. As ready as he was going to be, he put the bottle back into his bag, and started off towards the Genome warehouse.

CHAPTER 6

A network of security cameras watched the building and its surroundings. It was set up all around the fence which surrounded the warehouse on all four sides. The fence wouldn't be a problem; it was simple chain link, and Nathan had long ago taken the habit of carrying heavy wire cutters in his bag to allow quick escape during his explorations of local dumpsters. That still left the problem of the cameras.

The chain link fence which divided the two properties was only about two feet from the wall of a paper warehouse, but on the Genome side, there was the alley between him and the door, about the width of a car. Still, it was the shortest distance between the fence and any door.

He walked on the sidewalk, going around the block of buildings, making his way to the paper warehouse as nonchalantly as he could. The streets were still empty, though the sun was starting to show over the rooftops. He wondered if the warehouses shared the same hours of operation as the market; he sighed inwardly, thinking he should have checked that before he left. Who knew how long it would be before people started showing up for work?

He ducked into the alley on the northern side of the paper warehouse as soon as he had reached it. It was so close to the fence that went around the three sides of the buildings that it was hardly practical, and looked like it was scarcely ever used. Discarded food containers and colored plastic bags carpeted the ground so thickly it was almost ankle deep, and Nathan had to slow his progress considerably to avoid making too much noise. He wasn't entirely sure he really needed to be careful, deserted as the place was, but he wasn't going to take a chance.

He made his way slowly to the ideal spot behind the Genome warehouse, the occasional empty bag of chips crunching under his feet and making him jump. When he reached it, he stayed there for a few seconds, pressing his back against the brick wall of the paper warehouse, catching his breath. The place was still deserted.

He looked up at the fence. It was about ten feet high, with barbed wire coiled over the top to prevent anyone climbing it. A surveillance camera swiveled slowly on top of the corner post, overlooking the alley. Nathan breathed deeply, and laid a hand on the fencepost. He hoped he could reach the camera from here; the post was metal, but there was no guarantee that he would be able to reach the camera's systems. Besides that, he had never tried to speak to a camera before. He hoped they were as easy as electronic locks were: if this didn't work, his mission was over before it had even begun.

To his intense relief, the fencepost was as conductive as it looked, and he found the camera's mind right away. Once there, it took him a few seconds to understand how to interface with it, but once he did, he found that it was networked, and that he could access every other camera linked to it. He closed his eyes to see the images coming from the cameras more clearly, and started to scan through them.

Most of them were set over the huge storage area on the main floor which contained mostly large, reinforced metal crates and refrigerated containers. Most of them also bore large tags with colorful, arcane symbols. Other cameras seemed set over offices, and an apparently bare hallway, on either side and at the end of which were solid metal doors, with narrow windows at about eye level.

He sighed. It was obvious that he couldn't see the whole building. For one thing, he hadn't seen a single security guard, and he knew there had to be some. At least, there were computers on the desks in the office area. He could only hope the whole company would be on the same network.

The computer controlling the network of cameras was one of the simpler ones Nathan had encountered. He could have probably reprogrammed it entirely in a matter of minutes; however, it was simple enough that it would take anyone with any skill at all the same amount of time to reverse what he had done. He might not even have time to make it to a computer before they got the cameras back online. He hated to have to physically harm the little computer; machines had always been kinder to him than people, but Annie was at stake.

He barely had to concentrate to find the computer's power supply. Electricity had always been easy to find; it was drawn to him like a pin to a magnet. The power filled his body like adrenaline as he drew it; when he had stored enough, he directed it into the computer. The surge was so powerful he felt the camera that was his link fry with the computer it was networked to; he could hear it sizzle above him. He smiled at himself as he let go of the fencepost; damage this extensive would call for new equipment; he had all the time in the world, now.

He pulled the wire cutters out of his bag, and was through the fence in a few quick gestures.

His breath was shallow and he could feel his heart beating in his eardrums by the time he reached the small back door. His hand trembled as he touched the electronic lock's chip card slot. Electronic locks were the first kind of artificial intelligence he had ever interfaced with, and none of them had any secret from him. This one was no more complex than any he had encountered before, but nervous as he was, he still had to try twice to get it to open for him.

The hallway beyond was short, bare and metallic; there was only another door at the end, with its own electronic lock. Nathan walked to it and pressed his ear against the cold metal of the door anxiously. When he heard nothing on the other side, he touched the lock, and opened the door carefully.

The acrid smell of chemicals greeted him on the other side, and he covered his nose and mouth instinctively to prevent himself from gagging, wrinkling his nose. The door led to a landing in the middle of a metal staircase. On Nathan's left, the stairs went up to a metal walkway that went along the wall; he couldn't see what was up there. On the right, the stairs descended into the large storage area Nathan had seen on the cameras.

At the bottom of the stairs, on the left side, was a wall with two electronically locked doors. He took a step toward it, and the door closest to him opened. He froze; a security guard was just coming out of the room, twirling his keycard by its retractable cord. He turned calmly to close the door and make sure the electronic lock clicked back into place. He hadn't seen Nathan.

Nathan held his breath and moved slowly and carefully to go press his back against the left wall on the landing, out of the guard's direct line of sight. The pounding in his chest was so loud that he thought surely the guard would hear it. Even if that wasn't true, what would Nathan do if the guard decided to head upstairs? There wasn't a single place to hide.

He refrained from breathing a sigh of relief when he saw the security guard miraculously turn to walk further into the warehouse to the second door. Nathan waited until the man had vanished into the other mysterious room before he bolted up the stairs. He hoped there was only one guard.

The metal walkway upstairs seemed to go all the way across the building, to another flight of stairs. The right side of the walkway was open over the storage area, with a simple metal railing to prevent falls. On the left were three entryways; two of them were doorless openings, the third was another electronically locked door.

The first door led to a small kitchen, but the second one opened onto a large office space in which were about half a dozen desks facing the walls, separated by gray felt partitions. Nathan smiled to himself and was about to walk in, when he heard a sound coming from the far side of the walkway. He turned his head, straining his ears; there was the very distinctive sound of boots on metal stairs, and it was getting closer. Nathan thought for an instant about running back the way he came, but just then he saw the top of the guard's head bobbing over the edge of the stairs, and he jumped into the office.

Nathan searched frantically for a place to hide. There was no closet, no curtains, not even a coat rack. He glanced under one of the desks; he would be spotted for sure, even behind the chair. Unless... He frowned, pulling the chair away to get a closer look. The metal filer was not part of the desk's original design, and it didn't reach all the way to the wall. It was a pretty small space, but then again, Nathan was pretty small.

He dove under the desk, squeezed himself behind its small filer, and contorted an arm out to pull the chair back in place. As its wheel was hitting his foot, he heard the guard's footsteps on the walkway stop right outside the opening that led to the office. Nathan drew in his breath and held it, not wanting to make a single sound. He saw the guard's booted feet walk past his hiding place, inches away from him.

The few seconds the guard took to walk around the room seemed like hours to Nathan. He wanted to scream, and had to press his hands over his mouth to make sure he wouldn't. When the guard walked out of the room at last, Nathan let out a long, shuddering breath through his nostrils, his hands still clamped over his mouth.

He closed his eyes, concentrating on his hearing. He counted to a hundred in his mind after he heard the last of the guard's steps going down the stairs before daring to move. Letting go of his mouth, he reached for his bag, and his trembling hands fumbled with the childproof bottle cap. He almost dropped all the stims inside when he finally got the bottle open.

He waited for the small pill's effects to kick in before pushing the chair away from the desk to let himself out. By the time he was standing, he was full of chemical confidence again. He quickly reached for the computer on the desk. Its screen lit up when he accidentally hit the mouse, so he didn't even need to turn it on. He just found a jack, and connected his mind to it.

He'd gotten lucky: it seemed all of Genome's computers were on the same network after all. He swam in the data flux for a little while, going from file to file, unable to find the thought that would bring him to Annie specifically. One thing was for sure: they were doing research on ghouls, and had been for a very long time; Nathan couldn't stop finding information on ghouls.

After filtering through what had to be thousands of files, he finally found what he was looking for. It seemed that they were capturing ghouls from Three Walls and shipping them off to their location in the crater. His heart leapt when he found the next information: the ghouls were stored in the warehouse between shipments; the next shipment was scheduled for today. Could it be that Annie was right here?

Nathan felt sick to his stomach as he let go of the jack. What was he doing here? He should have been trying to find a new squat, staying as far away from places like this as possible. What if he encountered an army of ghouls? Or scientists? What if he got killed? Even worse, what if he got caught?

What if he never saw Annie again?

He sighed in resignation and leaned out of the door and into the metal walkway, making sure he was alone. He made his way soundlessly back the way he came, taking the stairs down to the storage area.

It was only about ten yards from the bottom of the stairs to the door he had to reach, but he stopped three times to look around madly, certain he had heard a sound. Each time, he found himself alone. When he reached the door, he stood, motionless, staring at it for what seemed like several minutes, afraid of what he would find on the other side. His hands were shaking again when he put them on the lock, and he noticed his heartbeat was filling his ears again, and his breathing was ragged.

The hallway beyond the door was long, with steel doors on either side, and one at the end. Each door had an individual electronic lock, and were extremely close to one another as if they lead to very small rooms. Each door had a long, narrow window at about eye level. He went to the first one, and had to stand on tiptoe to look inside.

He started when he took in what he saw; four ghouls, shuffling aimlessly, one of them clawing at a corner of the small cell. He was in the right place, at least, and the ghouls were indeed still here. His voice quivered with hope when he shouted, so close to his goal he forgot all thought of caution.

"Annie? Annie!"

He ran from cell to cell looking for her as he shouted for her; he stopped in the middle of the hall when he heard a voice.

"In here!"

He frowned, turning toward the origin of the sound. It was coming from a cell on his right, and it was definitely a man's voice.

He ran to the door and grabbed the edge of the small window with the tip of his fingers to balance himself as he got up on tiptoes. He almost shouted when he found himself nose to nose with a tall man; whose milky white were unmistakably dead. Nathan was about to turn and head to another door when the ghoul spoke.

"You're not one of them."

Nathan blinked. Even knowing Annie, he hadn't expected this. Were ghouls suddenly all developing the power of speech and thought?

"Them who?"

"The scientists."

Nathan blinked again. "Right. Uh, I'm looking for my friend. She's... well, she's got black hair, she's tall, and she wears a lab coat. But she's not a scientist. Well, not from here, anyway. They took her and brought her here and..."

"Yeah, I know where she's at. Let me out and I'll help you find her."

Nathan reached out to lay his hand on the electronic lock, but stopped himself at the last moment. The dead man saw him hesitate and rolled his eyes at him.

"Come on, dude! You can't just leave me here!"

Nathan's fingers hesitated inches from the lock. He frowned up at the ghoul.

"You won't hurt me?"

"I swear!"

"And you really do know where Annie is?"

"Scout's honor!"

The ghoul held up three fingers pressed together, his pinky and thumb meeting in the middle of his palm. Nathan had no idea what any of this meant, but the expression on the man's face was earnest. He let his fingers touch the lock, and the door clicked open at his thought.

The dead man grabbed the handle and yanked the door open, jumping out as though he thought Nathan might change his mind any second. For a moment, Nathan thought he'd been betrayed and the man was fleeing, but once the ghoul was through the door, he turned a smile on Nathan so warm it was unsettling to see on a dead face.

He was a good head taller than Nathan was, and up close, his skin was a dark, sickly brown-gray. His dreadlocked hair was gathered in a loose ponytail that reached halfway down his back. He was dressed in rags, but of a very different sort than Nathan's; his seemed much too clean to really be old, and seemed to be torn just the right amount, all in predetermined places.

"Thanks, little dude! I..."

The dead man didn't have time to finish his thought. The door leading to the storage area opened, catching both their attention. A short, balding man wearing a freshly pressed lab coat was walking in distractedly, his eyes fixed on the clipboard he was holding. Nathan's heart felt like it had suddenly stopped. The man raised his head and stared at Nathan and the ghoul. In a moment that lasted forever, none of them moved a muscle.

Then, time seemed to accelerate dramatically as the man ran back outside, screaming for security. Nathan was frozen to the spot, but the ghoul jumped on the scientist, punching him squarely between the eyes. The man fell backward, his clipboard clattering on the floor behind him. The ghoul grabbed the scientist and threw him out of the room, then shouted at Nathan over his shoulder.

"Close that door!"

Nathan felt his legs move, and was at the door before he had time to think about what was happening. He shut the door, and put his hand on the lock. He'd never tried to do this before, and he was surprised at how easy it was to delete all the codes from the electronic lock's memory.

He turned to see his new ghoul friend closing the door to the cell in which he'd been. Nathan couldn't see the scientist anymore; evidently, the ghoul had put him in the cell. The dead man glanced down at his wristphone and glared at Nathan.

"Couldn't you have timed your rescue mission a little better? People are coming in for work!"

"How was I supposed to know?"

The dead man shook his head. "Never mind. Let's find your friend and get out of here."

The door which led to the storage area rattled like someone was trying to pull it off its hinges, and someone shouted from the other side. "What's going on in there?"

Nathan looked at the ghoul. "Where is she?"

The ghoul nodded and headed toward the door that was at the end of the hall. Nathan followed, looking over his shoulder at the rattling door; there was pounding, now. The ghoul finally reached the door toward which he had been headed, and peered through the narrow window.

"Yeah, she's in there all right. Can you do your mojo on the door?"

Nathan nodded and touched the lock on the door without hesitation. He took a few seconds after opening the door to erase all the codes on that one, too, before walking in and closing the door behind him.

This room was not a bare cell like the other one had been; there was a tray with tools and instruments on it, most of which Nathan couldn't identify, a computer, and a table in the middle, on which lay Annie. The ghoul was leaning over her, pressing fingers against her throat. He shook his head, and his white eyes were sad when he turned toward Nathan.

"Sorry, man. She's dead."

Nathan frowned, and headed towards the computer. "Well, yeah, but she was already dead when I met her."

The ghoul's eyebrows shot up at this and he shook his head slightly. "You're an unusual little guy."

"Can you carry her?"

"Yeah, no problem. The bigger problem is, how do we get out of here?"

Nathan jerked his head toward the door. There was pounding on the other side; obviously whoever it was had managed to get past his first deadlock. They would be able to get through this door, too.

He turned to the ghoul. "What do you know about this place?"

The dead man shrugged apologetically. "Nothing. I've only been here since yesterday."

Nathan found a jack on the computer and linked with it. Having a very clear idea of what he was looking for this time, it took him only moments to find the information he needed. The warehouse had eighteen employees total, including security personnel. He was ridiculously outnumbered. However, there were far more ghouls held in the warehouse than the total number of employees. He gave his new friend and unsure glance.

"I think I have an idea... but it's a really bad one."

The ghoul was hoisting Annie up across his shoulders in a fireman carry, eyeing the door apprehensively. "Well, whatever it is, it's gotta be better than nothing, which is what I got."

Nathan sighed, and searched for the controls to the cell locks. He found the control that would release all the ones he wanted, and activated it.

The screams had started on the other side by the time he joined his new friend by the door. The dead man frowned at him, looking worried. "What did you do?"

Nathan went to stand on tiptoes to look through the narrow window. "I let all the ghouls go."

"You did what?"

Nathan couldn't see anyone anymore; just ghouls, shuffling and scrabbling their way out of the hall and into the warehouse through the open door.

"I let them go. I think they'll distract everyone enough for us to get away."

His new friend unexpectedly burst out laughing, and Nathan frowned at him. "What?"

"You're crazy. But you've got balls. I like you."

Nathan shook his head in puzzlement and looked back out. There wasn't a ghoul left in the hall. He took a deep breath. "They're gone. Let's go."

CHAPTER 7

Nathan let his new friend go ahead of him. Being already dead, Annie and the man were in no danger from the other ghouls. Nathan followed a few feet behind. The dead man leaned out the door carefully, looking around, and after a few moments, signaled for Nathan to follow him.

When Nathan reached the door that led to the warehouse, there were only a few ghouls straggling in it, too far from Nathan to be an immediate danger. He saw a body lying across an alley and started to feel guilty about the man, but his new friend's loud whisper pulled him out of his reverie.

"Hey! Little dude! Snap out of it!"

Nathan started and skipped to the stairs. The dead man had already reached the door that led outside, and was leaning into it to make sure the way was clear. Annie was still hanging limp across his shoulders. Nathan made it to the door as the dead man was stepping out.

It was as eerily quiet outside as it had been when Nathan came in, though now Nathan could see ghouls shuffling around the edges of the parking lot. They were spread out all over the place, but they would start to converge once the first one saw him.

The dead man carrying Annie surveyed the parking lot critically, apparently perceiving the potential danger as well. Nathan followed his gaze to a car which lay abandoned in the middle of the way, its driver side door open.

"Hey, man, can you work your mojo on a car?"

Nathan frowned uncertainly; he didn't know the first thing about cars. "I don't know. Do cars have computers?"

"Yeah, I think so."

"Then I suppose it's worth a try."

"All right. Give me a few seconds' head start and then follow me."

Nathan nodded, turning to look back inside. There was a ghoul approaching slowly, limping on a leg which twisted at an odd angle. Nathan stepped through the threshold and moved sideways, pressing his back against the wall; he didn't want to have to worry about things coming at him from behind.

He had a quick, nervous look around. The ghouls that were still outside had not yet noticed him. He turned his attention to the dead man, who had almost made it to the car. He was jogging easily, as if Annie weighed no more than a simple scarf. He reached the door, pulled the back driver's side door open and put Annie down on the back seat.

Nathan took a look at the parking lot again to make sure the way was still clear, and started running towards the car. He had only taken three steps when he had to come to a sudden stop, surprised. A ghoul had just wandered from the side of the building, putting itself in Nathan's path to the car. Nathan glanced around for the best way to avoid it, and noticed that the other ghouls had seen him, and were starting to converge in his direction.

At that moment, he heard an engine starting, and jerked his head around to see the car the dead man was now apparently driving come into motion. The tires screeched and smoked, and the car bounded forward, ramming the ghoul which was blocking Nathan's way so hard it bounced on the hood, rolled over the roof and landed clear on the other side of the car, twitching with the grace of a broken machine.

The car came to a spinning stop next to Nathan, who had to dodge it to avoid getting hit. Inside it, the dead man leaned over to open the passenger side door, grinning madly at Nathan.

"Keys were in the ignition! Hop in, little dude!"

Nathan didn't have to be told twice; he jumped in, dragging the door closed behind him. As soon as the door slammed, the dead man put his foot down on the accelerator and the car sped out of the parking lot so fast that Nathan found himself stuck to his seat, at an awkward sideways angle. The dead man managed to hit three more ghouls on his way out, cheering loudly every time he succeeded.

Nathan hugged his bag to himself, trying to remain upright, and to think of something else than the crazy dead stranger next to him, or the still form of Annie on the back seat.

The dead man calmed as they put some distance between them and the warehouse, and there no longer was a trace of neither ghoul nor pursuit. He slowed as he got to the intersection to Highland road, and looked at Nathan.

"Which way do we go, little dude?"

Nathan blinked and frowned. He hadn't thought ahead that far. In fact, he hadn't thought any further than finding the warehouse; everything since then had been improvised.

Where should they go? Annie didn't have a place. Nathan didn't dare go back to his squat. The dead man checked the mirrors impatiently and looked back at Nathan.

"So?"

"... I dunno."

The dead man stared at him in disbelief for a few seconds, then shook his head and turned right on Highland, laughing to himself. "You really suck at rescue missions, you know that?"

Nathan grunted unhappily. "Well, we're outside, aren't we?"

"Well, I gotta give you at least that. By the way, my name's Jeffrey."

"I'm Nathan."

Nathan glanced at Jeffrey to see if the dead man was expecting some kind of physical contact, but he didn't seem to be, concentrated on his driving as he was. Nathan finally worked up the courage to glance at Annie, on the back seat. She

76

was still motionless, her eyes closed. Dead. What if she never woke up?

He felt a pain in his stomach that was starting to become familiar, and he reached into his bag for the comfort of the little pink pills. Jeffrey glanced down as he opened the small bottle.

"What're those?"

"Stims."

Nathan expected Jeffrey to say something disapproving, but the dead man remained silent. Nathan swallowed the stim, and regretted not having brought some water. His throat was dry, and the pill stuck to it a bit before going down.

They drove for a little while longer, swerving off into the smaller streets, remaining in Outer Circle but getting closer to Inner Circle, the richest part of the city. They had reached a residential district.

The streets were narrow, and had nearly no potholes. They were flanked on either side by tall apartment buildings which seemed glorious and brand-new when compared to the ones found in Three Walls.

There were a lot of people in the area, more than Nathan had seen together in one place yet. Neighbors were speaking to each other from the street or their windows. Children were running after one another, jumping through a spinning rope or hopping over chalk drawings on the pavement in games that seemed arcane to Nathan.

He watched them, his face pressed against the window of the car, full of envy and wonder, until Jeffrey turned the car into a narrow alley, and all that Nathan could see anymore was a brick wall. He turned to frown at Jeffrey as the dead man was turning off the ignition.

"What are we doing here?"

"A buddy of mine lives here. I thought we could hide out here until we can figure out what to do."

Nathan nodded. He didn't really feel like being in the presence of yet another stranger, but he didn't have any other ideas, so he supposed he should be glad that Jeffrey had decided.

The alley was so narrow that Nathan could only open the door as wide as his body was, and had to squeeze himself through the tight opening to get out. By the time he was standing at the rear end of the car, the dead man had already retrieved Annie from the back seat, cradling her in his arms this time instead of throwing her across his shoulders.

Jeffrey walked down the alleyway to the back of the building. Nathan followed him, circling around the driver's side, where there was at least enough room to walk past the car without having to go sideways.

Jeffrey led him to a simple blue metal door in the black, which had no apparent means of opening from the outside, no knob, or even an electronic lock, just an intercom box. Jeffrey shifted Annie around in his arms so he could hold her with just one hand and a shoulder, and punched a key on the intercom.

"Call Liam," he articulated.

Nathan waited patiently, trying not to look at Annie. It was hard to stay in one place for too long; he felt more restless with each passing second. Jeffrey started talking into the intercom.

"Yeah, Liam, it's Jeffrey."

The voice on the other end sounded angry. "Jeff? Seriously? Where have you been?"

"It's complicated. I don't really have time to..."

"Don't give me that crap! Do you know how much I tried to reach you?"

Jeffrey sighed. "Don't get pissy with me, I'll explain everything! Just get your ass down to the back exit."

"I'm on my way."

He let go of the key and lowered Annie back into his arms. He then turned towards Nathan, smiling. "Don't worry, little guy. We can have a rest and then I'm sure you can figure out what to do."

Nathan nodded uneasily. He wasn't sure about that. There was no rest for him in a place with two strange men. And as far as what to do next, he had no idea. He gave Annie an anxious glance. He couldn't imagine her not waking up, and he felt completely paralyzed with her in this state.

The door opened so suddenly and violently that Nathan had to take a step back to avoid getting hit in the face. A pale-faced young man with tired, blood-shot eyes and a mess of dark curls glared at Jeffrey from beyond it, wearing black pajama bottoms with cartoon ducks printed all over them and a wrinkled, stained t-shirt that had once been white.

"You better have a..."

The young man's expression changed, his words trailing off, when he took in the sight of the dead girl in Jeffrey's arms, and the unknown boy next to him. His face slowly shifted to utter shock as he finally took a closer look at his friend.

"Jeffrey, what the hell is going on? What happened to you? Are you okay?"

"Just shut up and let me in, won't you?"

"Uh, yeah, sure."

The young man stood aside, letting Jeffrey and Nathan through the door before closing it behind them. Their steps echoed loudly as the young man led them up a few flights of stairs and to another door. Before opening it, the young man turned to Jeffrey and looked at him, his face full of concern and shock.

"What's wrong with your eyes?"

"It's a real messed up, complicated story."

The young man sighed and pushed the door open. They stepped into a much quieter, carpeted hallway. There was the distinctive smell of age in there, yet the blue paint on the walls seemed fresh, and the place seemed to be cleaned regularly.

Nathan hadn't been in many places that were this clean; at least, none that had been meant to live in.

They stopped in front of an elevator. As the young man pressed the top one, he turned toward Jeffrey, frowning at him. "Aren't you going to tell me what happened?"

"Not right now."

The strange young man snorted angrily. "You've been missing for like, a week! You leave with Felicia to go score some M, and nobody ever sees you again. You don't call me, you don't answer my texts..." He shook his head. "We missed two gigs!"

The elevator dinged and the doors opened. As they stepped inside, Jeffrey looked at his friend. "I lost my phone. As for the rest, you probably won't believe me."

"Try me."

"So, about that party... Felicia and I thought the best place to get M would be in Three Walls. We got turned around and stopped in an alley, and the next thing I know, we're being picked up by these guys in a van. I thought they were hitters, and I kept screaming that we weren't ghouls, but the bastards used a stun gun to knock me out. I woke up in this lab. They put me in some sort of machine and I passed out again. I woke up on a pile of dead bodies. Like this."

"Dead bodies?"

"Yeah. Bunches of them. I couldn't see anyone else moving. Which is why I guess nobody was really watching. I took the chance to escape."

Nathan looked at Jeffrey, confused. "If you escaped, how come you were in that place?"

Jeffrey looked annoyed, and a little shameful. "It took a while to get back to the city. I was feeling... I dunno, tired, I guess, but not exactly. They caught me again as I reached the city and made my way through Three Walls, last night. It's stupid, and I don't want to talk about it."

Nathan shut his mouth, though he had more questions. Had he been pursued like Annie and he had? Jeffrey's friend returned to the charge with questions of his own, though.

"So... what's wrong with you?"

Jeffrey grimaced, uncomfortable. The elevator came to a stop with a lurch that made Nathan feel queasy, if just a moment, and the doors opened. The stranger crossed the hall to lead them to one of the doors, swiping his keycard through the electronic lock, looking at his friend as he punched in the code.

"Seriously, Jeffrey, what's the matter with you? You look dead."

Jeffrey looked at him angrily before stepping through the door that had just been opened. "I think I am."

Nathan ducked under the young man's shocked stare to follow Jeffrey inside, but stopped after a few feet, staring around himself in amazement. The place was huge, with high ceilings, and tall windows which faced the sun. The main room, which the front door opened to, was in itself as large as Nathan's entire squat had been. The floors were light wood, spotless and free of splinters.

The couches looked plush and brand new, and faced the largest screen Nathan had ever seen. The opposite wall was decorated with posters of musicians Nathan didn't recognize. Behind the couches was a small table, covered with a pile of papers, and a row of six guitars lined up under the posters.

There were two doors on each side. Jeffrey was walking towards the one that was the furthest away on Nathan's right side. Nathan heard the front door close, and realized that Jeffrey's friend was now staring at him.

"So, who are you, anyway?"

"Uh, I'm Nathan."

"Okay, what I mean is, what are you doing here?"

"I... was helping my friend. I'll go check on her."

Nathan hurried to the door behind which he had seen Jeffrey disappear. It was a large bedroom. A double sized bed was the main feature, on which Jeffrey had laid Annie down, her head resting on a pillow. She could have been sleeping. Maybe she was. Nathan wasn't sure he'd ever seen her sleep; he didn't think so. He went to stand next to the bed, unsure what to do, staring down at her. Jeffrey was doing the same on the other side of the bed, arms crossed. He noticed Nathan and looked up at him.

"You okay, little dude?"

Nathan shrugged. "Why hasn't she woken up yet?"

Jeffrey shook his head. "I dunno. I dunno what keeps me going. Why I think. What's the difference between me and a ghoul? Hell, what's the difference between a ghoul and a corpse, anyway?"

Nathan sat on the chair, helpless. "How should I know? She's the expert on that."

"Too bad we don't know how to wake her up and ask her."

They stayed quiet for a few more moments, and Nathan got up to drag his chair closer to the bed. Jeffrey watched him, and looked back down at Annie. "So, she your girlfriend or something?"

Nathan frowned. This was completely unknown territory. He'd come across the word in the past, but he wasn't really sure what it meant, so he moved to a safer word.

"She's my friend."

Jeffrey rubbed the back of his neck, and stood. "All right, I guess I'll leave you to it... I gotta catch up on some stuff."

Nathan nodded distractedly, staring at Annie. He hardly paid any attention to Jeffrey as the dead man walked out. It had been a very long time now, hadn't it? Shouldn't she wake up by now? He wished there was something he could do.

Absent-mindedly, he reached into his bag and dug out his camera. He pointed it at Annie, but for some reason, couldn't make himself take the picture. There wasn't anything else that looked that interesting to him in the room, so he started flipping through the pictures on the memory card. He started from the most recent he had taken, and was shocked when the first thing he saw was Annie's body, sprawled in the dump, bullet hole through her throat. He had taken this one when he first laid eyes on her. It seemed like a long time ago, now, but he realized it had only been a few days.

He had come to the dump looking for parts to work on one of his many projects when he'd stumbled upon a group of raiders attacking her shack. They'd left her for dead, among the garbage, like that was what she was to them. Nathan had waited until he was sure that they were gone, and he had felt compelled to go and see the girl, then take the picture.

He wasn't exactly sure why; just that he had a horrible feeling in the pit of his stomach at the sight of the body, but he couldn't turn away. He remembered thinking how absurd it was that in the next few hours she might rise as a ghoul or be eaten or buried in trash, and no one would know she had existed. At least, he would.

He had gotten too close, and she had reached out suddenly from apparent death and grabbed his arm. He had felt his energy draining into her, and he remembered seeing her wounds closing.

He frowned, and looked away from the camera, and back at Annie. She could use his energy to heal herself. Maybe there was something he could do, after all.

He reached out a hand to touch her arm hesitantly. Her sleeves were, as always, rolled up to her elbows, and her forearms are bare. Her skin felt cold, and stiff. Had she been this cold before?

Nothing happened. He closed his eyes to concentrate. He was able to transfer electricity to his body; maybe he was able to output his energy into her body? He tried to recall the feeling he had had when she had drained him, that time, and attempted to reproduce it. At first, this yielded nothing but a headache, but as he relaxed and focused, he felt his fingers tingle, and there was a feeling not unlike breathing out underwater as the energy left his body, slowly at first, then more and more rapidly, until he was no longer in control. He let out a panicked little moan, and lost consciousness.

CHAPTER 8

Waking up was slow, difficult, and painful: Nathan's whole body tingled like it had pins and needles. His tongue felt swollen, his vision was blurry, and his stomach hurt. He recognized Annie's voice before he had regained enough of his senses to even wonder where he was.

"Nathan! You're awake!"

He turned his head towards the sound. His muscles felt like they had rusted, but his eyes finally focused on her face, leaning down over his. Her hair was untied, and her smile was so radiant, that for a moment Nathan thought she'd managed to bring herself back to life, somehow. But her eyes were still milky white. It didn't matter much, though. Nathan couldn't remember being happier about seeing anything in his life. His smile made the skin of his face feel tight.

"Annie! You're all right!"

She smiled warmly at him, running her fingertips down the right side of his face. "Thanks to you, I hear."

Her touch felt odd. Not because it was cold; Nathan was getting used to that. Rather, it almost felt like electricity did. It made his skin tingle pleasantly and stirred up a strange, enjoyable feeling somewhere beyond the pit of his stomach.

She stood, still smiling. "I'll get you some water. You sound thirsty."

He watched her skip out the door in wonder, the memory of her touch clear on his cheek. He was thirsty, and water sounded divine. But at the same time, he didn't want her to be away. He tried to move his limbs, but they wouldn't budge. Strangely enough, this sensation brought little fear: Annie was all right, she was near, and she would be back at his side in a matter of seconds.

He looked at his surroundings, now that his eyes were working properly again. He was in the same room as when he passed out, lying in exactly the same place as Annie had been. Someone had undressed him; he wasn't wearing his own clothes anymore, but a pair of gray sweat pants and a t-shirt that were both too large for him.

The door opened, and Annie walked back in, carrying a glass of water. She was still smiling brightly; seeing her happiness made him feel warm and confident, a little like the stims did, but different, and better.

She sat back down on the bed and helped him up, bringing the glass to his lips. He drank in small sips, because it seemed the weakness of his body extended to his throat, and he had a hard time swallowing without choking on the water. Still, he felt better after drinking, and she put the glass down before lowering him back in a lying position.

"Better?"

"Yes. But I'll feel even better if you just help me to an outlet."

She chuckled and shook her head. "Right. I almost forgot you could do this."

She reached down to pick him up, and lifted him easily, bringing him to an outlet in a corner of the room, not too far from the door.

The electricity felt wonderful as it went up his arm and spread to his body, like his blood had finally started flowing again, the strength returning to his limbs. He let out a long, satisfied sigh, and grinned at Annie.

"Now I feel better."

She smiled and stood, extending a hand to help him up. He took it, even though he didn't need to, and was again dismayed at the contradictory sensations of the cold of her skin and the pleasantness of her touch.

"Are you hungry? I think Liam ordered some Chinese food."

Nathan made a face. "Like those noodles from the market?"

"No. I think you'll like this."

He followed her out the door and into the large living area. Jeffrey and Liam were apparently playing a video game, waving their arms in front of the huge screen. Liam had dressed, and seemed much happier than before. Nathan glanced at the screen, and saw that their avatars were monkeys engaged in a tennis game which involved using a screaming squirrel as a ball.

Jeffrey made a high motion with his hand, and Liam scrambled, lost his balance and fell flat on his face while his avatar ran uselessly to the side. The screen displayed a scoreboard, which made Jeffrey's avatar start a little dance, while the squirrel ran around it with pompoms, screamed his cheers in an annoyingly shrill voice. Liam cursed, and Jeffrey grinned at him.

"Looks like I still got it!"

"Yeah, right! You're probably using one of your new superpowers to cheat or something."

"Hey. If I have superpowers, there's nothing new about them."

Liam rolled his eyes at this, and stood, dusting himself off. He picked up the television's controller, and switched it from game to music, lowering the volume enough to maintain a conversation in the living room. Jeffrey then turned to Nathan and Annie, grinning. Nathan thought he seemed remarkably happy, for a dead man.

"Our little hero dude is awake!"

Nathan blinked, and had a quick glance towards Annie. He wasn't sure why, but he wanted to see her reaction at being called a hero. She just smiled softly at the tall dead man, before turning to Nathan. He had the familiar feeling that something was expected of him again, and decided that it was an answer to Jeffrey's statement.

"Uh, yeah."

Jeffrey chuckled. Liam sat on the couch, keeping his eyes on the screen, but the curious glances he kept stealing towards Nathan and Annie betrayed his interest. Eventually, Annie looked towards him, and he looked away toward his smartwatch.

"Should be just another half hour before the food gets here. I got beer, though, if your friend wants it."

Nathan didn't have time to consider the offer. Before he could say anything, Annie answered for him. "No, he doesn't. I'd be grateful if he could use your bath, though."

Liam turned his attention to Nathan, looking him up and down, and wrinkled his nose.

"Yeah. He looks like he hasn't had one in years. Towels are in the bathroom. It's that door."

Nathan frowned, starting to feel uncertain. The conversation was taking an unknown turn, and he wasn't sure he liked it. Annie turned to him, smiling, and motioned to the door that Liam had pointed to.

"Why don't you go have a bath, and we'll wait for you here."

Nathan looked over his shoulder at the direction where he was supposed to go, and then took a hesitant step toward it, before stopping and looking uncertainly at Annie. He almost asked his question, but then glanced at Jeffrey and Liam, who were both watching him, and the words stuck in his throat. Annie understood anyway, at least the question, if not the embarrassment. She had a second of disbelief and surprise, before shaking her head in a resigned fashion.

"You sit in water and wash yourself. With soap."

Liam's expression remained carefully neutral, but Jeffrey raised an amused eyebrow, still watching Nathan, who scratched the back of his head uncomfortably. There had been a decontamination room in the lab, which he thought was much like a shower, from what he'd heard of it. But he'd never had a bath before, and he didn't like the sound of it.

"Um... I'm fine. I'll just stay here and wait for the food."

Annie raised her eyebrows, but Liam made a disgusted face and spoke before she could.

"No way, dude. If you're going to be wearing my clothes and sleeping in my guest bed, you're gonna take a bath."

Jeffrey still seemed amused, but he nodded in approval, adding: "Yeah, man. You stink."

Nathan felt his cheeks heat, and he tried to glare at them, but found himself incapable of sustaining anyone's stare. "I do not!"

Jeffrey burst out laughing at this, and Annie and Liam shared a look, and said nothing, until Jeffrey finally spoke, standing. "All right, little man. Come on, I'll show you how it's done."

Nathan tried to protest, but Jeffrey was already leading him by the shoulder in the direction of the bathroom. Nathan let him, glowering at his feet, much too embarrassed to say anything.

The bathroom had a huge mirror on the right side, above the sink, in which Nathan stopped to stare at himself when he walked past it, completely fascinated.

This was the first time he'd ever really seen his reflection, other than in a spoon or a dirty window. He looked very different from what he had imagined. For one, he did look as dirty as the dirtiest people he had seen in Three Walls. His face had grime encrusted into it in places, making it look darker than it was. His hair wasn't shiny and silky like Liam's, or even Annie's, but seemed almost wet with grease. It was no wonder Annie had thought he looked sick, too: his eyes were sunken in, his cheeks were hollow, and it only seemed worse because of the downy stubble growing all over his chin and cheeks.

He stared at himself until he heard the sudden torrent coming out of the tub's faucet when Jeffrey turned on the tap. He jumped, startled, and turned to see the big man sitting on a toilet that was clean, white and unbroken, leaning over a bathtub that was equally white and unmarred, and large enough for two people to sit face to face comfortably.

Nathan stepped closer and looked over the edge of the tub suspiciously. The water did look clean, remarkably so, in fact; it was much cleaner than any water he'd had to drink in Three Walls, even rain water.

Jeffrey put his hand under the pouring water, and for an instant, Nathan thought he saw his happy-go-lucky expression make way to one of grief and dismay. But it was gone as soon as he saw it, and Jeffrey turned the smile back to him as he said:

"Hey man, can you come see if the water's all right? Seems my sense of touch isn't what it used to be."

Nathan crouched to immerse his fingers in the bath water. He pulled them out immediately with a cry of shock. "It's burning hot!"

Jeffrey nodded, and fiddled with the faucet. When Nathan put his hand back in the water it was finally better, and they watched the tub fill quietly for a few moments before Jeffrey broke the silence. "So, you've really never had a bath?"

Nathan shook his head again. Jeffrey simply shrugged, and stood to get a small piece of cloth, and a towel. He handed the washcloth to Nathan along with two plastic bottles he retrieved from the edge of the bath.

"You wet that bit, put that stuff on it, make it foam, and then you scrub yourself 'til you're the color you're supposed to be. This one's for washing your hair."

Nathan took the items and looked at the bath uncertainly as Jeffrey stopped the water. The large man raised an eyebrow at him. "Well, come on, dude, take off your clothes and get in!"

Nathan put the cloth and bottles down on the edge of the tub, and quickly got out of the clothes that were not his, leaving them on the floor. The water was an exquisite temperature; it warmed his whole body almost instantly, making him feel calm and content. He didn't think he'd ever had a physical sensation that was so pleasant. He closed his eyes, sighing happily, and leaned back against the wall of the tub.

"Feels pretty good, huh?" asked Jeffrey.

Nathan nodded, not bothering to answer, or even look at the other man. They stayed silent a while longer as Nathan enjoyed the warmth, but when the water started to cool, he followed the instructions he had been given and started to wash himself. Jeffrey looked at him from his seat on the toilet.

"So what's the story with you and that girl?"

"Annie? She's my friend."

"You said that."

The conversation stopped for a moment, because Nathan had to put his head under the water to wet his hair. It felt even better to have his whole body under the warm water at once, but he didn't like knowing that he couldn't breathe, so he didn't linger there. He started shampooing when he sat up again. The shampoo smelled wonderful, fresh and sweet, like nothing Nathan had smelled before.

"So... she says she's like a scientist, and she's been working on a project to... make herself alive again?"

Nathan turned and tilted his head to look at Jeffrey, but a drop of shampoo rolled into his eyes. "Ow!"

Jeffrey had a sheepish smile. "Oh, yeah, sorry. You might want to keep your eyes closed while you do that. That stuff stings."

"Thanks for the warning," grumbled Nathan, rubbing his eyes.

"So, anyway, she says you might be instrumental to her success."

"Well, I'm trying to help, anyways."

He had to put his head under the water again to rinse his hair. When he sat up again, Jeffrey was looking at him intently. Nathan frowned at him. "What?"

"You think you can help?"

"I dunno. Annie thinks so."

Nathan stood out of the now lukewarm water. It had turned brown, and even had small specs of dirt floating to the surface. Nathan remembered how clear it had been before he stepped in, and simply couldn't believe all that stuff had been on him. Jeffrey handed him the large blue towel so he could dry himself.

"But, if you can, you'll do it?" asked Jeffrey.

"Yes, of course."

"So, if you do it for her... I mean..."

Jeffrey's voice trailed off. Nathan removed the towel from his head so that he could look at him, and saw that the large man's expression somewhere between expectant and hesitant. Nathan finally understood what he had been driving at.

"Oh, well of course if we can do it, we'll do you, too."

Jeffrey grinned, relieved. "Great! You know, you're pretty cool, for such a grimy dude."

Nathan smiled, and dropped the towel to the floor, reaching for his borrowed clothes. After he had pulled them on, he noticed Jeffrey was examining him critically, and he frowned uncomfortably. "What?"

"You need a shave."

"A what?"

Jeffrey chuckled and started rummaging through the drawers under the sink. "Shave. It's when you get the hair off your face."

Jeffrey put a plastic plug on the hole at the bottom of the sink, and filled it with water, while Nathan touched his chin, looking at himself in the mirror. The hair there was golden and soft, but unevenly distributed on his face. He'd never given it much thought before.

"Why do I need to remove it?"

"'Cause you look scruffy. And weird. I'll show you how it's done. First, you wet your face."

The tall man followed his own advice, then handed him a black plastic razor. Nathan frowned at it and stood closer to Jeffrey, taking the strange object in his hand. Jeffrey took an aerosol can, shook it, turned it upside down, and squirted a dollop of shaving cream onto his palm. Then he handed the can to Nathan.

"Take some cream, and put it on your face like that."

Nathan started by splashing some water on his face, and then imitated Jeffrey, smearing sweet-smelling white foam all over his chin, neck, and under his nose.

"All right. Now you have to be careful when you do this. You want to press hard enough to get all the hair, but not too hard, or you might cut yourself."

Nathan watched attentively in the mirror as Jeffrey shaved the better part of his left cheek. They both looked funny with their foamy white beards, and Nathan found himself smiling. When he finally lifted the razor to his own face, his hand trembled slightly. He hated hurting himself. To his surprise, though, it went smoothly, and when he pulled it away, the line it had left was soft and free of hair. Jeffrey nodded his approval, smiling.

"All right. Rinse the blades in the water, and do the rest of your face."

He wiped his own face clean with a towel as Nathan continued to shave, slowly and carefully. It went very well until Nathan got to the awkward space between his chin and lower lip. When he dragged the razor there, he felt a sharp pain and pulled the razor away abruptly, hissing through his teeth. A tiny drop of blood was forming at the place where he'd hurt himself, mixing with the foam next to it. Jeffrey ripped a tiny piece of toilet paper and handed it to him.

"Stick that on there until you're done. It'll stop soon enough. Don't worry, it happens all the time."

Nathan stuck the little piece of paper to the cut, and resumed with even greater care than before. The bleeding had stopped when he was done, though, and he could rinse and wipe his face clean. He looked at himself in amazement. He hadn't thought such simple things could change someone's appearance so much.

His hair was almost dry by then. He saw that it was a dark blonde that was almost golden brown, the same color his beard had been. It almost reached his eyes; Nathan thought he'd be due to cut his hair soon. This was the only grooming he had ever really performed on himself, and only because it annoyed him to have hair in his eyes.

Jeffrey was rinsing the dirt away from the bathtub when he noticed Nathan was done. He looked him up and down, and nodded in satisfaction.

"Much better. Come on, I bet your food's here."

Jeffrey picked up the towel Nathan had used, threw it in a hamper by the door, and led them both back to the living room, where there was indeed an exotic smell. There were paper bags and cardboard containers on the table in front of the television. Liam was sitting on the floor next to it, eating, while Annie was staring at a small notebook on her lap. They both looked up, and Annie had a surprised smile. Jeffrey grinned at her and slapped Nathan's back amicably, making him stumble a little.

"What do you think? Looks good, doesn't he?"

Annie nodded in approval. "How do you feel, Nathan?"

Nathan smiled and looked at the food. He felt ravenous, though the bath had also relaxed him quite a bit, and he was starting to recognize the first signs of fatigue in his body.

"Good. Hungry. Where's my bag?"

Annie's smile faded, if only a little. "In the guest room. Looking for your stims?"

Nathan nodded, heading towards the door before she could say anything about how stims were bad for him. His bag was on the desk, intact. There was still no trace of his own clothes, though his pills were there, apparently untouched. He took one, and sat on the bed to wait until the effects kicked in before he went back to the living room, where Annie was explaining something to Jeffrey in a tone that was patient and just a bit hopeless.

"We were a large team. And there is really complex equipment involved. And some components that are hard to get."

94

He sat down on the floor next to Liam, who had finished eating and was now engrossed in a music performance on the huge television. Nathan looked at the different foods on the table. There were quite a lot of things to choose from, meats he couldn't identify, mixed with vegetables he had never set eyes on before, all swimming in sauces of various colors. Nathan tasted the red mixture. It was sweet, and bready, with little tiny bits of meat in the middle; he started eating with increasing appetite.

Jeffrey let out a frustrated sigh. "Well, what's out next move, then? How's this guy supposed to help? Do we make him swim the flux for more info?"

"He has already. That's not where we'll find the information we need. I only need a little more; I'm already far in my calculations, but am stumped. If I can just figure out where I went wrong last time I managed to experiment, I know I'm almost at a solution."

She retrieved the notebook she had been looking at from where it lay on the ground, and handed it to Jeffrey. Jeffrey took the notebook from Annie's hands, leafing through it.

"This is all my research from the past nineteen years," she said.

"Is that even writing? It looks like just a bunch of gibberish to me."

Annie rolled her eyes at him. "They're equations."

Jeffrey shook his head in resignation and handed the notebook to Nathan, who wiped his hands on his borrowed sweatpants hastily before taking it. The pages were deeply embossed with Annie's strong handwriting, and made an odd crackling sound as he turned them.

They were covered in arcane combinations of symbols of which Nathan had no comprehension. He stayed quiet a little while, turning the pages, fascinated with this object which contained so much knowledge and yet was so hopelessly out of his grasp. He had never learned how to read. He understood all

95

information as a computer did: virtually. At length, he looked up at Annie's hopeful eyes, and shook his head sadly.

"I'm sorry. I have no idea what this means. I can't really read anything when I'm not swimming."

She nodded, sighing. "I didn't think so. Well, looks like I'll have to think of something else."

Nathan took a spoonful of a mixture of some meat, nuts, and something that looked like sprouts. This one had a subtler taste that was neither sweet nor salty, but a little of both. The sprouts were surprisingly crunchy, and contrasted well with the wet texture of the other ingredients. Nathan let out a satisfied sigh as he chewed. He'd never had food this good before.

Jeffrey shrugged. "Well, someone's gotta have information somewhere."

Nathan swallowed the bite he had been chewing on so he could speak. "They had a lot of information on the computers at the warehouse."

He took a spoonful of a bright yellow meat. This one tasted sweet, and sharp at the same time, and he had another sigh of happiness before noticing that both Annie and Jeffrey were staring at him in mild shock.

"What?"

"You mean you actually found what we need?"

Nathan shrugged, starting to feel a bit defensive. "I dunno. I guess it could be. I didn't see."

"Well, did you take some files?"

"Well... no. ...I guess I was preoccupied."

They stared at him for a few more seconds, and Jeffrey burst out laughing, slapping his thighs. Nathan felt his cheeks heat a little.

"What?"

"Dude, for a smart guy, you don't seem to think ahead much."

CHAPTER 9

Annie and Jeffrey helped Liam clear away what was left of the food. Nathan went to retrieve Oliver from the guest room, powering him up as he made his way back to the floor in front of the couch, where he sat down and linked to the flux. He had tried sitting on the couch after his meal, and found that even though it was comfortable, he couldn't adopt the positions he was used to by sitting on the floor, and had opted for doing just that.

By the time Annie and Jeffrey joined him, minutes later, he had long found what he was looking for. Liam went to sit on another couch, remaining uninvolved, and yet obviously curious. Nathan turned Oliver around so that his screen faced them; it wasn't like he needed it, anyway. "Here they are."

He had to close his eyes to make sure he was bringing up the right information on the screen. Speaking while swimming was something he'd never tried, and he found it surprisingly difficult.

He found the maps, and displayed them on the screen tiling the windows so they could be seen simultaneously. He had never preoccupied himself with screen displays before, and it required almost as much of his concentration as speaking.

"This is the warehouse. I'll assume we know enough about that one already. This is an office building in Inner Circle"

As he named the places, red circles appeared on the corresponding map locations. He enlarged one window, which showed satellite pictures of the office building.

Like every other building in Inner Circle, it was incredibly tall and sleek. It looked like it was made entirely of glass, and the whole structure seemed to shine. It had three skywalks connecting it to its neighbors; Inner Circle had a vast, complex network of these skywalks, connecting building to building on the higher floors, so much so that one could virtually cross all of it without ever setting foot outside.

"It's on the tenth level," continued Nathan, making the virtual visit engine twist so they could see around the building. "It's right in the middle of Inner Circle, but there are a lot of ways to get in."

Jeffrey frowned and pointed to two other dots on the map, a hundred miles from the city, one right at the edge of the crater, at the limit of tolerable radiation, and one inside of it. There wasn't much there, just two small villages, and then, the lab.

"What's that?"

Nathan licked his lips, and hesitated before replying. "That's their lab. But I don't think we should go."

Jeffrey blinked. "Why not? Obviously I don't mean the one in the crater, but what about the one outside of it? I got a cabin not too far from there. We could hide out there and have a little vacation."

"It's big, and they do their research there, so it's probably well-guarded," lied Nathan. He was trying to think about another convincing argument for them not to go to that place, but Annie spoke up before he could, and he opened his eyes to look at her as she spoke.

"Nathan's right. It's too dangerous out there, and too secluded. We'd be found right away." Annie and Jeffrey were both watching Oliver's screen attentively. Annie had a little smile when she looked up at Nathan. "You really did your homework. When did you look all this up?"

He shrugged, letting go of the jack and the flux to ease his speech. "When you disappeared. I knew what to look for, so... yeah."

Her smile widened, and she lowered her face to the screen as if to hide it. "So you really did come to rescue me?"

Nathan nodded. His plan had been ill-conceived, and it had only succeeded because of his miraculous encounter of Jeffrey. He wasn't sure he wanted to take the merit for it, but it did seem to please her.

She smiled warmly at him, touching his forearm lightly with her cold fingers. "Thank you," she said.

Nathan felt his cheeks heat and heart beat a little faster. He cleared his throat, looking away, wondering what was wrong with him. "Um," he said, "from what I could tell from the computers at the warehouse, I'm pretty sure the whole company's on the same network."

Jeffrey nodded seriously, if enthusiastically. "So we can go to any of the three and we'll have access to the others?"

"Should be."

Jeffrey leaned in to look at the screen closer. "We shouldn't go back to the warehouse. They'll be prepared, this time, and they already know how to handle ghouls. The lab in the crater..."

Nathan shook his head vigorously, interrupting him. "We can't go there," he repeated anxiously.

Annie's features contracted slightly in that thinking expression she had when she was figuring something out. Nathan couldn't be sure if she would have said something then, because Jeffrey went on almost as if he hadn't been interrupted. "Then I guess our best bet is Inner Circle."

Nathan frowned. He would have rather gone back to the warehouse, whether or not they expected them. It had seemed very poorly guarded.

"Isn't that going to be dangerous? I mean, we'll stand out and be spotted, won't we?"

Jeffrey snorted. "Speak for yourself. I work there. Well, I should say, I used to. Now I guess I can go be dead there."

Liam chuckled, shaking his head. Annie raised an incredulous eyebrow at Jeffrey. "You work in Inner Circle? That's serious money."

"Well, I used to live there, but we moved here because it made us a lot less visible." Jeffrey grinned, obviously expecting something, then looked at them in amused confusion. "Really? I mean, I know you guys have had a lot on your mind, but you still haven't figured out who I am?" Nathan and Annie shared a puzzled look, and Jeffrey chuckled. "That's refreshing, anyway."

Liam smirked at Jeffrey. "See what I told you before? I'm the cute one that plays bass. No one even knows you're there."

Jeffrey glared at him, but very little of his anger was genuine. "Shut up, douche, if they don't know who I am, they don't know who you are, either." He shot a glance at Annie looking slightly worried. "Right?"

She only shook her head. "We really don't know either of you."

It's was Liam's turn to look incredulous, and mildly shocked. "We're Zombies Eating Tomatoes!"

Nathan and Annie looked at each other, and turned puzzled expressions towards Liam, who put down the beer he'd been drinking. "The rock band! You know, *Rubbing my banana?*"

Nathan blinked, his confusion deepening. "Rubbing your what?"

Jeffrey started laughing again, but Liam insisted, still full of disbelief. "The song! It's our hit single! Doesn't number one on the flux for three consecutive weeks mean anything anymore?"

Liam started humming a few bars from a song Nathan had never heard before. His voice was slightly off, and the humming hardly even sounded like anything. Jeffrey ran out of breath to laugh with, which didn't stop him: he just kept right on shaking with unheard laughter, doubled over, and holding his stomach. Liam glowered at him, red-faced, standing up.

"Shut up!"

Jeffrey waved a hand to signal his incapacity to stop his hilarity. Liam rolled his eyes, looked back at Nathan, who was looking at Oliver again, and Annie, who simply smiled politely. Liam picked up his beer to drink a deep sip, and then put it back down and stood.

"I'm going out."

He walked to the door without another look behind. Jeffrey calmed his laughter and took a deep breath to speak. "Awe, come on, Liam, don't be so sensitive."

Liam grabbed a coat from the wardrobe next to the entrance and put it on. "I need a real drink. I'll be back later."

He slammed the door behind him when he walked out. Jeffrey shrugged and turned to Nathan and Annie. "Don't worry about him. He's going through a lot, and..."

He trailed off. Annie finished for him, her voice soft. "And not everyone has the same ability to deal with their lives being disrupted. Or with large and potentially permanent changes in loved ones."

Jeffrey shrugged noncommittally, saying nothing. Nathan wasn't sure what they were talking about, but he could feel the silence becoming heavy and uncomfortable, so he said something. "So you really are famous?"

Jeffrey picked up the half empty beer can that Liam had left behind, looking at it longingly, nodding. "Yeah. We hit it big a couple months ago. But don't worry; we're still the same low-lives we used to be before."

He brought the can to his lips, and Annie leaned forward to stop him, putting a hand on his forearm. "Don't drink that. You can't digest anymore. You have no idea the trouble it is to get stuff out of your stomach again. And if you don't, it rots there, and draining human life won't help at all with that."

Jeffrey sighed, putting the beer down. "Yeah. Well. Anyway." He seemed to look around for something to use to change the subject, and his eyes fell on Oliver. "Right! So we better make up our plan. We raiding this Inner Circle building, or what?"

Annie nodded. "It does seem like the best idea."

Jeffrey looked up at Nathan, leaning forward in his seat, putting his elbows on his knees. "So what do we know about it, anyway?"

Nathan blinked, and looked down at Oliver, though he already knew he'd told them everything he thought was relevant about the building. "Uh, what else do you need to know?"

"Everything we can! What else is in the building? What are the exits and entrances? How many guards are there, and at what times? How strong is the security?"

Nathan sighed and pulled Oliver onto his lap. "All right, give me some time, and I can probably find out all that."

Jeffrey grinned and stood. "Well, get cracking, dude! You're my only hope of ever drinking beer again!"

Annie rolled her eyes almost imperceptibly. She and Jeffrey both watched Nathan for a while after he had turned Oliver back on, plugged him in, and linked with him. Jeffrey eventually turned on the television at a low volume, and started flipping through the channels, eventually settling on the same music channel Liam had.

It took a long time for Nathan to find everything they needed, since he couldn't directly access the company's databases. He had to rely on outside information, and so had to double and triple-check everything to make sure what he got was right. He wasn't exactly sure how long it was that he spent swimming, though he was aware that at some point, Liam came back, and he and Jeffrey disappeared somewhere together.

When he finally let go of the jack, Nathan's whole body felt numb and heavy; it was pitch black outside. He rubbed his eyes, yawned and stretched. Annie looked up at him when he stood. She was still sitting on the couch, next to him. Jeffrey had reappeared, and sat a little further away, fiddling with one of the guitars.

Annie put down the notebook she had been scribbling in. "How goes the search?"

"I'm all done. I don't exactly have everything, but I have everything I can get from the flux."

"That's great!"

She grinned at him. Did she seem impressed? Nathan found himself smiling. Sleep was starting to creep into his limbs, slowly, and he stretched again, this time reaching for his bag. Annie watched him, and shook her head slightly in disapproval when she saw him retrieve the small plastic bottle.

"It's very late, Nathan. If you're tired, you should sleep."

He snorted. He had thought that rescuing her might at least make her stop telling him what to do, but it seemed he was out of luck for that one. At least, she didn't press the issue, and stayed quiet as he opened the bottle. There were only two more pills left, and he found himself hesitating. The fatigue was strong, and though he could worry about refilling later, when he was out, he wasn't sure where he would go to find it.

Jeffrey put his guitar back on its stand and got up to walk to the couch, looking at Nathan expectantly all the way. "You're really something, man, but the lady's right, you oughta get some sleep. I'm sure there's a lot of time before we have to act."

Nathan shook his head, stuffing the pills back into his bag without taking one. "I should stay awake a while. We might as well take the time to formulate a real plan. I mean, there's probably something I haven't thought of, and I'll need to do more research, and if we wait until I sleep, I won't have time."

Jeffrey shrugged dismissively and slung himself over the back of the couch to sit on it.

"Suit yourself. I'm good to stay up. I haven't slept since I died." He looked at Annie then, raising an eyebrow. "Do you sleep?"

She shook her head. "I haven't slept in nineteen years."

Nathan raised his eyebrows. Who was she to tell him to sleep, then? He shook his head and put down Oliver on the

103

table, so he could stretch his legs and help the blood flow return to his feet. He then turned the screen towards Annie and Jeffrey, putting his fingers on one of Oliver's jacks to link with him so he could present what he'd found.

The Genome office was on the tenth floor of the building. Starr Planetary Holdings occupied the lower levels, and the floors separating Genome from the bank were occupied by law offices. It would be difficult getting to the office from the ground floor through all this. Fortunately, this wasn't the case for some of the skywalks connecting the building to others that surrounded it, on the fourth, eighth, and twelfth floor.

The ones on the fourth and twelfth floor led to a megaplex which was located right next to it. The megaplex was a huge, twelve floor commercial and entertainment center; its top five floors were theaters. The third skywalk led from the Starr Planetary building to a smaller condo tower.

Nathan had no details about security systems or personnel. He did know there were high-security metal gates separating the megaplex from the tower, but physical barriers were almost nonexistent when it came to the condo tower.

His mouth was dry and pasty from talking by the time he let go of the jack. Jeffrey and Annie were both frowning thoughtfully, their white eyes glued to Oliver's screen, which had been displaying what Nathan had been able to find of blueprints, satellite pictures and other relevant information as he spoke. He tried clearing his throat, but it only pushed him into a fit of coughing, and he reached for the can of beer Liam had left there that afternoon, taking a large gulp of its contents. He made a face as it went down his throat; it was bitter and warm, and it tasted awful.

Jeffrey was the first to speak, looking at Nathan intently, and waving his index finger at the screen vaguely. "These security gates, can you get them open?"

"As long as they have electronic locks, it shouldn't be a problem."

"And the cameras?"

"If we find them before they see us, I can deactivate them."

"Then I think I've got a plan."

Annie and Nathan turned to look at him. He was quiet for a moment, and then nodded decisively. "We go to the megaplex, we find a place to hide until after closing, and we get to the other tower from there."

Nathan frowned worriedly. "At night?"

"Well, yeah! We can't do it while everyone is around."

Nathan nodded, anxiety knotting his stomach. This new breaking into buildings habit was one he hoped wouldn't last too long. Annie rubbed her chin thoughtfully, looking at Oliver's screen, and turned to Jeffrey.

"Wouldn't it be easier to come from the condo tower?"

He shook his head and pointed at Nathan with his thumb. "We've got a technopath, and where there's big steel impenetrable doors, there's usually no guards. It's the least likely place for a break-in, so they won't be expecting us to come from there."

Annie sighed. "I suppose you're right. When should we go?"

Jeffrey shrugged. "We can go later tomorrow. A couple hours before they close. It'll give us a chance to prepare."

Nathan frowned. "Prepare? What do we need to prepare?"

"Well, we should get you some clothes that fit you. Something that doesn't look like someone else's cast-offs. We'll stand out a lot less that way."

Nathan looked down at himself, confused. He was still wearing Liam's sweatpants and t-shirt. They were, without a doubt, the cleanest, newest clothes he had ever worn. He didn't dare ask what was wrong with them, though: he thought he looked enough like an ignorant idiot without adding to it at every chance he got. Annie nodded her agreement.

"I think it's the best idea we have. You're sure you want to do this, Nathan?"

He blinked, surprised. The question hadn't occurred to him. Once it had been suggested that they go, he had taken it for a fact that they would. "Well, of course. I mean, we have to, don't we?"

"You don't have to. Jeffrey and I can go alone."

"Well, of course I do! We need that information, and I was too much of an idiot to get it from the other place. Besides, I'm the one who can get to it the fastest."

Annie smiled, but kept on insisting. "It'll be dangerous."

Nathan shrugged, trying to appear braver than he felt. "Getting you out of the warehouse was dangerous. I managed that."

Jeffrey grinned. "You sure did. Besides, this time, you'll have our help, and an actual plan."

Nathan shifted. The thought of going in that building made him sick to his stomach with fear. He knew with absolute certainty that he wanted to be nowhere near that place. Yet, at the same time, he wanted desperately not to be afraid, to be ready to enter that building, to do what was necessary, to do everything that was necessary to make Annie alive again. He concentrated on that feeling, and when he looked up at her and nodded, his resolve was stronger that it had been before.

"I want to do this, Annie. I know I can."

CHAPTER 10

Nathan woke up. He was lying on his side, on black leather; he could feel a wet spot around his mouth where he had drooled. He sat up abruptly, wiping his mouth with the back of his hand, and analyzed his surroundings.

He was still in Liam's living room, lying on the couch which faced the television. The room was dark, and he was alone. Someone had put a blanket over him. Oliver lay on the small coffee table, his screen dark and lifeless. Nathan reached out to grab him, his heart jumping to his throat, but he had only left him unplugged again, and Oliver had run out of battery power.

He heard laughter coming from the kitchen. The sound was so unfamiliar that it startled Nathan to his feet, and he was standing there with Oliver clutched tightly to his chest for a few seconds before he recognized Annie's voice. He put Oliver down on the coffee table again and slowly made his way to the kitchen.

Yellow light spilled out of the doorway. Nathan could hear Annie and Jeffrey speaking softly on the other side, their voices hushed. He paused, and tried to listen to what they were saying, but he couldn't make out the words. Whatever it was, it seemed they were having a lot of fun, and he felt left out. He could hear them laughing again when he walked in.

They were sitting at the table, leaning over it towards each other so they could talk at the lowest volume possible. They turned simultaneously when they saw Nathan walk in, their identical white, dead eyes meeting his own. Annie smiled brightly at him. She had let her hair down, and the dark mass of curls framed the heart-shaped face perfectly, making the deathly pallor of her complexion almost pretty.

"Nathan! You're awake! Did you sleep well?"

Nathan frowned at her suspiciously. "You didn't drug me again, did you?"

Her smile melted into a frown, and he knew that she hadn't; he felt bad for mentioning it.

"No, I didn't," she said. "You just fell asleep while you were swimming. I brought you a blanket and we let you sleep, that's all."

"Oh."

Nathan sat down at the table, glancing at Jeffrey before turning to Annie again. "What were you talking about?"

She shrugged and stood, walking to the refrigerator. "Nothing important. Would you like something to eat?"

"Sure!"

She opened the door of the black fridge, peering inside. It was very sleek and modern, and, like everything else in the kitchen, had the air of not being used very often. Nathan turned his attention back to Jeffrey, and found the dead man watching him with a curious expression. Nervous again, he coughed and took another look around.

"Where's Liam? Did he go out again?"

Jeffrey looked away, frowning, as though this were an uncomfortable subject. "He's in bed. It's still the middle of the night."

Annie brought a plastic plate to the microwave, and shoved it inside, punching in a few keys. "You know, Nathan, most people spend their entire night sleeping. Every night."

Nathan considered this for a second. "You don't. You never sleep. Except for that time I got you from the lab."

She stared at him, expressionless, until the microwave oven let out a long beep. She stayed quiet and motionless for a little while longer before retrieving the plastic container from the oven and bringing it to him.

"I can't sleep, Nathan. Neither can Jeffrey. I wish I could, trust me. Humans need their food and sleep to get the energy they need to walk and talk and repair their bodies. Ghouls don't."

She sat back on her chair, putting the plastic container in front of Nathan. There was a mixture of a few of the meats and vegetables they had ordered the day before. Red, yellow and brown swirled together in the container, the various smells wafting together towards his nose to become something new, sweet, tangy and delicious. He picked up the fork and started filling his mouth as she went on.

"Our bodies work differently. We can only get our energy by stealing it from living beings. It's how we repair them, and how we keep ourselves from decomposing. As for what happened in the lab... well, they did all sorts of experiments on me, and, honestly, I just thought they'd killed me for good this time. When you woke me..." She shook her head, and shrugged. "I don't know what it was. But I can tell you it wasn't sleep. I can't sleep. I've tried often."

Nathan nodded. All this sleep talk was starting to make him tired again, and he reached in his pocket for the small plastic bottle. The few pills left in it made a distressingly light rattling sound as he opened it. There were only two of them left. He had no idea how to get that kind of a drug outside of Three Walls, and Annie had made it clear they should not risk going back there, broad daylight or no.

Sighing, he closed the bottle without taking a pill, and looked up to see Annie and Jeffrey still watching him, the first one amused, the other curious. Nathan looked down at his meal, but the sudden knot in his stomach had taken his appetite. He just needed to find out as soon as possible where he could get some stims in Inner Circle. He wasn't going to ask, though, not Annie, not about this. It wasn't that he didn't trust her. In fact, he wasn't sure why he felt that way at all, but he felt very strongly about it.

She didn't say anything as she watched him put the bottle back in his pocket. After a few seconds, she smiled at him, though he thought she seemed slightly worried.

"Are you sure you'll be all right to do what we planned to do tonight?"

"Of course!"

But as she mentioned it, the knot in his stomach tightened, though he struggled to keep his smile. For some reason, it seemed important that she not know how scared he really felt.

She seemed satisfied: she nodded once, and waved encouragingly at his food. "Eat, then. You have a big day ahead of you. You'll need all your strength."

The rest of the night was particularly difficult for Nathan. Without his usual high dose of stimulants, he found himself nodding off more often than not, which wasn't helped at all by the fact that his companions grew quiet every time his eyes started to close.

At long last, though, the sun rose, its light helping to keep Nathan awake. A few hours after that, Liam emerged from his room, his face puffy and his eyes barely open, his hair standing up on his head in many different directions. After a few cups of coffee, Liam turned out to be awake and in a good enough mood to keep Nathan awake too.

Liam seemed to be just as lacking in conversational skills as Nathan was, so he offered to teach him how to play one or two video games. At first, Nathan tried to play the game like he interacted with everything else that had programming, by linking with it and trying to swim. To his great surprise, however, this didn't work at all.

What was projected on the screen was much more complex than a simple image file, and there was too much information at once for Nathan's mind to analyze. He had no choice but to use his hands instead of his mind, and fumbled uselessly with both the controller and the body part, the one as unfamiliar as the other to him.

All of this kept Liam in a fairly good mood, as he managed to win game after game. It didn't bother Nathan at all, and even when Liam was dancing and taunting him with his every victory, he was glad for the distraction from the stress of having to go without stims, or the sense of impending doom that his evening plans brought.

When Jeffrey came to inform them that it was time to go, all of Nathan's worries returned with full force, and his legs felt like they would buckle under him with every step as they made their way down to the parking lot under Liam's building. He finally took one of his only two remaining pills in the car, as Liam drove them into Inner Circle.

Where there were obvious differences between Outer Circle and Three Walls, Inner Circle was a whole world of its own. As they got nearer, the buildings grew taller, and sleeker. Above their heads, a dense network of streets, electrified railways and skywalks formed what looked like an enormous spider web that nearly blocked out the sun. In fact, several of the lower level streets needed artificial lighting even during the day.

Everything Nathan could see was brilliant, new, and looked almost seamless. Even the streets were smooth, though the circulation was much heavier than in Outer Circle. At first, most of the cars and trucks they encountered were hitter patrols, but the deeper in they went, the less hitters they saw. There were people everywhere, filling the sidewalks and skywalks, dressed in brightly colored, brand-new clothes of all styles and fashions.

Liam slowed the car in front of the megaplex. The building seemed as wide as an entire neighborhood, and was at least large enough to contain the entire block where Nathan's squat had been, yet it rose high against the sky, its dark glass structure connected to other buildings and streets on many different levels. It had huge doors on the ground floor at semi-regular intervals, with brightly lit, colorful signs displaying the name of the store to which they led.

Liam chose the least busy corner to stop and let them out, between two entrances. Still there were quite a few onlookers when the three of them climbed out of the car. Nathan noticed the passersby were giving him strange looks, and wondered why.

He heard Jeffrey speaking, and turned to see him crouching beside the passenger door, talking to Liam through the open window. Annie was standing, looking up at the tall building and the network of passageways overhead. She had relinquished her lab coat, and stuffed it in her bag, so she wouldn't look so conspicuous. Under it, she wore a frayed turtleneck that must have been black a long time ago, and faded blue jeans. Her clothes looked clean despite their obvious age; Nathan found himself wondering how long she'd really had them.

With her lab coat off, Nathan noticed more curves to Annie's body than he had imagined. She was leaning on her right leg, her left knee slightly bent, her right hip propped up, accentuating the pleasant turn of her waist. Nathan became aware that he was staring at the same time he noticed that she was looking at him, one of her eyebrows arched high over the rim of her sunglasses, her lips stretched in a slight, amused smile.

Nathan felt his face heat, and his heart pound harder in his chest. He cleared his throat and directed his attention to Jeffrey, who was walking back toward them. He clapped his hand on Nathan's shoulder with a grin. "Ready, man?"

Nathan shrugged, and Annie nodded, turning her smile toward the large man. "Yes! Let's start by getting Nathan some clothes."

He frowned as he followed her towards the door. "I still don't see anything wrong with the ones I have on now."

Annie looked down at his sweatpants before she walked through the door. The cuffs had been rolled up to keep him from tripping, and they were so baggy that Annie had had to

112

double-knot the drawstring so they wouldn't fall off Nathan's waist. "They're too big. You look like a clown."

"A what?"

She chuckled, waving dismissively with her hand. "Never mind."

The megaplex had to be the cleanest, brightest place that Nathan had ever seen, cleaner even than the lab had been in. The black, gray-speckled stone floors were so polished that he could see his reflection in it, as though he was walking on some great dark mirror.

There was also glass everywhere; Nathan had never seen so much of it in one place before. The shops had walls and doors made of it, and not only was none of it broken, but all of it was clean and brilliant.

The stores themselves were bursting full of fascinating, colorful things. Nathan wanted to stop at all of them. He had loved going to the dump to rummage; finding new things to bring back to his squat and play with had been one of his favorite activities. But there were so many more things here, with the great exception that every single one was clean and useable, and Nathan didn't have to dig through a pile of rotting gray sludge to get to them.

Annie didn't let him stop anywhere, at first. She led him by pressing her fingers on his arm gently, looking around, her brow furrowed. It had to be hard to see in the dim light with her sunglasses. She went into a few stores, but they only seemed to cater to women. After a few unsuccessful tries, Jeffrey finally decided to lead them to a store called *Rock Shack*, which he swore would be perfect.

It was large, and a lot less decorated than the other stores. The clothes in it seemed almost drab compared to what Nathan had seen so far, mostly in varying shades of black and blue. They were perfectly clean and a bit stiff to the touch, like they were new, but they looked a bit worn anyway. Most of the pants were faded and ripped, though when Nathan examined them closer, he saw that there was sewing around the tears to keep them from spreading further.

Nathan turned a puzzled expression to Jeffrey after he had thoroughly examined a pair of jeans, the legs of which had a series of horizontal tears, all perfectly aligned, centered, and of the same length.

"Are these new or old?"

He heard Annie try to suppress a laugh, and turned to see her hide her smile behind her hand. Jeffrey turned to look at him, appearing surprised but a bit sad at the same time, like he couldn't believe what he was hearing. "Of course they're new! Why would you think they're not?"

Nathan squinted at the jeans. "They've got holes in them."

"Well...!" Jeffrey turned to Annie for some support, but saw that her shoulders were shaking with suppressed laughter. "It's a style!" He turned back toward Nathan, his expression almost pleading. "It's cool!"

Nathan shrugged and looked around. "Can we try and find stuff that hasn't got so many holes in it? I don't like to be cold."

Jeffrey threw his hands up in the air. "Fine! I'll find you pants. What size are you, anyway?"

Nathan blinked, confused, and held his hands about a foot from one another. "About this wide?"

Jeffrey's expression remained neutral, but it took him a few seconds to answer. "Right. You guys look for pants. I'll find you shirts."

He turned around and disappeared between two racks of black shirts with colorful band names printed on them. Nathan could still see the top of his head bobbing over the clothes. He watched him go, and turned toward Annie, unsure. "Did I make him mad?"

She smiled and started to walk towards a rack of pale cargo pants, letting Nathan catch up to her. "I don't think so. He's got a lot on his mind, you know."

Nathan considered this a second. "Did you know him from before?"

She stopped, looking at him with a quizzical smile. "Whatever made you think that?"

"Well, you seem to get along really well."

She resumed her leisurely pace, shrugging again. She remained silent until she reached the rack, and started looking through its contents. "He's nice. And easy to talk to. Beside which, we have a lot in common."

"Because you're dead?"

She looked up at him sharply, and then had a quick glance around herself to make sure no one had heard. The store was busy, but not crowded, and they seemed to be alone in their corner. She shook her head and went back to looking at the pants.

"Among other things."

Nathan sighed and turned to find Jeffrey, though he couldn't see the tall man anywhere. "What other things?"

She shrugged with her left shoulder, pulling out a pair of green pants with her right hand. She held them by the hanger in front of Nathan's waist, pursing her lips, a critical expression on her face. "Things... he reads, a bit. We have similar tastes in fiction."

She hung the pants over her left forearm, and resumed going through the rack. Nathan glared at his feet. He felt something strangely close to anger, and couldn't explain why. He just suddenly wished he had something, anything, in common with Annie. Something better than what Jeffrey had.

When he looked up again, he spotted Jeffrey heading back their way, holding three or four black shirts over his arm. "Look, buddy! I found you the perfect shirts!"

He held one up by the shoulders for Nathan to see. On the chest was printed a large, colorful illustration of two ghouls. They were all wearing studded leather coats, and their faces were grotesquely misshapen and a sickly shade of green. Their mouths were red with the juice from the tomatoes they were eating, dripping down their chins and all over their chests. The ghoul in the top left corner had crazy dreadlocks which stood up in all directions, and the one at the bottom had short, curly black hair.

Nathan frowned down at the drawing. "What's that?"

"It's one of our official shirts!"

Jeffrey caught the wrists of the shirt's long sleeves in either hand, and flipped it to show Nathan the back. The sleeves and the back had a word each printed on them in bold, square red letters, so that when he held the sleeves at a right angle to the rest of the shirt, the words formed an expression. Nathan frowned at it.

"What's it say?"

"'Zombies eating tomatoes', of course!"

Nathan smiled, thinking about the dreadlocked ghoul printed on the front. Even as a real ghoul, Jeffrey looked much better than that. "Oh! Your band! They sell that here?"

"Of course they do! I told you man, we're famous!"

Jeffrey shoved the rest of the shirts in Nathan's arms, grinning. Annie did the same with her pants, and led Nathan to a small stall where she made him not only try on every piece of clothing they had picked out, but also come out of the stall wearing them so he could parade for her while she looked at him critically before giving her approval. Nathan didn't protest all the while, though he thought she was making fun of him again.

She had insisted he buy four shirts and two pairs of pants, even though he couldn't understand what he would do with more clothes than he could wear all at once. He had to wear the shirt Jeffrey had picked for him and a new pair of green cargo pants, because Annie had thrown away his old clothes while he was changing.

Jeffrey led them to the third basement of the megaplex, where there seemed to be only food vendors. There were so many different places with so many different smells that Nathan didn't know what to do. He wanted to try everything there was, but he knew that even if he did manage to get only one bite from each place, he would be full before he had gone through half.

Annie must have noticed his hesitation, because after only a few short seconds of standing with no obvious indicator that Nathan would make a choice, she turned to Jeffrey with a smile. "It's been too long for me to really remember what things taste like. What do you recommend?"

"Hmm..."

Jeffrey looked around at the stalls, and apparently spotted one he liked at the far end. He took Nathan by the shoulder and started leading him to it enthusiastically.

"That little place over there makes great curry. It's some kind of Asian. Do you like curry?"

Nathan had no idea what curry was, but when they got to the green and yellow stall, the smell made his mouth water. What Jeffrey ordered for him was a light yellow, and served on top of white rice. The flavor was like nothing he'd ever had before. The meat was fresh, tender, and spicy enough to sting his tongue. It was balanced perfectly by the bland flavor of the rice, which eased the burn, and the spices made his chest feel warm.

They sat at a table while he ate, Annie and Jeffrey watching him in silence, as they usually did. As he scraped the last of the food from the bottom of the Styrofoam container, he thought about the two old, dented cans of beans he still carried in his bag. He couldn't believe he had thought that stuff was so good when he had first come to Three Walls. It was much better than the food at the lab, but what he had tasted since he had met Jeffrey made him realize all the wonderful possibilities of taste he had been missing out on until now.

He sighed in satisfaction when he was done, and dropped the plastic fork he had been using in the now empty container.

Annie was watching him, smiling, leaning her head in her hand. "Was that good?"

He nodded, somehow unwilling to admit just how good. Jeffrey glanced at the clock on the commercial display screen.

"The megaplex will close in an hour. We should get going."

CHAPTER 11

The empty bathroom echoed Nathan's sigh as he checked the time on Oliver once again. They had elected to wait in the bathrooms, hiding in stalls until one hour after closing time. As he needed Oliver to be functional later on, he could not use him to connect to the flux, which meant the hours he had to remain hidden, still and quiet inside the stall could not be spent doing anything else than waiting, and dreading the moments to come.

Being alone with his thoughts quickly became so unbearable that he actually started to look forward to the moment when he would finally be breaking into the Genome offices, just so he could be doing something. He tried to resist as long as he could, but after about an hour, the craving was so bad he was about to pull all the hair from his head, and he finally gave in and took his last stim. It was another eternity after that until Jeffrey finally knocked on the wall separating their stalls to signal that the time had come.

They had chosen the toilets on the twelfth floor as their hiding place. There were fewer cameras on that floor, since it was mostly occupied by 3D theaters and there were a lot less things to steal. Though separate, the men's and women's bathrooms exited through the same wide opening. Annie wasn't there yet, so Jeffrey waited for her in the common exit while Nathan snuck his way down the hall to take out the first security camera.

It was located in a corner of the tiny hall which led from the theaters to the bathrooms, and looked out at the entrance booth for the theaters. It was high, and out of Nathan's reach, but there were arcade games under it, and so Nathan climbed on top of a life-sized plastic replica of a motorcycle to lay his hands on the diminutive camera. He closed his eyes and concentrated.

Here, too, the cameras were networked; he was able to disable them the same way he had when he rescued Annie. He wanted to shout with joy as he hopped down from the motorcycle's seat. It was almost too easy; their path was clear all the way to the skywalk that would take them to the Starr Planetary building, where the Genome offices were located. When he was back on the ground, he noticed that Annie had emerged from her hiding place and was now speaking with Jeffrey. He waved to get their attention, and they joined him quietly. Jeffrey eyed the camera suspiciously. He and Annie had taken off their sunglasses to better see in the gloom.

"Did you manage to take it out?"

"I managed the whole network. We don't have anything to worry about until we get to the security doors."

Jeffrey frowned and chewed on his lips. He seemed dissatisfied with Nathan's answer. "What is it?"

"Well, won't they think it's suspicious that their whole network's out of order?'

Nathan shook his head. "I used a power surge, and that's all it'll look like. I don't think we need to worry about it."

"Still, when you open the doors, won't they figure it out?"

Annie clicked her tongue irritably, interrupting them. "It doesn't matter. We can't worry about that anymore. Let's not waste the precious time we have left."

Jeffrey nodded reluctantly, and Nathan turned to lead them to the skywalk. They walked between the theaters on a quiet carpeted hall, between theater entrances, passing what seemed like a smaller version of the huge food court they had eaten at earlier. Everything was now closed, of course: the stalls had been locked with metal shutters and there were only a few lights remaining on. Nathan grew nervous as they made their way to the pair of steel doors which led to the skywalk, adorned only with an elaborate electronic lock on the right side.

Nathan stared at the lock uncertainly for what felt like a very long time before laying his left hand on it. It was a bit more complex a lock then the ones he had encountered in the Outer Circle warehouse, but to Nathan, it was all the better. The more programming there was to a gadget, the more complex a dialogue he was able to establish with it, and usually, this also meant there were many ways to accomplish his goals. After a few seconds, the little light on the panel switched to green, and the door started to slowly pull itself open.

He turned to the others. "It's done."

"Good. Let's go," said Annie.

Nathan watched Annie as she stepped towards the opening that was forming between the doors. There was something grim about the expression on her face, and it scared him a little. She cursed when she was halfway through, and withdrew right away, ducking behind the wall turning an annoyed glance at Nathan.

"There's a camera on the other side of the walkway. It's looking straight at the door!"

Nathan leaned into the opening to look, and his heart sank. There was a camera, exactly like she said. Unless they were incredibly lucky and the guard in charge of looking at the screen was asleep or absent, he would be seen on his way to it. There was nothing else to do; he ran down the skywalk to the camera, hoping that if he hurried, he could go unnoticed.

When he got to the camera, he didn't even take time to catch his breath before climbing up the side window and disabling it. He finally slumped down to the ground then, breathing hard, as Jeffrey and Annie caught up to him. "Did you get it?"

"Yeah, it's all good."

"Were you able to tell if we'd been seen?"

Nathan shook his head. "No. Sorry. I can't tell if someone's watching the monitor. There wasn't an alarm that I could feel anywhere, though."

"I suppose that's all right. Can you open this door?"

He turned to look at the metal gate on this side of the skywalk. It was identical to the one on the megaplex side, thick and with no handles, complete with its own electronic lock. Nathan's hand trembled when he lay his fingers on the lock. He wished he had more stims; this was starting to be more reckless and dangerous than he had bargained for.

The door unlocked easily, and this time Annie was more careful, stepping to the side as the steel gates slid open. She peered through them before walking in to where they led, which was a short, wide hallway, at the end of which was a small, empty booth and three security turnstiles. Annie and Jeffrey were tall enough to jump them, but Nathan had to crawl underneath to get through.

They then found themselves facing a spacious, oval-shaped lobby. At one end was a row of elevators, while facing it was a long, elegant desk which echoed the shape of the lobby, placed under an elaborate golden company logo set in the wall.

Nathan hurried to the desk; there was a computer there. He turned it on, and had to wait for it to boot before he linked with it. It took him only a few seconds to find what he was looking for. He was still a little out of breath as he spoke.

"It's not linked with the Genome systems. We have to get to their offices. But I found a map of the building, I think I can get us there."

Annie nodded, folding her arms. She looked like she was thinking hard for a moment, then she nodded again, but more to herself, this time.

"We've gone too far to turn back now. Can you work the elevators?"

Nathan shrugged. "If they've got a computer, I guess."

"Then let's go!"

Nathan rushed to the elevator panel, touching it with his fingertips. It was a simple panel with two buttons, one that pointed up, and one, down. The panel itself wasn't conductive to anything he could link with, so he tried just pushing the down button. It lit up and stayed lit, so he waited anxiously while Annie and Jeffrey joined him to stand in front of the golden doors. A faint whirring sound was heard, grew louder, and finally a soft bell chimed and the golden doors rolled open.

Once inside, Nathan tried pressing the button for the tenth floor. It didn't stay lit, and the elevator didn't budge, so he lay his hand on the panel, sighing. There was a link there, at least, and the programming was very simple. It was only a quick moment before he had convinced the system that the elevator really wanted to be on the tenth floor.

It gave the same nauseating lurch when it came to a stop as the one in Liam's place had, only this time it felt to Nathan like it was much, much worse, since his stomach was already tight to begin with. He stifled a moan as it came to a stop, but Annie apparently heard him anyway, turning to frown at him as the doors started to roll open.

"What's wrong?"

Nathan didn't have time to answer. As soon as the doors were open, there was a shout of surprise on the other side. Things started happening very fast, then, and Nathan felt like he could do nothing but watch, frozen in place. Jeffrey jumped forward, arms raised, shouting something that Nathan didn't understand. There was a loud clap, and the sound of an electric discharge, and Jeffrey crumpled to the floor like he was made of rags. Annie sprang in front of Nathan, shouting at him to stay back, and started running. Only then did he see the security guard pulling another electric stun gun from his belt.

Annie had almost reached the guard, and for a moment, Nathan thought she would actually get him before he could fire it, but he managed to draw it in time. Annie had to change her trajectory, jumping to the side. Nathan ducked behind the elevator's wall, his heart racing, his breath short. He heard the clapping sound again, but it was a moment before he could bring himself to look. By the time he did, Jeffrey was back up on his feet, and reaching for the security guard, who was backing away. Annie was scrambling to her feet, and Nathan heard her shout.

"Jeffrey, no!"

But Jeffrey ignored her, and grabbed the guard by the forearm. The man started twitching, dropping the useless stun gun. Annie, finally standing, raced toward Jeffrey.

"Stop!"

Jeffrey let go, and the guard let out a feeble, strangled moan, which transformed into a guttural sigh as he fell into a heap on the floor. Nathan let out a deep breath he only now realized he had been holding. He swallowed with some difficulty and made himself look down at the inert form of the guard Annie was crouching over.

"Is he dead?"

Annie nodded, looking grim. She stood up, not looking at Jeffrey. The large man had a look of mild shock, staring at his hands. "I... I couldn't stop! It... it just..."

"I know." Annie's voice was soft, yet there was something dark to it. "It's hard to control at first. It'll get easier."

Nathan stood in the doorway, very still, unsure of what to do, still shocked at the man's death. Annie turned to him sharply, interrupting Jeffrey who was opening his mouth to speak.

"Snap out of it, Nathan. We have work to do."

Nathan hesitated. It seemed to him like every step they took made things a little worse, and he wasn't sure he wanted to go any further. "Are you sure this is still a good idea?"

"Do you want to come back later?"

Nathan lowered his head. For some reason, the harsh tone of her voice hurt. He had thought his concerns were legitimate.

He looked around with his head still lowered, afraid to meet her eyes.

The small hall the elevators opened onto contained nothing but a security desk next to a door, which had on it one of the finest, most elaborate electronic locks Nathan had ever encountered. It took him longer than usual to get it open, and Jeffrey and Annie had been standing behind him for some time holding the dead man between them when he finally unlocked the door.

There was no one beyond it, just a long, white hall with three doors on either side and a camera at the end, pointed at the entrance. Nathan looked up at the camera; it was impossibly high, and there was nothing to climb on, besides which they had surely been seen by now.

"Do you want me to take care of it?"

Annie shook her head. "It'd be a miracle if they don't know we're here yet. Let's not waste any more time with this. Just do what you need to do as quickly as you can."

Nathan headed to the end of the hall and the last door on his right; he took care of the electronic lock and walked in. To his relief, this room, at least, was exactly as he had expected. It was a small laboratory, full of elaborate machinery that Nathan had rarely if ever seen before. All of it was linked to a row of five computers which shared a single screen, in the corner of a long, bare metal counter.

Nathan headed to the row of computers lined up under the metal counter. Everything was bolted into the floor, and there were no jacks in front. He had to stretch to fit his arm in the space between the wall and the side of the computer so he could finally reach one of the jacks in the back. He closed his eyes to help himself concentrate on ignoring the discomfort in his neck and shoulder as he linked with the network.

He swam through the data flux for a little while before he found a bundle of files which were encrypted. He wasn't sure that it was what he needed, but he couldn't find it anywhere else, so he opened Oliver to start uploading the files to him. It went smoothly at first, but when he was halfway done, he realized something was wrong.

The sensation of swimming was not unlike a sort of vibration which resonated with the swimmer's mind. That was what Nathan used to send his thoughts out to resonate with the pertinent information. The vibration was always slightly different from network to network, but it was always consistent within itself. Here, however, it felt like there was more than just the one vibration. It wasn't the cacophony that the flux was, more like two rhythms that were almost in sync but not quite, one of them fainter than the other. It was something Nathan had never experienced before, and he was tempted to spend more time to figure out what was different about this one, but he didn't dare distract himself from the task at hand.

He was almost done transferring the data when the second vibration became suddenly strong, overwhelming him like a sort of feedback, numbing his mind and body, making his teeth chatter.

Nathan. Nathan blinked. Why had he thought about his name? It must be the lack of stims. He closed his eyes and tried to concentrate again. *Subject 372.* He shook his head, trying to get some focus. Where had that thought come from? He hadn't thought of that name for years. He tried to concentrate, but his mind was becoming fuzzy with the buzz of the wrong vibration. He was thinking about breaking into Genome, and the information he had come to get. He thought about the lab where he had been a test subject, and how he ran away. He thought about all the things he didn't want to be thinking about, and he couldn't control it. Something was drawing the thoughts out of his head, and it was leaving him completely incapable of formulating one of his own.

Nathan.

Oliver. His friend. He was still connected to Oliver. He thought about what knowledge he already had about the experiments Genome had been conducting on ghouls.

Nathan. You're not alone. Concentrate on my signal.

He had come here with Annie and Jeffrey. Oliver was just a computer. No, Oliver was his friend. Oliver was talking to him right now.

You're still connected to me. If you try to come into my hard drive maybe you can get away.

Get away. It was something he had to do. He tried disconnecting from the network, and his head filled with pain. He screamed.

Don't disconnect. Come to me. I can put up a firewall.

He could feel Oliver's presence on the edge of his mind, and fled to it. He could feel rage, furious and blinding hot, though he was certain it wasn't his own, and he couldn't think enough to be afraid of it. And suddenly he was wrapped up in Oliver's familiar, comforting hard drive, only to be ripped from it a second later, thrown back into his own body by Oliver's powerful firewall.

He sat up, gasping for breath, looking up around himself. He had fallen on his back, away from the computer, and his nose was bleeding. His head hurt enough for him to be sure his brain had exploded. He got to his feet with some difficulty, and noticed the distinctive sound of people fighting on the other side of the door. He picked up Oliver, almost falling over, and had to lean heavily on the metal counter to maintain an upright position.

He only managed to stagger to the door, and poked his head out in time to see Annie pick up a guard by the collar with one arm, throwing him five yards further to collide into two others. Jeffrey was struggling with a few of his own; it seemed to Nathan that the white hall was now black with security uniforms. Annie, after throwing her man, looked over her shoulder and spotted Nathan. The look she gave him was desperate.

"Get away, Nathan! Run!"

Nathan took a step back, and had to lean against the wall to support himself as he walked as quickly as he could bring himself to. He wanted to help, he didn't want to just leave her, but what could he do? Even if he had been any good in any sort of physical confrontation, he could barely stand right now. He went in the opposite direction, trying to think. He knew the hallway formed a sort of L shape, and the other end opened to an emergency staircase. Annie and Jeffrey were going to be all right. Weren't they?

Every step was agony; his limbs tingled like they had been asleep too long and he couldn't get the blood flowing again, and his heart pumped miserably and much too hard, his head swimming, his forehead covered with sweat.

When he finally reached the corner, he saw that the other hall was empty, and his heart lifted a bit. He found the energy to stagger a little faster. It seemed easier with every step as the door that would lead him to the stairs, and safety, got progressively closer.

He was almost there, only at arm's length, when the door burst open with such violence that he fell backward on the floor. He stared up dumbly as three security guards and a young man who wasn't wearing a uniform poured out of the door. One of the guards drew a stun gun, and aimed it at Nathan. There was the clap of the shot, and Nathan felt a pinch on his arm. Before he could panic, the electricity poured into him. Electricity.

He grinned, drawing and converting it, his limbs feeling better and stronger already. He stood up with an agility he hadn't thought himself capable of, the guard staring at him, shocked. He didn't even have time to turn and run, before another of the guards decided to use a more traditional means of capture, and punched Nathan on the side of the head. He felt himself falling for a brief moment, but he was unconscious before he hit the floor.

CHAPTER 12

The first thing to come back to Nathan was his sense of pain, telling him that his head was killing him, that all his muscles ached, and that he was lying face down in an uncomfortable position on a cold, hard floor, which seemed to be moving.

"So he's the one?"

"I don't know. It's hard to tell. It's not like we see what the other looks like when we're swimming."

He could hear the voices, but he didn't recognize who they belonged to, and he couldn't tell where they were coming from. He tried to move. He felt sluggish and confused, and his body was no better than his mind. He could hear a motor, and feel a vibration. He had to be in some kind of vehicle.

"Well, you better hope he is. Seems he's some kind of valuable."

His eyes hurt when he tried to open them, but as soon as any light hit them, the pain in his head quickly made him forget about any other. This time he did moan, and his voice came out hoarse and raw through his parched throat. At last, his eyes opened all the way, and he saw he was lying on his stomach on a textured metal floor, his hands cuffed behind his back. He didn't seem to have his bag with him, and he felt panic rising to his throat. Where was Oliver? What had happened to him? What about Annie? Was she safe? The thought of her possible capture brought almost physical pain to him. His stomach tightened, his throat clenched, and he felt the now familiar sting of tears in his eyes.

"Shut up. I think he's waking up."

The voices were coming from behind him. He pushed himself up with his legs to roll over on his side so he could see where he was, exactly. There were two men seated in the driver's compartment. It was obviously them he was hearing; there was no one else he could see.

"What? You afraid of what he might hear? Twerp's not exactly in a position to repeat it to anyone."

He couldn't make out what they looked like; he could only see the back of their heads, and even that, only with some difficulty. One was wearing a black wool ski cap, and smoking a cigarette, judging by the cloud of acrid smoke that surrounded his head. He was the one who had just spoken, with a gruffer, lower voice. The other seemed younger, though Nathan could only judge by the sound of his voice; all that he could see of the man was a mane of curly red-brown hair. He sounded annoyed when he answered the ski-cap man.

"Seriously, I thought you'd have learned not to underestimate technopaths by now."

"Yeah, if it even is the one you think."

"It's likely. I think the other ones were ghouls, anyway."

There were no windows in the back of the van, only the same textured metal covering the walls and ceiling. He couldn't see his bag anywhere. The truck hit a bump which made him bang his head against the floor when he fell back onto his stomach. He groaned in pain and anger, and tried to sit up, but he couldn't push himself up high enough with his hands tied behind his back. He struggled until his efforts caught the attention of the man in the hat, who gave him a look through the rear-view mirror.

"Hey, keep still back there, if you know what's good for you."

"Where is Annie?"

"How the hell should I know? Now be quiet or I'll punch your lights out again."

Nathan closed his eyes and took a deep breath to keep from panicking. For some reason, he felt that if he could just find out whether or not Annie was safe, his own fate would be less terrifying.

He tried to remain quiet for the rest of the trip, which proved to be much more difficult than he had thought. For starters, the trip was incredibly long. They must have been taking him very far, perhaps even outside of the city. The pain in his stiff muscles just kept growing worse, exacerbated by the cold metal floor, his awkward position, and the immobility in which he was forced. After about half an hour, the urge to empty his bladder started blocking out all other thought, even the pain, and he finally worked up the courage to raise his head and address the drivers.

"I have to pee."

"Not my frikkin' problem, kid," said the man in the hat.

"Come on! I really gotta go!"

"You think I'm gonna fall for a cheap trick like that? Hold it in!"

The young one rolled his head backwards on his shoulders, letting out an exaggeratedly annoyed sigh. "Come on, Jack, let the guy piss. Just pull over."

"He's trying to run away or some shit!"

"Or he just wants to piss. Come on, pull over."

"Fine. But if he escapes, it's your ass, not mine."

The van jerked and bounced, slowing down on uneven ground as it pulled over, gravel crackling under its tires. When they were fully stopped, the red-headed man jumped out of his side of the van. Nathan could hear him walk around the side all the way to the back doors. Daylight almost blinded Nathan when the doors were pulled open. He hadn't quite recovered his sight by the time the other man was helping him up. He seemed slightly older than what Nathan had expected from the sound of his voice. Nathan thought he was about Annie's age, or at least the age she had been when she died, or maybe a little older.

He pulled Nathan to his feet easily, and had to help him stand and hop down from the back of the van, because Nathan's feet had been asleep through half the drive.

Nathan blinked, unable to shield himself from the light which blinded him. Once his eyes got used to the light, panic seized his chest, knocking the breath out of him.

They were on a long, empty stretch of road that went on of as far as Nathan could see on either side. It passed through what looked to have once been a thick forest, though all the largest trees were now lying flat on the ground, uprooted, apparently fallen all in the same direction. The trunks were blackened, and mushrooms had started to grow on them. New trees were growing in all sorts of shapes, heights, foliage and colors. Most of them were deformed, crooked and bloated.

Nathan recognized the place instantly; they were close to the crater, and the lab. Nathan had been through these woods before, years ago, when he escaped. He had sat among these trees, eaten their strange fruit and fought off the small, mutated animals which lived within them.

The young man was removing Nathan's handcuffs. Numbly and automatically, he rubbed his aching wrists, stretching his stiff shoulders, only now realizing that the man was saying something.

"... so no funny business, all right?"

Nathan felt himself nod and take a step forward. It was as though some kind of automatic subroutine had taken over, and his conscious mind had shut down. His brain finally started to boot when he was relieving himself on the side of the road. The young man was smoking a cigarette, leaning against the van casually, five yards away from Nathan, too far to reach and grab him if Nathan ran. The growing forest was full of places to hide; Nathan had never had to look very far to find one when he had escaped. Maybe, just maybe, if he planned it right, he would be able to get away this time too.

He took great care to keep his movements slow and casual as he fastened his pants, then he stretched comfortably before bolting into a run. He head the man curse and shout after him, but he never turned back, only ran faster, his heart pumping madly, his mind filled with the debilitating fear he had of going back to the lab.

He never heard the shot; he only felt the stabbing pain in his thigh where it hit. He screamed when he tripped, getting his feet caught in the limbs of a fallen tree, falling on his arm against the trunk. There was a dull snapping sound, and then the pain in his leg disappeared, replaced by the white hot agony that his forearm had become. He screamed as loud as he could, grabbing his injured arm, which sent a new wave of pain through his body. He understood only then that the sound must have been his bone snapping inside his arm, and not the tree, like he had thought.

Desperately, he tried to get back to his feet, but found that his legs wouldn't work. He looked down at them and let out a strangled sob when, instead of finding a bloody gunshot wound in his thigh, he found the red dart of a tranquilizer gun sticking out of it. He looked up to see that the man was running towards him and had almost caught up. He tried crawling away using his good arm, but he hadn't even moved an inch when the drugs reached full capacity, and he lost consciousness.

He was still very much in pain when he woke up. His leg and arm hurt dully, his mouth was even drier than it had been before, and his head felt like his brain had expanded and was now slowly cracking his skull to escape. He was lying on his back, this time, and he could feel cold metal through the thin fabric of his t-shirt. He opened his eyes slowly. A bright light blinded him when he opened his eyes.

"Stay still."

The voice was low and terribly familiar; it sent a rush of adrenaline through Nathan's entire body. He tried to sit up, and had half a second to realize his wrists and ankles were tied down to the table before agonizing pain from his left arm ripped a scream from his throat, which was so completely dry that the screaming immediately turned into alternating coughing, wheezing, and moaning.

"I told you to stay still."

Nathan turned his head toward the voice. His eyes were blurry with tears from the coughing, and he had to blink rapidly to get them back into focus. He was lying on a steel table, held down by brown leather straps. A familiar-looking old man with a bald head and a white beard was sitting on his left side, squinting down through gold-rimmed spectacles perched on the tip of his nose. Nathan followed the man's eyes to his own left arm, which was now purple and swollen. The man was covering it with strips of a white, wet stuff Nathan had never seen before.

"...Doctor Malavoy?"

The old man kept his eyes on his work, but nodded once to himself. "Good. Your memory is intact. I'd hate to think there had been brain damage. Who knows what you've been putting in your system."

Nathan let his head roll back on the table so he was looking up at the ceiling, a familiar tightness squeezing the air out of his chest. It was true. He was back at the lab.

The realization hit him with such force that he had to bite back a sob. For a short moment, he wished his two captors had had real guns, and had killed him when he tried to escape. Tears filled his eyes again, and rolled down the side of his face and into his ears. Doctor Malavoy glanced up at him over the rims of his glasses before resuming his work.

"There's no need to be melodramatic. There are plenty of worse places to be. I would think you might have seen one or two of them in your time away."

135

Nathan shut his eyes tightly and breathed in, trying to make himself stop. He had gotten away once, after all. He'd be able to do it again, surely. Besides... "Where is Annie?"

"Who?"

"My friend. Did you capture her?"

"Not to my knowledge."

Nathan wanted to feel relieved. If doctor Malavoy knew nothing, then perhaps that meant that Annie was still safe, still free. But the knot in his stomach would not go away. He looked around for something to calm himself, but the examination room contained nothing to reassure him; every time his eyes fell on some familiar piece of equipment, his chest felt tighter.

"...what's going to happen to me?"

Doctor Malavoy didn't look up as he shrugged. "I'm to examine you to see what you've been doing to yourself. Then we'll want to analyze your abilities. This is extremely exciting."

"What is?"

"Well, apparently you're a technopath of some talent. You shouldn't have hidden that from us."

The fear was spreading like a cold wave through Nathan's body. Did Malavoy seem angry? Was he saying they would have to do more tests on him? Or to run the ones they already, had, again? All of them?

"I... I didn't know! I wasn't hiding anything, really!"

Malavoy finished putting the last strip on Nathan's arm, and stood with his bowl of water, walking away from the table. "We shall have to see."

Nathan tried to catch his breath enough to talk. "What kind of tests are you going to do?"

"Well that depends on how cooperative you are."

Nathan bit back the urge to shout how cooperative he wanted to be. He didn't really want to cooperate; he wanted to be brave, but he was terrified. Malavoy watched him struggle with himself for a little while before shaking his head in resignation.

"That's too bad, 372. You should know we don't wish to hurt you."

"My name is Nathan."

Malavoy had a small smile as he walked back towards Nathan, holding a pair of scissors.

"What does it matter what I call you?"

"It's my name. Laura told me."

"Well, you can get used to being subject 372 again. Doctor Laura Chandler no longer works with us. She hasn't for a long time. But you were probably aware of that long before you escaped."

Nathan closed his eyes. Doctor Chandler had been the only thing that made this place bearable. She had been kind to him, treated him like a person, and even taught him his name; he was reassured to find out that the reason she had stopped coming was not because she had been bored of him, at least.

He felt fingers lifting the shirt from his belly, and opened his eyes to see Malavoy cutting the front of his new Zombies Eating Tomatoes shirt. He tried to squirm away, but the restraints held him firmly in place.

"Hey! Stop! What are you doing?"

"Well, we need to dispose of these. Who knows what kind of contaminants are all over them? Besides, I need to take them off to examine you. Now, stay still or you'll hurt yourself again."

Malavoy stopped cutting for fear of accidentally hurting him. The phrase reminded Nathan of Annie again. That, on top of the incomprehensible emotion he felt at the loss of the shirt Jeffrey had just gotten him, made his throat tight and his voice shrill as he spoke.

"Please, doctor Malavoy, let me keep it! I've got nothing else! I'll be good!"

"You'll be good because you need to be. Now stop squirming or I'll sedate you."

Nathan tried to control his breathing, to regain his composure, but this time, he didn't succeed. He closed his eyes to at least have the illusion of privacy as the tears rolled down his face, while the blades cut through the printed face of a ghoulish Jeffrey eating a tomato.

CHAPTER 13

The examination itself wasn't too painful, though it was long and invasive, and left Nathan feeling empty and defeated. He didn't fight or protest when Malavoy pricked and poked him, and drew what seemed like buckets of his blood. He didn't even try to run when his restraints were undone, didn't react when Malavoy dressed him in a pale green gown, and followed docilely when he sent him off with two guards.

After taking him to be disinfected, they put him in a tiny room that was just large enough for him to lie down comfortably. Its walls, ceiling and floor were gray concrete, and there was nothing inside, though the guards did leave him a bucket. It had only a plain metal door, with a plain metal knob that locked with a plain metal key, and no electronics at all. There wasn't even a light bulb in the cell, and Nathan was left in complete darkness, with only his bucket for company.

He spent a long time in dazed silence. It might have been fifteen minutes or three hours, he wasn't sure, but after a while the panic returned in full force. He felt his way to the door and pounded on it with his good hand. Then, he pulled on the doorknob uselessly until his fingers hurt. After that, he scraped at the door with his nails until they were broken and bloody and the pain in his left arm was unbearable. His energy eventually ran out, and he had to give up. He hadn't had any food or water since the dinner at the megaplex, and it wasn't terribly long before he could no longer stand without his head spinning.

The lack of stims didn't help, either. When he realized he couldn't take his drugs to stay awake, he broke down, curling up in a ball on the cold concrete floor, shaking and sobbing in utter despair, until his throat felt raw, his face sore and puffy. The urge to vomit overtook him, several times, though only bile came out, burning his already sore throat.

Exhaustion finally overtook him, and he started slipping in and out of sleep. He woke up a half dozen times, terrified at having been asleep, at waking up in a strange place, at being in pitch darkness, and, of all things, at being alone.

He was plagued by horrible, incessant nightmares. In some, he was torn apart by ghouls, or strapped to a chair to be cut, probed and burned. In others, it was Annie who was in his place, and he had to watch as they hurt her, killed her or turned her into a feral beast.

He sweated heavily in his sleep, which was incomprehensible to him, because in his waking moments, he was frozen to the bone from the bare cement, his flimsy, Velcro-tied cotton gown doing nothing to keep him warm.

It felt like days before the door of his little room opened, blinding him with outside light. He barely made out the shadow of a man against the light, coming in and dropping a few things on the floor. Then the man was gone, and the light, before Nathan's eyes had any chance to adjust. He reached with his trembling good hand in front of him, feeling the ground until his fingers hit the rim of a wide, shallow metal bowl. He tried to grab it, and the tips of his fingers sank into something soft and lukewarm.

He made a face and wiped his fingers on the front of his gown. It didn't matter that he couldn't see it; one touch was enough for him to recognize the tasteless gray sludge he had eaten all his life, before escaping the lab. He ignored it, thinking with regret of the delicious food he had tasted at Liam's place, and the megaplex. He felt again for the cup of water, but his hand trembled too much and he ended up spilling it. He was tempted to suck it off of the floor because he was so thirsty, but the cement absorbed it right away.

Later still, the door opened again. This time, he managed to shield his eyes in time, and crawled away from it, huddling in the far corner, wrapping his arms around himself. The stuff that doctor Malavoy had covered his broken arm with had hardened, and his arm felt tight in it.

The shapes of the three men blocked out some of the light. Nathan blinked and squinted, but he couldn't see who their faces. One of them stepped forward, and when Nathan heard the man speak, his blood froze in his veins, and he couldn't breathe for a few seconds.

"The prodigal son returns."

"Doctor Wilkerson?"

Nathan's voice was barely a whisper. He couldn't move. His heart felt like it had slowed, and couldn't pump any more blood to his brain. Though his eyes could not yet see him, his mind pasted the well-known features on the shadow; the scraggly, brown comb-over, the horn-rimmed glasses, the large, hooked nose. He felt the man smile more than saw it.

"You remember me. I'm flattered. Will you remember how much easier your life will be if you follow me willingly?"

This was a discussion they'd had time and again. Every time Nathan had wanted to test a limit, Doctor Wilkerson had seen to it that he forget any notion of defiance. Nathan knew intimately how futile it was to fight back, and the only thing there was to do was what he was told. Yet every molecule in his being revolted at the thought. He could barely hold back the urge to scream as he rose to his feet, slowly and with great difficulty. His limbs were weak, and he trembled uncontrollably; he had to lean on the wall because his legs wouldn't support him.

Wilkerson nodded with a satisfied expression. Nathan's eyes had gotten used to the light by now, and he could see the ugly little man. He'd grown balder, and his skin sagged considerably more than the last time Nathan had seen him. He was also much smaller than he was before, and for some reason, this made Nathan feel better, if only a little.

The guards had to help him walk all the way down the hall as they brought him to a small exam room that looked very familiar to Nathan. It had a table equipped with leather straps on one side, a counter with a computer and all sorts of instruments on the other, and, in the middle, the dreaded chair. When he saw it, the little strength he had left in his legs vanished, and he stumbled. The two guards who were helping him walk caught him before he fell, and they had to drag him the rest of the way. They dumped him unceremoniously into the chair, and didn't even bother to do up the straps, just standing on either side of him. He eyed them suspiciously, then turned his attention to Wilkerson.

The short, balding man was stooped over the metal counter. Nathan tried to lean forward to see what he was doing, but one of the guards pushed him back into the chair roughly. He could hear the clinking of small glass bottles. He took a deep breath, trying to calm down. If they weren't tying him to the chair, then the chances were good that what they were planning would not hurt. When Doctor Wilkerson approached him with a syringe, though, he felt like he might soil himself. He had to lick his lips to moisten them before he spoke.

"What's that?"

Wilkerson stopped to consider him for a few seconds, and for that time, Nathan believed that he would actually answer him, but Wilkerson simply turned his gaze to the guards.

"Restrain him."

"No!"

Nathan sprang from his chair, but the two guards grabbed him by the wrists and shoulders, pinning him down on it. He should have been no match for them, especially in his current state, but he realized with some satisfaction that it took the two strong men some time and effort to do up the restraints, and he even managed to kick one in the face as they tied his legs.

The guard cursed and raised a hand to return the favor, but Wilkerson stopped him.

"Don't damage the subject. Am I going to have to hire more of you just to restrain an undersized boy?"

The guard shot Wilkerson an angry look, and, for a second, Nathan was very pleased with himself. Then Wilkerson turned to him. Though he knew very well just how useless it was, he twisted in his bonds to get away from the needle, but he couldn't even manage to give the doctor any pause at all. The needle gave a pinch that was no more painful than he remembered as Wilkerson jabbed it in his thigh. He watched as the ugly man brought down the plunger, and felt the fear squeeze his heart as he watched the transparent fluid disappear into his body. Wilkerson took the empty syringe back to the counter and dumped it in a bright yellow plastic container. Then he turned to the guards and dismissed them with a gesture, picking up a folder and a clipboard.

He browsed through the folder as the guards left the room. The one that Nathan had kicked glared at him as he exited, but Wilkerson didn't spare him a glance as he leafed through the folder. It lasted long enough for the drugs to take effect. Nathan started feeling groggy and disoriented by the time Wilkerson was paying attention to him again, coming closer with a small flashlight, which he shone in and out of Nathan's eyes while peering at them. Apparently satisfied with the results, he put the flashlight back in the pocket of his lab coat, picking up the clipboard again, this time with a pen.

"You've been away for some time, 372."

"My name is Nathan."

Nathan frowned, trying to focus. He hadn't meant to say that. He had thought about it, wanted to say it, but he hadn't actually meant to. His head was spinning, and he had a hard time seeing straight. Wilkerson ignored him, and went on.

"I'm told you are a proficient technopath."

"Yes."

His speech was a bit slurred. His mouth and tongue felt numb, yet he felt like the words were spilling out of him unbidden. He tried to concentrate, and he felt dizzy and nauseated. He saw Doctor Wilkerson scribble down notes on his clipboard.

"You can swim the flux? And control computers?"

"Yes."

"Can you control other types of machines?"

"Cameras. Elevators. Electronic locks. If it has any programming, I can do it."

"We found a sentient computer in your bag. Did you make it?"

"Yes. Is he all right?"

As always, Wilkerson ignored his question. He kept his eyes on the notes he was writing, not even sparing a glance to his subject.

"Who taught you how to use your talent?"

"228B."

This time Wilkerson did look up, slightly puzzled, reaching into his pocket for the flashlight again.

"That was the number of your cell."

"It was the name of the lock."

The doctor raised his eyebrows, shook his head slightly, and resumed his questioning. Nathan let the words dribble out of his mouth, thinking about Oliver, fighting the stinging sensation in his eyes.

"How did you escape?"

"I asked 228B to open the door."

Wilkerson paused briefly to scribble more notes on his clipboard. Nathan's head rolled on his neck. He didn't have enough energy to hold it up anymore. He managed to get it to lean back on the chair, but the position forced him to look at Wilkerson. The sight of the ugly, hook-nosed face protruding from the lab coat sickened him even further. The coat reminded him of Annie, and he realized how he'd come to associate its sight to something good. Seeing the thin, balding man wearing one seemed absurd, even though he'd never seen the man without one.

"You look stupid in a lab coat."

Wilkerson gave him a mildly puzzled look before concentrating on his file again.

"No one helped you escape?"

"Just 228B."

"How long have you known you could do this?"

"Since the day I left."

"Interesting. You'd never responded to any of our tests before then."

Nathan had a memory of all the times he'd been hooked up to a computer in the lab. The computers had been so simple, and the attempts to get him to respond so transparent, that he'd refrained from answering, finding every little way he could to rebel against them.

"I could always hear the machines. I just didn't want to talk back."

Wilkerson frowned, pursing his lips. "What else can you do?"

Nathan gritted his teeth and tried to fight the urge to speak, but the words burst out of his lips. "I can draw electricity from power outlets and convert it into something I can use to make myself feel better."

Wilkerson scribbled into his file again. "Interesting. How do you use this ability?"

"I just touch something that conducts current, and I recharge."

"Can you use it to heal your wounds?"

"I've never tried."

Why couldn't he have just said no? It was inevitable now. Wilkerson put down his pad and pen, and walked to the door. "Where are you going? I don't want you to do experiments on me!"

The doctor didn't even pause as he walked out, leaving Nathan alone. He was a long time coming back, and Nathan was almost grateful when he did, because he had started to doze off. He instantly woke up when Wilkerson walked back in, though. The short man was carrying a simple, long extension cord. When Doctor Wilkerson got closer to him, he could see that the female end had been cut off, and the cable stripped to reveal the metal wire inside. Wilkerson gave Nathan that end to hold. Two guards were following him in, coming to stand on either side of Nathan.

The doctor turned to him when he reached the outlet in the wall above the counter. "I want you to absorb as much energy as you can, and I really mean until you can't anymore."

Nathan nodded, grasping the stripped wire in his right hand incredulously. Was that it? He wasn't going to be hurt? Wilkerson was just going to let him recharge? He almost felt like smiling. This was too easy, surely something more terrible waited just around the corner. But at least, for the next few seconds, he would feel much, much better.

Wilkerson plugged in the male end and turned to look at Nathan. The energy surged through Nathan's body, spreading the pleasant tingling sensation to every inch of his skin. It was powerful, stronger than it had ever felt before, but Nathan believed it was because he was so tired to begin with. He drew it into him, making his head feel better, chasing the sleepiness away, relaxing his muscles. He might have stopped there, but then he felt the tingling sensation intensify and concentrate in his injured arm, and the more energy he consumed, the better and more alive he felt.

He opened his eyes when he felt sated, and cut himself off from the surge of power in his hand with a simple thought. He let out a sigh of satisfaction and started when he noticed Doctor Wilkerson peering at him, close to his face.

"Is that all you can take?"

"Yeah. I feel better. Am I healed?"

Wilkerson went back to the counter to unplug the extension before examining Nathan in more detail, starting with his eyes, face, and ending with his injured arm.

"No. You're not. You don't feel pain?"

"A little still in my arm, but not much."

"Hmm."

The doctor wrote down in his clipboard and Nathan let go of the metal wire, letting it drop to the floor. It was too bad. Electricity had only ever made him feel better, but the feeling hadn't lasted too long. He was still in the same situation he was before. The moment had been good, though.

They ran a machine over his arm to look at his bone and make sure it really hadn't healed, and when they were sure, Wilkerson let the two guards bring him back to his cell. The one Nathan had kicked pushed him roughly inside, and kicked him once in the stomach with his booted foot while his companion waited by the door. It took Nathan some time to catch his breath after they left, and by the time he did, the door opened again. A silhouette Nathan could not distinguish against the back light picked up his untouched bowl of gruel, and lay down a fresh one, accompanied by a fresh cup of water. Nathan was already scrambling towards it when the door closed and left him again in complete darkness. He stopped then, and felt the rest of the way carefully with his fingertips, afraid to spill the cup's precious contents again. He found it and lifted it to his lips. The water soothed his dry tongue and cracked lips, though there wasn't enough to really make a difference.

He didn't touch the food, though he was very hungry. He didn't think he could have digested it, anyway; his stomach felt like it was being squeezed. The pain and anxiety of losing Oliver and Annie were starting to dull, slowly replaced by the pain of not having stims. His arm and belly still ached, the floor he was lying on was humid and freezing, his teeth were chattering from the cold his flimsy cotton gown did nothing to stop, but none of it would have mattered right now if he could have had just one of the little pink pills.

Beyond the withdrawal, the hours spent alone in the darkness brought their share of anxiety; sleep, in particular, was even more terrifying than he remembered. There were the nightmares, of course, and the anxiety of wondering if he was still alone when he awoke. A few times Nathan thought he heard or felt something move next to him, but he couldn't see a thing; the darkness was so complete that his eyes simply could not get used to it. He called out, but never got an answer.

All he could do was think, about Annie, about stims, about Oliver, and what experiments they would do to him tomorrow. He tried not to think, but he couldn't help it, no matter how hard he tried.

They finally came to get him again, after what seemed like an eternity. There were only the two guards, who took him to the decontamination room, where they stripped him and threw him unceremoniously in a stall. Nathan was at least used to the treatment again by now and covered his eyes before he was showered with the high-speed jets of hot water, disinfectant, hot water again and air to dry him off. For some reason, though, his skin felt very sensitive, and this time it hurt a lot more than usual. When the guards pulled him out of the stall and shoved a new green cotton gown in his hands, his skin was bright red, and felt raw and burned. It hurt when he pulled on his new garment.

The guards shoved him along to a room Nathan knew well. It was empty, gray, and cold, like everything else in this place, furnished with nothing but a metal table and chairs, and a mirror on the wall. He'd spent a large part of his childhood there, being submitted to all sorts of strange tests. These tests were the easy ones, though, and almost never hurt. They mostly involved having to guess the picture on a card he couldn't see, being connected to a computer, or trying to move objects with his mind.

This time, though, there was a small computer with no screen, to which were connected two headsets that had neither headphones nor microphones. Wilkerson was not there, though Nathan imagined he was behind the mirror with Malavoy and the others. To Nathan's surprise, however, the young man who had been with the guards who shot him with the tranquilizer gun during his trip back to the lab, was sitting in the chair with no restraints, fastening one of the headsets to his own head. He smiled up at Nathan when the guards strapped him to the chair.

"We meet again, it would seem. Remember me?"

Nathan started to nod, but then one of the guards tried to put the second headset on his head and he dodged it. The young man seated across from him let out a laugh.

"You're afraid of a swimmer's headset? What kind of amateur are you?"

Nathan felt himself flush and glared at the man. He'd heard of the things before; they were supposed to make your access to the flux easier and faster, while leaving your hands free to do whatever else you wanted. He let the guard put it on his head, curious as to what was happening. Did they want him to swim, now? To what end? And why was that guy linking as well?

When the headset was fastened to his head, he could feel the inviting hum of the computer, and couldn't resist linking to see if he couldn't find his way to the flux. After all, they already knew about what he could do, what was the harm?

The computer was not linked to any circuit, and its hard drive was completely empty, with not even an operating system installed on it. It didn't even have any wireless access to the flux, which seemed very strange to Nathan. Why make a computer that couldn't connect to it? He'd never encountered anything like this before; he direly wished, not for the first time, that he was able to connect to the flux without physically touching a machine. That's when he felt it.

It was the same strange vibration he had felt last time he had linked with a system, at the Genome offices near the megaplex, and finally realized that it was the man's mind he could feel there with him. He looked up at the stranger seated across the table from him.

His red-brown hair puffed up stupidly over the headset, forming a funny-looking, mushroom-shaped lump on top of his head. His eyes were closed, and his face wore an expression of intense concentration. Nathan felt the shift in the vibration he had the first time, when he had lost control of his thoughts. He closed his eyes to better focus on it, and felt the vibration push, discreetly, against his own mind.

He steeled his brain to block it, thinking with all his might of Annie, which was the first and strongest thought to come to him. He concentrated on her, thinking of her laughter, her strange dead eyes, the way her hair had looked when it was untied and cascading down over her shoulders, the pleasant curve of her hip. The image was perfectly clear, and he could feel the vibration was no longer bothering him.

He opened his eyes to look at the other man, holding to the picture of Annie in his memory with everything he had, and saw that the stranger was now gritting his teeth, squeezing his eyes shut in intense concentration. Nathan could feel him fighting at the edge of his mind still, though it didn't feel hard at all to keep him out.

Nathan smiled to himself, and at the struggling man. Could he do the same thing that the man was doing? Tentatively, he probed with his psyche against the vibration that was the other man, and felt him try to drive Nathan out. He pushed harder, putting all his mental strength in it. Sweat was starting to bead on the other man's forehead, and his knuckles were white from gripping the armrests of his chair. Nathan drew a deep breath to keep his strength, feeling more and more self-assured as he watched the other man struggle. He kept thinking of Annie, and pushed the thought into the stranger's mind, sending it out to resonate just like he would on the flux. He felt a resistance, at first. It was strong, but when Nathan concentrated hard, he managed to bend it, and eventually, break it.

The other man screamed at that point, and seemed to convulse in his chair, throwing his head back. The resistance was completely gone, and thoughts started flowing back to him. There was very little that concerned Annie. At first, Nathan had to sift through various images of different women, doing things that were vague and incomprehensible to Nathan, but very pleasurable.

He focused his stream to be more specific, and a single memory made it back to him. He was surprised to find himself looking at his own limp body being dragged by a security guard, in the hall of the Genome office they had broken into. Then there was noise on the other side of the hall, and he turned to see Annie and Jeffrey, headed his way. His heart leapt, and he wanted to go to them, but this was only a memory, and not even his own, so he turned to run the other way, leaving the remaining two guards to take care of the ghouls.

Nathan opened his eyes to see the door to the room he was really in burst open, and Wilkerson, Malavoy, the two security guards and two other doctors Nathan didn't really remember pour through it. Nathan broke his link with the computer and the other man's mind before it could be done for him. As he had thought, the guards rushed towards him, yanking the headset from his forehead, but the doctors all ran to the other man. As Nathan followed them with his eyes, he could see why.

The man was twitching in his seat, making strangled little noises, his eyes rolling back into his head, his nose bleeding profusely. Though the doctors all seemed to be fussing over the stranger, Nathan couldn't help but notice that they kept stealing horrified glances at him. The expression on their faces was something between fear and shock, like the one on the faces of the bandits when Annie had killed their leader. It was like they saw him as some kind of monster. It didn't matter what they thought of him, though. After all, they had never treated him like anything even close to human. Besides, it was all right now; he had managed to glean one last thought from the man as he broke the link with his mind: they hadn't caught Annie.

CHAPTER 14

He was alone in the darkness for another eternity. It seemed this time, it was much longer than before. The door to his cell opened and closed more than half a dozen times so that someone could bring him a fresh bowl of horrible gruel, so he supposed it was at least a few days. At first, he felt strong, heartened by his victory over the other technopath. He could take this, he could take anything they had to throw at him. But time wore on, and he stayed alone, in the dark, with nothing else than his thoughts and the terrible, tasteless food that made him gag even when he was starving. His newfound self-confidence quickly dissolved, and he found himself sinking back into despair. This time it had an edge of bitterness and anger. Hatred was starting to replace the fear that he had always felt towards this place, towards these men.

The cold, damp floor kept him awake when nothing else would have, and for that he was almost glad. Sleep was a terrible time, bringing with it increasingly terrifying nightmares, full of needles, ghouls and security guards with tranquilizer guns. Waking up was even worse. Every time, he was still in a place worse than his dreams, cold, hard, and so dark he couldn't tell whether he was alone or not. By the second day, though, he was shivering so bad that his skin and muscles ached, and he longed for the days before his escape, when he'd had a more comfortable, glass-walled cell that had light and a mattress, even a blanket. The pain got so bad that second night that he found himself wishing he'd never escaped in the first place, even though that meant he'd never have been free, never have made Oliver, never have met Annie.

He was insanely grateful when they came to get him again. He didn't care where he would go, or what would be done to him, so long as he got to be out of his cold, dark cement cell. He had never been left alone this long before. Four guards came to get him, this time, and they acted like he was dangerous, even though they had to pick him up and carry him because he no longer had the strength to stand on his own.

His head hurt from the light, but he was so dizzy he could barely feel it. His skin was what felt the worst, though. It felt raw, and every time it touched anything at all, it sent a wave of pain and shivers throughout his whole body. He was dreading what the disinfection room would do to him, though he was almost looking forward to it, if only to stop being so cold.

The heat was, of course, too intense and too brief to do any good to his frozen bones, and all it did was make him scream with agony when it hit his aching skin.

He was barely conscious as they carried him into the radiation lab. He had a hard time keeping aware of his surroundings, and he could only tell where he was only because he spied the large, round contraption in the middle of the room. Wilkerson and Malavoy were both there, working on a control panel next to it. Malavoy turned to look at him and the guards, pointing to the tray that had been pulled out of the machine.

"Put him there, and leave us when you're done."

Nathan didn't even try to struggle when they strapped him down on the large sort of tray that went in the round chamber. He knew this test. He'd had it a lot in his youth. All the machine did was slide him into a large white cylinder that made a lot of noise and took pictures of his brain, and it didn't hurt at all. The guards tightened the Velcro straps around his wrists and ankles, and then turned and left the room.

Malavoy walked to him, holding a syringe. Nathan needed all his strength just to keep awake, so he didn't try to struggle, just watched him come. Malavoy injected him in his left arm, just above the cast, in the crook of his elbow, and took advantage of the moment to examine the injury a little bit, then put a hand on Nathan's forehead.

"Well it looks like the swelling's gone down. He seems to have a fever, though. Must be something he picked up on the outside. What do you think?"

Malavoy was looking across Nathan to the machine, so Nathan turned his head to see that he was addressing Wilkerson, who was writing in his clipboard.

"Get him some antibiotics."

Malavoy nodded and walked away. Nathan kept his eyes on Wilkerson, who didn't look back. When Malavoy returned, he injected Nathan again, but this time, to Nathan's great surprise, the doctor actually spoke to him.

"You surprised all of us with your little... demonstration, the other day."

Nathan tried to concentrate, but his thoughts felt murky, and strangely disconnected. "Demonstration?"

"Of your ability as a technopath, of course. That was quite impressive."

Impressive? What was he saying? Malavoy reached for a strip of Velcro with a dial on it, which he wrapped around Nathan's upper arm.

"You mean what happened with that guy, on the computer?"

"Yes. You gave our technopath quite a run for his money."

The image of the man, moaning, twitching, and bleeding came back to Nathan, this time with none of the satisfaction he had felt when it had just happened, only an empty, sick feeling.

"Is he all right?"

Malavoy shrugged, and squeezed the rubber pump, making the pressure build up in the Velcro contraption around his arm until it cut off the circulation, then slowly let out.

"He'll be fine. He's recovering, and there's no fear of permanent damage. We've never seen anything like it, though.

It's too bad there aren't means of recording a technopath's level yet. You'd probably be off the scale!"

He unstrapped the Velcro strip from around Nathan's arm and put it back in its place. Nathan's body rocked slightly with the movement, and the motion brought with it a strong wave of nausea. He didn't know if it was from the fever or Malavoy's injection, but he was growing dizzier and more disoriented. Malavoy went on, shining a flashlight into Nathan's eyes, one after the other.

"We never thought you'd develop such amazing abilities. It's not exactly what we hoped for, but it is an interesting development. It's a wonder we were never able to detect this earlier. Obviously, we need to improve our methods."

The words echoed in Nathan's mind, but he wasn't sure why. They seemed incredibly important, suddenly, but the thoughts spun in his head like everything else around him. He noticed that Wilkerson had finished doing whatever it was he was doing and was now watching him intently. The meaning of the words started to sink in, and he turned back to Malavoy.

"Did you make me like this?"

Malavoy shook his head, smiling. "Of course, we did! You're one of our longest-running projects. And it actually turns out you might be a success. But I'm surprised she didn't tell you that."

Nathan felt faint. His heart felt like it wanted to stop, and beat itself out of his chest at the same time. His breath was short and shallow. He wasn't sure it was all the drugs, though. His eyes had a familiar sting in them.

"She? Who, she?"

"Doctor Annie White, of course."

Nathan stared at Malavoy, utterly confused. Were they talking about Annie? His Annie? But Malavoy just kept on talking. "I should have thought of it when you were asking after an Annie, when you first came in. Of course, we never imagined it could be the same Annie."

Nathan stared at him. He held on to his incomprehension, because what he was understanding couldn't be true. Why was he talking about Annie? Had they caught her, after all?

Malavoy walked over to take the clipboard Wilkerson was now handing him. Nathan realized with some discomfort that Wilkerson was still staring at him with that intense thoughtful expression.

"We thought she had been terminated by now," Malavoy continued. "We certainly never thought she might continue her experiments after all that. But knowing her, I suppose it was only to be expected."

Nathan stared at Malavoy dumbly for a few seconds. Was he saying that Annie had been working with these men? Here? Doing things like this?

"You mean Annie worked for you?"

"She did. It was her ideas that carried this project."

This couldn't be. Why would Annie work on a project that hurt people? That hurt her?

"You must be mistaken. I mean, how are you sure it's the same Annie?"

"There's no mistake about it. You put the thought of her so strongly in Stewart's mind that it was all he could think about for a whole day afterwards. Getting him to swim our data flux and associate the relevant information was easy enough. It seems your Annie is our doctor White."

Nathan's entire body felt numb, and he had a hard time breathing. She had told him she worked in a lab, and she had recognized the logo on the van, but he never imagined that she could be doing things like what had been done to him, that she could have been associated with the people who made his life so miserable. Malavoy seemed amused at his expression.

"You seem surprised. I should have known she wouldn't tell you. I can't imagine you'd have let her get close if you had known her true intentions."

"What? What are you talking about?"

157

Malavoy opened his mouth to answer, but suddenly the lights went out, immediately replaced by the two emergency bulbs in the corner near the door. The two doctors exchanged troubled looks, and Wilkerson nodded at Malavoy.

"Go see what's happening. If there's any sign of trouble, bring back some muscle so we can move him."

Malavoy nodded, put the clipboard down and walked out in hurried steps. Wilkerson went to the machine to check its screen, but it was dark, and he muttered a curse under his breath. Nathan watched him for a while, and asked the question that burned his lips, no matter how little he thought his chances of actually being answered.

"What did Malavoy mean about Annie's intentions?"

Wilkerson looked down at him, and an annoyed expression crossed his features. For a second, Nathan thought he would just be ignored like he always was, but Wilkerson actually answered him.

"You were the most exciting project we had when she left. It only makes sense she would try to continue her experiments on a prize subject like you."

Nathan's head swam, and he stared at Wilkerson. He felt like he might pass out any minute now. Was he saying that Annie was part of the people that had... made him? That all she wanted with him was to keep up the very experiments he had escaped?

"She's my friend. You're wrong!"

Wilkerson looked at him, nose wrinkled, like he was looking at something particularly unpleasant.

"Idiot. It was her research that started the project, didn't you hear? She was head of research, the team leader, right up until she left and I took the position. If it hadn't been me, it would had been her, and your life would have been no different."

Nathan didn't have time to react. As Wilkerson finished his sentence, a loud explosion out in the hall shook the walls, floor, and the machine Nathan was still strapped to. Wilkerson almost fell. He caught himself on the machine's screen, and gave a panicked look around.

"We have to get you out of here."

Wilkerson started to remove the Velcro strap that held Nathan's right wrist in place while Nathan's senses came back to him, full of the last statement Wilkerson had made.

"Annie's my friend!"

Wilkerson sighed as he finished with the strap, and turned a very annoyed expression towards Nathan. "Are you still going on about this? Just shut up and be still so I can finish untying you."

"No!"

Nathan's breath was still short, and his head swam, but he found the strength in his distress to focus on Wilkerson, even though the rest of the room seemed to be spinning. The doctor only glared at him through his glasses. His voice was a hiss as he spoke.

"You naïve little imbecile! I'm trying to keep you safe, in case you hadn't noticed! Don't think I won't sedate you some more if that's what it takes!"

The old man reached into the pocket of his lab coat, and retrieved a syringe from it. When Nathan saw it, a sudden surge of adrenaline cleared most of the fuzziness from his head. Without thinking, he reached out with his free hand and grabbed Wilkerson's wrist before he had time to remove the syringe's protective cap. The old man gave a startled shout, and tried to pull free. Nathan had almost no strength left; he thought Wilkerson would break free for sure, but then he felt energy at his fingertips, buzzing right under the surface of the doctor's skin, and he drew.

Wilkerson gasped, and started to fall, shaking convulsively. Nathan found that with the energy flowing into him, he could hold the man up by the wrist without a problem. He wanted to stop, but the feeling was so incredible, that he just couldn't bring himself to. He was revived, and all his pain was dissolving, even the dull, constant ache from his broken arm.

Wilkerson's face was growing ashen, his eyes were rolling back, and he was making pathetic little strangled noises. Nathan made himself open his hand and let go of the man, who fell all the way to the floor and didn't get up again.

Nathan took a deep breath. He felt better than he ever had in his life. His arm felt completely healed, and he felt awake, aware, and ready to run for miles. He hurriedly undid the straps that restrained the rest of his limbs and hopped down from the table. He looked down at the inert shape of Doctor Wilkerson with some horror, remembering the man that Jeffrey had killed. Annie had said it was hard to stop. She had said ghouls stole energy to regenerate themselves. Nathan looked at his hands. What did that make him?

He approached Wilkerson cautiously, and turned him over. The man was very still, and gray, but he was still warm. Was he dead? Had Nathan killed him? Nathan had no idea how to find out. He crouched there miserably, for a few seconds, trying to decide whether or not he'd stopped on time, until Wilkerson let out a sigh and stirred slightly. Nathan jumped back, startled. He was alive, then. Breathing out his relief, Nathan scrambled to his feet and headed for the door. Something was happening out there; maybe it was his way out.

The door wasn't even locked. Outside the hall was dark, with only the emergency light at each end. Nathan turned to his right and ran to the end of the hallway. He knew exactly where to go. He was on familiar ground, even after all those years.

The hall formed a T with another one that went along the outer wall of the wing; Nathan had to cross it to get to the doors. He flattened himself against the corner wall, and leaned out his head to peer into the hall he had to cross. It was just as dark and deserted as the one he was in, so he jumped across it to pull the door open. He grasped the handle, yanking the door open and throwing himself through it. He bumped his face on something soft right on the other side, and he staggered backward, looking up at what it was.

His mouth hung open with shock for a few seconds when he realized he was looking up into Jeffrey's dark, grinning face. He was still gaping up at him when he heard the sound of something heavy dropping to the floor. He barely had time to see that Annie had dropped what looked like a large bag before she threw her arms around him, embracing him tightly.

"Nathan! You're all right!"

She held him tightly for a few seconds. She was cold, but she didn't smell a much like death as she usually did. Her hair tickled his nose slightly.

She let go of him, holding him by the shoulders to look at him. She seemed happy with what she saw until she noticed the cast.

"What happened to your arm?"

Nathan looked down at the cast on his left arm. "I fell on it. It's a long story. I think it's better now." Annie looked up at his face again, puzzled. Nathan didn't give her a chance to ask her question before he replied. "That's a long story too. Can we just get out of here first?"

Annie nodded and picked up the duffel bag, retrieving a gas mask from it and handing it to Nathan before swinging the bag's strap over her shoulder.

"Here. You'll need this. Are you all right to walk?"

"Sure! I could run! I feel great."

"All right. Follow me. We can't go back. This way."

She pointed down the hall with a metal baseball bat Nathan hadn't noticed she had. He saw now that Jeffrey had one, too. He put on the gas mask as he listened.

"Down that way is an emergency exit. It should take us only a few yards from where our driver's waiting."

She started to walk without expecting a reply, and Nathan and Jeffrey fell in behind her. They ran down the deserted hallway, and turned to the left at the end, in a direction Nathan didn't know. He followed her down a flight of emergency stairs. Two floors and a metal door later, they were outside.

The sky was overcast, but the light was still bright enough to hurt Nathan's eyes, if only for a few seconds. Annie was looking around, as if searching for something. There was a shout somewhere to their right, and by the time Nathan turned to see the four security guards draw their weapons, Jeffrey grabbed him to shield him from the guns. Annie threw something that looked like a small metal can at the guards. The moment it hit the ground, the can started releasing a thick gray smoke that quickly surrounded them. She threw another one, and turned to Jeffrey.

"Come on! Move!"

She started running the other way, followed by Jeffrey, who pulled Nathan along. Nathan tried to keep up with the large man's strides as best he could, stumbling more than once. Jeffrey picked him up gently each time, until a beaten up old brown car drove up in front of them. Annie stopped to look back, while Jeffrey opened the back door to stuff Nathan inside.

The driver was not Liam, as Nathan had expected. Instead, it was some stranger, whom Nathan had never seen before. Nathan was suddenly very aware of the green cotton gown that was all he was wearing. But the man's attention was diverted when Jeffrey sat in the passenger seat. Nathan turned to see what Annie was doing, and saw she was throwing another can in the direction of the guards. She opened the door to get in to where Nathan was sitting, and he scooted over to make room for her. She dumped her bag between them and retrieved a small textured metal ball with some kind of mechanism on top. The car got in motion as soon as the door was closed.

"Slow down next to those trucks there," she said as the car made its way to the side of the complex, where a small parking lot stood. "As soon as I've thrown these, step on it!"

She pulled a pin out of two of the metal spheres and threw them between the trucks. The tires screeched as the car they were in pulled away. A few seconds later, Nathan clapped his hands over his ears as the trucks went up in a large explosion. When he opened his eyes and lifted his head again, he noticed that Annie was leaning over him, as if to shield him from the blast. She let him go and sat back up quickly when he noticed, and turned back to look at her handiwork. Nathan followed her gaze to see that the trucks were burning, and the security guards that had been running to the trucks were recoiling from the fire. Feeling very stunned, he sat back down in his seat, and noticed that Jeffrey was giving him an appreciative grin.

"What?"

"Man, your girlfriend is real scary when she's pissed off."

Nathan looked at Annie, who had either not heard or was pretending not to have heard, just looking out her own window thoughtfully. Nathan frowned down at his knees, thinking of what Wilkerson had said about her.

"Yeah... I guess she is."

CHAPTER 15

They drove on the road that went through the forest for over half an hour, until they came to a small dirt road that crossed it, and turned on it at Jeffrey's indication. They were quiet, and the mood in the car was tense as they made their way on the bumpy road. Nathan watched the strange forest. It was thicker here, the ground overgrown in yellow, purple green and red vines and underbrush. The trees were also varied in shapes and colors, their limbs strange and inconsistent. Once in a while, Nathan thought he saw a house in the woods, but he wasn't sure. Eventually, they came to a much smaller road that went around a lake, and there he could see very clearly many small wooden houses of varied designs perched all around it.

The car stopped not too far from there, at a small, brown wooden house which faced the lake. Jeffrey got out of the car then, and leaned back in through his open door to speak to the driver while Annie and Nathan climbed out a little more slowly.

"Thanks again, dude!"

The driver snorted. "Yeah, you can keep your thanks. And screw this half my debt stuff, after this kind of kamikaze shit, I owe you nothing anymore."

Jeffrey shrugged. "Sure, whatever. Take the thanks anyway. This wouldn't have worked without you."

Nathan watched Annie as she hoisted the heavy-looking duffel bag over her shoulder. She had been very quiet all the way, barely even looking at him. He wondered if she was mad at him for getting himself caught.

The car drove away, and Jeffrey bounced back up towards them, searching his pockets. He retrieved a set of keys held together on a ring which sported a cartoon bird with orange and blue feathers. He grinned at them as he made his way to the side door. He unlocked and opened it, then turned to grin at his friends.

"Welcome to *casa del* Jeffrey!"

Jeffrey strolled inside proudly, flipping a light switch on. Nathan and Annie followed him through the door, looking around.

The interior was even better than Liam's apartment had been. The kitchen and living room were all in the same, open space, separated only by a small island counter. The far wall, which faced the lake, was made almost entirely of glass. Nathan could see a great set of sliding doors in the middle. Stairs descended into a basement in the far left corner.

Everything was made of the same wood Nathan had seen on the outside wall, and lamps hung from the large wooden rafters that separated the square frame of the walls from the slanting roof.

Jeffrey grinned proudly at Nathan's expression. "Not too shabby, huh?"

Annie went to drop her duffel in front of one of the couches, sitting to open it. "Why do you have a house so close to the crater, anyway?"

Jeffrey shrugged, a little hurt, turning toward her. "It's not a house. It's just a cabin. I have a studio in the basement. It's really fashionable, you know. All the cool people have them."

Annie chuckled, rummaging through the contents of her bag. Unsure what he should do, Nathan went to sit on the couch opposite her.

"How'd you find me?"

Annie smiled at him, but did not meet his eyes. "Well, it wasn't too hard to figure out where they'd take you once they got their hands on you. The hard part was coming up with a plan to get you out again."

Nathan nodded. He was starting to get tired again. "Well, whatever it is you did, it worked."

"It helped that you were already getting out, apparently. How did that happen, anyway?"

Nathan shrugged uncomfortably, remembering the disturbing conversation he had had with Malavoy and Wilkerson, and the way Wilkerson had moaned and twitched when he stole his energy.

"It's kind of a long story."

She pulled out a gray plastic bag from the depths of her duffel and tossed it to Nathan. "We have ample time for long stories."

Nathan caught it, almost falling out of his seat. He opened it to peer inside, and recognized with some delight the extra clothes Annie had made him buy at the Rock Shack. He pulled out a pair of faded blue jeans that were crisp and new, and a fresh Zombies Eating Tomatoes t-shirt. This one had a picture of Liam and Jeffrey, made up and dressed like grotesque ghouls, standing very rigid and knee-deep in tomatoes in the middle of an otherwise empty field.

He pulled on the clothes gratefully, removing the green cotton gown and tossing it to the floor. He noticed that Annie was still staring at it gloomily as he finished dressing and sat back down on the couch. She looked back up at him then, though her expression was neutral.

"So?" she said.

He blinked, confused, and remembered she wanted him to tell her how he had escaped. He shifted in his seat and cleared his throat. "Well... it's..." He noticed that Jeffrey was leaning on the small island counter, his chin propped in his right hand. He continued, hesitant, staring at his fingers which fiddled with the frayed material around a hole in the knee of his pants. "I... doctor Wilkerson..."

He couldn't make himself say it, for some reason. Everything that had happened, that was still happening, seemed so fantastic that it could not be real. It felt more like a dream than reality. But if he said it out loud...

Annie was frowning at him. Nathan knew she was realizing something important, and he felt like an idiot for not telling her. "I was left alone with Wilkerson. He... passed out, and I ran."

Annie watched him intently. "...passed out?"

Nathan looked down at his hands. His left forearm was still encased in the cast. "I touched him. I touched his wrist... and I drew his energy. Like I do with electricity."

He couldn't bear to look up at her and see the expression on her face that would no doubt show how horrified she was. Her voice was very quiet when she answered him, ice ages later.

"Did you kill him?"

Nathan shook his head enthusiastically. "No! No, I checked, and he was still alive!"

He looked up at her then, and was surprised to see not shock and horror painted on Annie's face, but just concern. "Are you all right?"

Nathan wanted to say he was fine, but he just managed to shrug. He swallowed to try and dismiss the knot from his throat and then tried to clear it, with no success. He looked down at his arm.

"My arm is okay now. But I'd really be better if you could get me some stims. Either of you got any?"

Annie shook her head, and Jeffrey shrugged. "I can always make you some coffee, but that's as close as I've got."

Nathan nodded, sighing. He wished he had stopped to search the lab before he left. They had all sorts of drugs there. "I'll take the coffee."

Jeffrey nodded once and started to make it. Annie gave Nathan a tentative smile. "I've got something that could make you feel better."

She pulled out a garbage bag from her duffel, and put it down on the rug gingerly, like it contained something fragile, or precious. Nathan frowned at it. "What is it?"

"Why don't you find out?"

Nathan let himself slide to the floor, intrigued, and reached out to pull the bag closer to him. Its contents rattled a bit as it slid across the fluffy rug. Nathan opened it and pulled out a diminutive hard drive, a motherboard, and the casing of a very small computer. He grinned at it when he recognized it.

"Oliver! You found him!" He hugged the hard drive to his chest, and put it down next to the other parts, looking into the bag. "Do you have a screwdriver?"

Jeffrey turned to reach into a cupboard in the kitchen, pulling out a miniature toolbox.

"I have more tools downstairs, but you should find what you need in here."

Nathan got up to take the box from Jeffrey, and found what he needed. He immediately set off to work on rebuilding his friend under the watchful eye of Annie and Jeffrey.

He ended up drinking the whole pot of coffee in under an hour, and asking for more. After much convincing, he got Jeffrey to put on another pot. Annie insisted that Nathan should have some food, but when Jeffrey went through his cupboards, they found next to nothing for Nathan to eat, except for something called popcorn, which was deliciously light and salty. Nathan enjoyed it immensely, except for the fact that it kept getting caught in his teeth.

He took much longer than he really needed to repair Oliver. He knew how to do it, he had upgraded him many times, but this time he was filled with a sense of dread. What if it wasn't Oliver when he put him back together? What if they had broken him? Erased him? What if Oliver was mad at Nathan for leaving him to be hurt? And what would happen when he ran out of excuses for not talking to Annie?

Eventually, he could no longer reasonably put it off, and he finally put the last small parts in. Then he plugged Oliver in, and, taking a deep breath, booted him.

The booting sequence seemed to go exactly as expected, but Nathan held his breath until the operating system had loaded. When he didn't hear Oliver complaining, he called out hesitantly.

"Oliver?"

"Don't bother me. I have a million diagnostics to run."

Relief washed over Nathan as he heard the familiar, annoyed voice. He sighed and leaned back against the couch. "All right, tell me when you're done."

He noticed that Annie was still watching him with a thoughtful expression, though now she was also smiling. He looked back down at Oliver quickly, uncomfortable again. Fortunately, that was the moment Oliver chose to declare that his diagnostics were complete, but that he couldn't establish a connection to the flux. Nathan looked at Jeffrey, who was reading a magazine, sitting next to Annie.

"I can't get a connection to the flux. Is your booster down?"

"I'll check it tomorrow. I haven't been here a while, and sometimes possums nest in it."

Nathan nodded, a little disappointed. "All right. I guess it'll give me time to go through the files we got from the other lab."

Annie leaned forward, looking eager. "You mean you actually got them? And you think they're still there?"

Nathan nodded enthusiastically. "Definitely. Oliver would have never let them through if he didn't know them. They would have to wipe him from the hard drive before they accessed or erased the files. If he's still there, so are they."

Jeffrey grinned broadly and turned to Annie. "Hear that? We still got a shot!"

Nathan looked back down at Oliver. He seemed to be unable to stop thinking about the things Wilkerson had said about

169

Annie. In his heart he knew they couldn't be true, and yet... there was so much he didn't know about her.

"Are you all right, Nathan?"

He looked up and realized they were both watching him. He wondered how long he'd been lost in his own thoughts as he gave a short nod and moved his fingertips to one of Oliver's jacks, linking with him.

The files were indeed there. In fact, everything was in its proper place. The only thing that was amiss was Oliver's fretful attitude. Nathan had to spend a lot of his time and energy reassuring him, and by the time he got to the files, he was starting to feel very tired. He discovered then that they were heavily encrypted, and he let out a groan of annoyance. He put Oliver down on the rug in front of him and stood.

"What's wrong?"

Annie looked up from the note pad she'd been scribbling on. Nathan was pacing where he had been sitting in front of the couch opposite her. He shook his head, folding his arms. Why couldn't those files just not be encrypted? Wasn't it already hard enough as it was?

"I don't know!"

"Is something wrong with the files?"

"They're encrypted!"

She let him pace a little more before going on. "And you can't decrypt them?"

"Yes I can! Of course I can! But it's difficult! And it's complicated! And why do I have to do everything around here?"

She frowned at him, looking puzzled. Jeffrey had gone down to the basement, and so they were alone for the first time since they got him out.

"What's wrong with you, Nathan? You've been acting strange since you got back."

Nathan went to the kitchen to pour himself the last of the second pot of coffee, even though it was cold by now. He felt stiff and jerky, like he wanted to punch something. He'd not felt like that very often in his life, but he knew what would make him feel better. He grimaced at his coffee, and resisted the urge to throw the cup across the room.

"I'm tired! I need stims!"

Annie sighed, visibly trying to contain her annoyance. "Well, you'll just have to wait until tomorrow. We don't have any, and we have to rely on Jeffrey's friends to bring us what we need."

He clicked his tongue irritably and drank down the bitter black brew in one sip, hoping it would wake him up a bit. Annie watched him and shook her head.

"Why don't you try to sleep a little until then? It would make the time go by faster."

"I don't want to sleep!"

He had almost screamed at her this time. She didn't look angry, though, just sad, as she turned her face to look away from him. His anger turned on himself then, and he stomped toward the sliding glass doors, reaching it just as Jeffrey appeared on top of the stairs that led to the basement.

"What's going on? What's all the shouting about?"

Nathan bit back a uselessly flippant reply, and simply walked out. He had to calm down. He wasn't sure if he'd be able to do it without the stims, or if he wanted to. He made his way near the shore, and sat down in the sand, watching the waves. He'd never been near a large body of water. He had only found a stream in the forest when he had escaped, and then he had been in the city.

The water looked black, forbidding and soothing at the same time. The breeze was very cold against the bare skin of his arms, yet sitting there in the sand watching the water felt calming, and he soon found himself feeling less tense.

After a little while, he heard the glass doors slide open, and turned, ready to tell Annie to leave him alone, but it was Jeffrey who was making his way towards him, holding a dark green jacket that reminded Nathan vaguely of a security uniform. When Jeffrey reached him, he dropped the jacket on Nathan's shoulders, and sat next to him. He leaned over and put an unopened beer can in front of Nathan's feet, then leaned back on his elbows and said nothing.

Nathan remained still for some moments, then slipped his arms through the sleeves of the jacket. It was too large for him, but it was warm, and that was all that mattered. He then reached for the beer. The can was cold, and Nathan had never had cold beer, though he'd heard about its merits. He opened it and drank his first sip hesitantly.

It was a little bitter, but much better than his first taste had been at Liam's place; the bubbles and cool temperature added a lot to its flavor. Jeffrey smiled at him. "Feeling better?"

Nathan nodded, if only slightly. He really was feeling better. The night air had helped clear his mind a little, and he didn't feel so angry anymore.

"So what's with the crabbiness, anyway?"

Nathan took another sip of beer, and frowned at Jeffrey. "The what?"

"You know, the moodiness. You seem pretty pissed off. And I don't think it's just the stims."

Nathan glared at him, feeling his anger spike. "It's none of your business."

Jeffrey chuckled a bit. "You really are a piece of work. You pissed at Annie?"

Nathan stared at his beer, not answering. Perhaps he was mad at her. How did he know he could trust her? Even if he did, what would happen when he turned her back to life? She wouldn't need him anymore, then.

Jeffrey sighed. "Don't be so hard on her, man. She's feeling really terrible about letting you get caught. You should have seen the way she shook down those guys to get her hands on the explosives. She cares about you a lot, you know."

Nathan snorted into his can as he drank more of its contents. Jeffrey raised his eyebrows at him. "Is that hard to believe?"

"No. She needs me. She said so."

Jeffrey remained quiet for a few seconds, then shook his head, smiling. "You're a dumbass."

Nathan scowled at him. "What?"

"You think she just needs you? I need you. I also happen to think you're pretty cool, but I wouldn't go into a killing rage or cry a whole night away because something bad happened to you. Which is what she did, by the way."

Nathan shrugged, but his anger was ebbing. Still, Jeffrey didn't know about all the things Wilkerson had said. The tall dead man nudged him with his elbow. "Come on, little dude. You like her too, don't you?"

Nathan frowned up at Jeffrey. "What?"

Jeffrey sighed a bit, looking up at the stars. "Look, all I'm saying is, if you got issues with Annie, you should tell her about it, instead of acting like you've got some kind of PMS."

"Like I got what?"

Jeffrey laughed again. "Someday, you're going to make some woman really frustrated, you know that?"

Nathan was so confused by then he had no idea what to say, so he resumed drinking his beer. Fortunately, Jeffrey caught on to his confusion, even though he kept laughing at him.

"Look, all I'm saying is, you gotta learn to talk to people instead of saying nothing's wrong and then acting like something is. Got it?"

Nathan nodded. It seemed like a convoluted way of saying something very simple, but then again, Jeffrey was a convoluted kind of person. Nathan watched him. He barely knew Jeffrey, but then again, he barely knew Annie, and Oliver wouldn't know what to say if he asked him.

"How do I know I can trust her?"

Jeffrey smiled, but there was nothing derisive about it, this time. He simply shrugged and turned his dead, white eyes toward the lake.

"You don't. That's not what trust is about. If you knew everything she would do, you wouldn't have to trust her. When you trust someone, you don't know what they're gonna do with that trust. They might be worthy of it, or not. You learn who isn't by trying."

Nathan sighed. This wasn't what he had wanted to hear at all. "Then why trust anyone?"

Jeffrey grinned. "Because you have to! If you don't trust anyone, then you're all alone, aren't you? I guess some people like that better. Not me. I prefer being hurt once in a while."

"You do?"

"Of course! The good times are worth it."

Nathan considered this. He had been alone, all these years he'd been in Three Walls. He'd had Oliver, that was true, but he had made Oliver himself, and he knew him too well to really have a conversation with him. No matter what, he would always know what Oliver would answer him, and since he had met Annie, and Jeffrey, he realized how lonely he'd been. He craved their company now almost like he craved stims, and the rare occasions he'd felt Annie's cold touch when she was trying to reassure him in his moments of distress were burned in his mind like some of the most significant memories he had.

He sighed heavily, and drained the last of his beer. Sleep was creeping up on him; he could feel it make his limbs and eyelids heavy. He yawned and put the empty can down in the sand. Jeffrey looked at him. "Ready to go back in?"

Nathan nodded and stood. The cold had somewhat stiffened his limbs, and he stretched as soon as he was standing, then looked down at Jeffrey expectantly. The dead man only shook his head.

"Go ahead. I'm gonna stay out here a little longer. I always loved the lake at night, so I'm going to take advantage of the fact that I can't feel the cold."

"All right."

Nathan thought about staying out here as well. He didn't really feel like heading back inside and being alone with Annie, but this time, it was a different sort of apprehension he felt, which didn't feel quite so bad. The breeze picked up, making him shiver through the thin coat, and making up his mind for him. He walked back to the sliding glass door, trying to walk in as quietly as possible.

Annie noticed him anyway; after all, she was sitting on the couch facing the door. She seemed about to say something, but then hesitated, and remained silent. Nathan cleared his throat nervously, and went to sit on the couch in front of Oliver.

Annie looked back down at her note pad, but didn't resume her writing. Nathan noticed that she was watching him discreetly.

"How did you find him?" he asked.

"Sorry?"

She blinked at him, surprised by the question. He nodded his chin towards Oliver. "Oliver. They had him. How did you find him and all his parts?"

She looked down at Oliver. Nathan had the impression she didn't want to look at him as she answered. "I knew where he would be, so I went to get him. I knew you'd miss him."

Nathan stared at her for a long time, trying to decide what to say, or do, how to ask the things he needed to know. His head fell forward, and he realized his eyes had been closing on their own. He sighed. This wouldn't do; he would never be able to have an important conversation like this. He started to stand to get more coffee, and remembered he drank the last of it. He saw that she was looking at him again, and searched her dead white eyes for some kind of answer.

"I'm falling asleep," he finally said.

"I can see that."

There was no mockery or sarcasm in her voice, or at least, none that he could detect. He yawned, trying to buy himself a few more minutes.

"What will you do, if I fall asleep?"

She cocked her head on the side, her face taking on that puzzled, thoughtful expression he had come to know so well. "I don't know. Got anything in mind?"

He nodded and rubbed his hands nervously. "You know, the night you drugged me?"

He thought she looked a bit sad, and ashamed. "Yes."

"Can you do what you did that night?"

She frowned, visibly not understanding. "Drug you?"

He shook his head, a little annoyed that he had to say it. "Stay close to me. You know, when I sleep."

She smiled then, broadly and happily, and her eyes seemed so bright that Nathan thought he could almost see the color they had once been. She stood, extending a hand to help him up.

"Come on. Let's go find you a bed."

CHAPTER 16

The stairs led to a basement that was made of the same wood that was all over the rest of the cabin; it had a TV room in a small open area on the left side, and a few closed doors on the right side.

The first door was locked, so Annie moved on to the next one. This one opened onto a small bedroom. There were posters all over the walls, of musical groups that were not Jeffrey's band, with names that Nathan couldn't read in various bold colors at the bottom of the picture. There was a large pile of clothes in a corner, though there were so many other clothes scattered all over the floor along with objects of all kinds: headphones, papers, shoes, and a few electronic gadgets Nathan didn't recognize. The bed was the only place relatively free of litter, save for a couple of shirts. It was large enough for two people, and had a bright orange comforter that looked warm and inviting, even to Nathan.

Annie shook her head when she took in the mess, but Nathan could see that she was still smiling. She walked to the bed, and removed the few pieces of clothing from it, tossing them on top of the pile in the corner, then shook the wrinkles out of the blanket, and fluffed the orange pillows. Nathan watched her, standing still until she was done. When she was, she lifted a corner of the comforter and smiled up at him.

"All right, why don't you come lie down and make yourself comfortable."

Nathan nodded, and went to slip under the blanket. It was thick and soft, and he felt his eyes close as soon as his head was on the pillow. He saw Annie reach for the light switch, and his heart sent a surge of adrenaline through his body that woke him right up.

"No!"

She turned to him, surprised and puzzled. Nathan sighed with relief and laid his head back on the pillow.

"Leave the light on. I don't want to be in the dark."

She nodded, and came to sit beside him on the bed. She seemed to be hesitating, frowning down at him thoughtfully, undecidedly. He watched her through half-closed eyes. His body felt heavy with sleep, and he wanted to surrender to it, but each heart beat brought a little bit of chemical fear to his brain, just enough to keep him awake, if barely.

At length, she ran a hand through his hair. "Are you all right, Nathan?"

He looked down at her hand, lying flat on the bed right next to his fingers. Even though they were not touching, he could feel how cold her skin was. His words were barely intelligible as they came out, but he found he could do no better than mumbling.

"Are you going to do experiments on me?"

She blinked, and frowned. The hand that was moving through his hair stopped to rest on his cheek. "I would never do anything to hurt you, Nathan."

It was enough, for now, anyway. The fear slowly vanished, and his eyes closed all the way. It seemed right after that, the nightmares came.

He was in one of the chambers they used for what they called 'stress tests'. He hadn't had a lot of those, but they were the most terrible. They took place in small places that looked like refrigerators with glass doors. They usually locked him in there naked, hooked to all sorts of machinery that measured the way his body and brain reacted by tracing squiggly lines on a monitor. The tests consisted in making it very hot, or loud, or sometimes removing the air from the container one way or another, and looking at what happened to him.

This time, though, they were making it cold, unbearably cold, so cold that everywhere his skin touched, all the places where the machines were connected to his body, seemed to burn. He could see the scientists on the other side of the glass, two of them, but he couldn't make out their facial features, just their silhouettes against the strong back light in which they were engulfed.

He screamed his pain, he screamed for help, and he screamed for Annie. He shouted her name over and over again, until one of the scientists got closer, and he recognized her face, Annie's face, with her dead eyes, writing down on a clipboard. He could hear laughter then, and saw Wilkerson was the other silhouette, and was pointing at him, laughing, his crooked teeth showing under his lips.

Nathan awoke with a scream, scrambling up to a sitting position. But he wasn't cold, and it wasn't dark, and someone was holding him, making soothing sounds in his ear. He took a deep, shuddering breath, and melted into Annie's embrace. It took him only a few seconds to regain his calm, and he realized his cheeks were wet, though he didn't really recall having cried. He rubbed his face, sighing, and Annie released him, looking at him.

"Nightmare?"

He nodded, not particularly inclined to discuss the details with her. He looked around, but the room had no windows. The light was still on.

"Is it morning yet?"

She looked over his shoulder. "No. But you've slept nearly six hours already. You must have been exhausted. Do you want to go back to sleep?"

He shook his head. He still felt tired, but he wasn't struggling to keep conscious anymore, and that was enough. He was sitting up, now, so he brought up his knees under his chin and hugged them, leaning his head on his arms to look back at Annie.

She hadn't put the lab coat back on, and she was still wearing the faded jeans and turtleneck she had on in the megaplex. Her hair was up in a ponytail. Fine curls escaped the elastic on the sides, and she had tucked them carelessly behind her ears. She lowered her gaze under his scrutiny, and her eyes fell on his left arm, which was still encased in hard, white plaster.

"What happened to your arm? You never said."

There was something like apprehension in her voice, like she was afraid of what he would say. He shrugged. "I think it was broken. It happened when I tried to get away from the van."

"When you what?"

She seemed surprised. He lifted his left arm to look at it. "I made them stop so I could pee. Then I ran and they shot me and I fell on it."

She smiled at him and shook her head. "You can be so brave, sometimes. You amaze me."

"'Cause I tried to run away?"

"Not many people in your situation retain so strong a sense of will, or identity."

He frowned and looked down. She picked up on his discomfort and leaned forward to put a hand on his left elbow.

"What's wrong?" she said.

He looked back up at her. He had to ask sooner or later, Jeffrey was right.

"Have you known a lot of people in my situation?"

She blinked and let go of him, taken aback. Then her expression grew pained, and she had a resigned sigh. "I told you. I worked in a lab."

He put his forehead against his knees, folding his hands on the back of his neck. So it was true. "You worked in *that* lab?"

"You know I did, Nathan."

"Did you experiment on me?"

He didn't look at her. He didn't want to see the expression she had when he asked her. He wasn't sure he would be able to deal with just hearing the answer.

"No," she said. "I didn't."

He turned to look at her then. Her face was sad, but not hurt. Was she saying the truth? "But you did on other people, though, right?"

She looked down shamefully. "Yes."

"Wilkerson said..." He frowned, wondering why he was still having trouble saying it. "He said you were part of the people that created me. He said... he said that... my life would have been the same." He stared at his knees again. "That if you'd have still been there, you would have done those things to me."

She touched his shoulder with her fingertips, gingerly. He risked a glance at her face and saw that she was looking very serious, intent, even. "He's wrong, Nathan. He lied to you."

"Why would he lie to me? He'd never even really talked to me before."

"He probably wanted something. They can be very coercive and manipulative. What else did he talk about at that time?"

Nathan thought for a second. "Well, not much else. He said I was naïve. Other that than, Malavoy did most of the talking."

"What did he say?"

"A lot of weird stuff. That I was a good technopath. That they made me like this. That I could be a success." He took a deep breath then, and said the important bits very quickly. "He said that you'd found me, that you knew who I was, that you just wanted to continue your experiments on me, that you were part of creating me, that you were in Wilkerson's place before."

She frowned, looking puzzled. "How did they know we were friends, anyway?"

Nathan scratched the back of his head, feeling his face heat a bit. Why was it so embarrassing to tell her that now, after everything else? "Well... it's complicated. I thought about you during a fight with another technopath. I guess they used it to find out who you were."

"And then they told you all that stuff about the way it would have been with me... and the stuff I supposedly wanted to do to you?"

He nodded. She shook her head, looking stricken. They stayed quiet for a long time, and he noticed her jaw seemed very tight, and her lips were pressed together in a thin line. Then, finally, she sighed.

"They were trying to manipulate you, Nathan. They were trying to win you over, or at least to discourage you from trying to run away again. From trying to find me again."

He felt tired again. What was he supposed to do if people were playing mind games with him to make him think things he wouldn't have thought otherwise? He could barely keep up with what he thought he was thinking on his own! What if Annie was playing mind games too? How was he supposed to tell? He shook his head and hugged his knees again.

She was watching him with a worried expression. "Nathan?"

"So, you're telling me that none of what he said was true?"

She shook her head, looking uncomfortable. "Well... more or less."

"What's true, then?"

She had that pained expression again, and she reached to undo her ponytail and do it back up nervously. Nathan waited patiently for the answer to his question. It took some time to come.

"I... did have Wilkerson's job before I left."

Nathan felt sick. So Wilkerson was right after all. Would he have hated her as much as he hated him? Would she have hurt him, terrified him like they did? She put her hand on his upper arm again, but this time he flinched away from her touch.

"It's not the same, Nathan. It wasn't the same back then. We did research strictly on ghouls, when I started out."

He looked up at her. How could it be true? He had been there all his life, and he was no ghoul. He was alive, anyway, as far as he really understood the term.

"I'm not a ghoul."

"I know. After a few years... things changed." She looked away, not really at anything, at what she was seeing in her mind. "We weren't getting the results that we wanted, and then... the directives... changed. I got in this to find a cure, Nathan. My mother had been turned into a ghoul, and I thought... I could prevent that kind of pain for someone else. But it didn't work."

She was quiet for a little while, but he let her go on. "After a while, it was no longer a cure they wanted. They wanted to give people eternal life. To change the process of becoming a ghoul, so that one would no longer... cease to be alive. That didn't work either. Not the way we expected, anyway. Wilkerson was sure that it was because of the subjects. We were testing on rats and monkeys, at that time. So he decided it was time to start testing on humans. Very few of us opposed it, and it was decided. The subjects started pouring in, old, young, men, women..."

Her lips moved soundlessly for two seconds, and she shook her head, remembering to draw breath. Nathan was motionless, riveted, afraid that if he said anything to interrupt, she might stop.

"They were all poor, and starving, from Three Walls and the wastes, mostly," she continued. "They didn't know they had come to give up their lives in exchange for a hot meal."

She paused then, as if unsure how to go on. Nathan watched her, but she never lifted her eyes to meet his. "We kept adjusting the formula, but we never grew any closer to what we were hoping for. People were always dead, no matter how much brain function they retained. So word got around in the communities about how our volunteers never made it back out again, and the volunteers stopped coming."

She paused to refill her lungs, and glared at the floor a little before starting again. "Even when they were volunteers, I was having second thoughts about the experiment. When they started taking people..."

183

Nathan frowned. "Taking people?"

She nodded. Her face looked paler than it ever had. She looked haunted, like she was waking up from a nightmare. "One day I came in to work, and the volunteers we had in the converter... they weren't volunteers. They were screaming. They didn't know how they got there, or what was happening to them."

"What happened?"

Nathan was mesmerized. He'd never known any of this; he didn't even know what a converter was. She looked sad. "They died. Some of them became like me. Most of them were just... dead."

"So, are there are a lot of others like you?"

"No. There weren't a lot in the first place who...changed. And they were always exterminated after study."

"You mean they were killed?"

"In a manner of speaking. They were already dead, like I am."

"But they didn't kill you?"

She looked grim again, and shook her head. "They didn't. I pretended to be a corpse. Then when they left me to be incinerated with the others, I escaped."

Nathan squinted down at the blanket, trying to add everything up in his mind. "But... why did they make you part of your own experiment in the first place?"

"Well, I was angry. I wanted to leave."

"Really? That's it?"

She had a small smile. "I just couldn't stand by and let them do what they were doing. There was a woman..." Her voice caught in her throat and she paused for an instant. "She was pregnant. She begged me to save her baby. I... tried to smuggle her out. I got caught. I threatened to go to the press if they didn't let her go, and I ended up in the same converter as she did."

184

She rubbed her mouth and chin with her hand, stealing a nervous glance at Nathan. "I think... I'm pretty sure she was your mother, Nathan."

He frowned and looked abruptly back up to her. All of his inner organs felt like they were being crushed, and his heart started to beat faster.

"My what?"

"Your mother. I think it was you who she was expecting."

"But... how could that be? Didn't you say she died?"

"I didn't. She became like me. Except she didn't know what was happening. She was taken for study."

He stared at her. Where could he have been? Why didn't he remember this? "What about me?"

She bit her lower lip, hesitating before she continued. "In the first few years after I was... converted, I had a friend on the inside who leaked me information she thought would be useful to turning me back to normal. In the files she leaked to me, I found your file. A baby who had been converted in utero, who remained alive while his mother turned into a smart ghoul. You were what everyone was excited over, the project of the decade. They tried to duplicate the experiment, once or twice, but... it never worked. You were the only one."

Nathan stared at her, mouth hanging open. "So you did know who I was when we met?"

She shook her head vigorously. "No, absolutely not! I didn't even suspect. I hadn't been in contact with Laura for ten years, I didn't know you'd escaped, or if you were even still alive! Besides, there were no pictures in your file. How would I have recognized you?"

He stared into space, feeling too empty to answer, or even be relieved. She glanced at him, saw he was staring, and went on nervously. "I didn't even start to suspect who you were until you told me where you grew up."

Nathan nodded a bit. "What about my... mother?"

Annie shook her head. "She was terminated after delivering you, according to your file. I'm sorry."

Nathan felt dizzy, and he lay back down on the bed, staring at the wooden ceiling. The lab had taken everything from him. He could have had a mother. He didn't even know what that meant, but he wanted one. Annie's voice was small, even hesitant, when she spoke to him again.

"Nathan? Are you all right?"

He shook his head. Slowly, anger and hate started to swim up to the surface, not yet surpassing the dull pain he felt in his chest. He didn't trust the steadiness of his voice to speak, so he remained quiet a very long time as did Annie. Nathan did not look at her to try to decipher the emotions on her face.

The empty feeling spread until he thought his whole body must be hollow, and he felt like he was nothing, even less than that, he was just a thing that men had used and played with to satisfy their curiosity. He'd never been anything else, he realized, though now he knew, for the first time, that he could have been.

After some time, she found the courage to put her cold hand on his shoulder again. This time he didn't pull away, but turned his head to face her.

"What's it like, having a mother?"

Her eyebrows almost met in the middle of her face when they rose in an expression of pain. She pulled him into her arms and embraced him tightly. He leaned his head against her shoulder, slowly feeling the heaviness in his heart reach his throat; he had to squeeze his eyes shut against the now familiar sting of tears, though it only succeeded for a very short time.

CHAPTER 17

When Nathan awoke again, his head felt heavy, and his eyes hurt and wouldn't open all the way. But Annie was still there, right where she had been when he had awakened from his nightmare, sitting on the bed next to him. She smiled down at him when she saw that he was awake.

"Sleep well?"

As he nodded, he realized that he had. He hadn't had a single nightmare in his second stretch of sleep. None that he could remember, anyway.

He had slept longer than he thought, and it was already late morning. When they went upstairs, they found Jeffrey chatting with Liam, who got up to greet Nathan warmly.

"There he is! The man himself!"

He gave Nathan's back two friendly slaps when he reached him, and Nathan found himself wondering why Annie was the only person he knew who didn't express her affection with hitting of some kind. Jeffrey laughed at him.

"Dude! Don't make that face! Liam's your best friend in the whole world right now."

Nathan looked from Liam to Jeffrey, confused. "He is?"

"He sure is. He brought you stims."

Nathan looked back at Liam, his heart leaping with relief and anticipation. "Really?"

Liam grinned at him and produced a small plastic bottle, full of tiny pink pills. As Nathan grabbed the pills from him and went to get some water to wash them down with, Annie shook her head at Jeffrey.

"You could have waited until I got some food in him."

Nathan shrugged and took a big gulp of water, swallowing a pill. "I'll eat later. I've got work to do."

Annie smiled at Nathan, but said nothing. He turned to go sit on the floor in front of the couch, where he'd left Oliver the night before.

The encryption on the files didn't seem half as complex as it had last night, when he had been exhausted and badly jonesing for stims. It was only a question of a few hours before he broke through the last of the codes.

Annie and Liam were cooking when he released Oliver's jack, or, rather, Annie was cooking and once in a while, she would pick up a spoon and feed some of it to Liam, who would shake his head and say that it needed more of a mysterious substance or other, like 'cumin' or 'paprika'. Nathan watched them in fascination from his seat on the floor of the living room until Jeffrey noticed him.

"Hey, you're done! How'd it go?"

Annie and Liam turned to look at him then, and he stood to join them in the kitchen, sitting on a stool next to Jeffrey.

"Good. The files are all decrypted so we should be able to use them now."

Annie smiled, and gave the dark, spicy smelling substance she was cooking another stir. "Great! Now, I'll definitely be able to find some kind of solution. I'm sure I'm almost there." She turned to give Liam another taste from her spoon. "So, what do you think? Is this ready?"

He tasted it, chewing it for a long time, rubbing his chin with his index and thumb, then gave a very stately nod. "Yes, I think it is." Then he turned to Nathan and grinned proudly. "Annie and me, we cooked!"

Jeffrey snorted derisively at him. "Annie cooked. If you had, you'd both end up just even deader than I am. Even with you just test-tasting, I'm not sure that won't happen."

Liam looked offended. "Hey! Annie made me general manager of taste, I'll have you know. I'm morally responsible, if this tastes bad! I take it very seriously."

Annie shrugged as she laid out the mixture in the middle of flat, round breads. "You heard him! So don't blame me if this is terrible."

"Oh no, trust me, it's good."

Liam turned a confident smile on Nathan while Annie folded the breads around the filling in the shape of a burrito, and served two to Nathan, giving the same to Liam.

"Here you go. My father's famous burritos. I remembered you really like burritos, right? If Liam did his tasting thing right, these should be a world better than those you had in Three Walls."

They were much spicier, thicker, and meatier than the ones he used to buy daily near his old squat. Nathan inhaled the first one, only then realizing just how hungry he'd been; this was the first real food he'd had to eat since being captured. He was glad to have someone eat with him, for once. Though Nathan was used to it by now, it seemed Liam found Jeffrey and Annie's habit of watching them while they ate disconcerting. As Nathan was starting on his second burrito, Liam glared at the ghouls.

"Ok. I can't eat with you guys just watching us like that. Can't you go do something else?"

Jeffrey shrugged and stood to go wash the dishes, while Annie went to sit next to Nathan, starting to examine his injured arm. Nathan let her, chewing slowly on his second burrito, until she seemed satisfied.

"You're sure this is healed?"

"Yeah, I've got no pain in it at all anymore."

"Hmm."

She let go of it and stood. "I'll get the equipment I need to remove it tomorrow."

Liam rolled his eyes. "You mean, I will."

She smiled at him. "Oh, come on, you're so sweet and agreeable."

"Yeah, yeah."

Nathan licked his fingers while she went to pick up Oliver and sit on the couch. She typed a few keys, and Oliver's voice was heard above an angry beep.

"Hey! You're not authorized to touch me! What kind of computer do you think I am?"

Annie raised an eyebrow at him, but before she had time to even turn to Nathan for help, he started laughing.

"Shut up, Oliver! It's just Annie. She's authorized."

There was another beep that sounded almost disgruntled, and Annie had a satisfied smile. "Thank you, Nathan."

She was still hard at work by the time they were done helping Jeffrey clean up, and they found themselves standing around her, unsure of what to do. She looked up from her work and arched an eyebrow at the three of them.

"Did you need something?"

Jeffrey looked at the other two, and shrugged at Annie. 'Well... can we help?'

She shrugged and looked from one to the other. "Any of you know anything about nuclear physics?" They remained quiet. "Meteorian biochemistry?"

They looked at each other, almost hopefully. Liam was the first to shrug, and Jeffrey shook his head. "I guess not."

"Then it looks like I'm on my own for now."

Nathan frowned. "You said I could help. You said you needed my help."

"I do. I will. Just... not with the science. But possibly with the application."

"The application?"

"I'll explain later. For now, though, I just need to compare my findings with theirs and complete my formula. So I suggest you find something to do."

To Liam's intense disappointment, Jeffrey didn't have any video games in his cabin. There also wasn't a computer other than Oliver, so swimming the flux was out of the question. Jeffrey did have a few movies, though, and they decided to put one on.

Nathan had never seen a movie before, and as he watched that one, he thought he hadn't been missing much. The story was about a man and a woman, caught in a neighborhood that looked a bit like Outer Circle. It must have been set right after the meteor, because ghouls were rising from everywhere and they didn't know what to do. But everything they did was the worst thing to do in the situation, and the ghouls were grotesque and deformed, with green faces, glowing teeth and melting eyes, not at all like real ghouls. Nathan thought the whole thing was stupid and ridiculous, and said so often enough that Jeffrey and Liam got tired of watching it halfway through.

Then, they decided that it would be a great idea to teach Nathan how to swim in the lake, since he was already great at swimming the flux. But the water was cold, and dark, and Nathan couldn't see what was in it. He was also uncomfortably reminded of the stress test in which they had filled the tank with freezing water and he couldn't breathe, so he refused to step in further than knee deep in the lake, no matter how the other two insisted.

After that, Jeffrey thought Nathan should learn how to fish, because, according to him, to be a man one had to know how to put meat on the table, whatever that meant. That was news to Nathan, who had thought it was a question of identity rather than deed, but he figured Jeffrey knew more about the world than he did, so he listened attentively as Jeffrey explained how to hook the worm and throw the line.

Since there was only one fishing line, Jeffrey and Liam went off further away with their guitars, saying they had a creative spell to take advantage of. They stayed there for the rest of the afternoon while Nathan sat on the wooden deck with the fishing pole in his hands. Nothing happened. He wondered if he was doing something wrong for the first hour or so, then unbearable boredom settled in, and he stared at the water moodily, not caring what happened, as long as something did.

The sky had started to turn red with the sunset by the time Annie emerged from the cabin, and Nathan reeled in his line gratefully, not giving his lack of success a second thought. Jeffrey and Liam also collected their sound recorder and their guitars, and they all reached Annie at roughly the same time.

It was Jeffrey who spoke first, visibly anxious for an answer. "So, have you figured it out?"

She nodded with a tired smile. "I think I have something that might work."

Jeffrey grinned and wrapped his arms around Liam and Nathan's neck, pulling them to him in a rough, happy hug. "Did you guys hear that? She's got it! So when do we go back to being alive?"

Her smile grew a bit more reserved, and she pulled a sheet of paper from her pocket. "Well, that may take a while more. I'm going to need a lot of components to build a converter."

Jeffrey frowned. "You gotta build a whole machine?"

She shrugged apologetically. "It takes really sophisticated machinery to convert the meteorian radiation into something we can use and control."

She handed the sheet of paper to Liam, who frowned, shook his head and whistled through his teeth. "I'm supposed to get all that junk? I don't even know what half of this stuff is, and the other half is worth more than my car!"

Nathan listened to them, thinking. He thought he'd seen Annie look at him a few times, nervously, in that way she had when she wasn't saying everything she knew. He frowned, trying to see what it was he was missing, and then, it hit him.

"This machine... it just converts that energy from the one kind to the other?"

Annie swung her head from side to side, considering it. "Well... put very simply, yes."

"It converts it into something that can heal, or harm?" She nodded again, and Nathan lifted his left arm, which was still a prisoner of its cast. "Well, then, can't I just do it? Why do you need a machine?"

Jeffrey and Liam shared a look, and then just stared at him. Annie made an unsure face, and shook her head. "It's dangerous, Nathan."

"Why?"

She looked uncomfortable. Jeffrey and Liam were now staring at her, waiting for her response. She sighed. "The radiation is normally lethal to humans. I don't think you can handle it safely. What if it kills you, or you turn yourself into a stupid ghoul? Besides, it's one thing to convert energy that is familiar to use on your own body, but transferring it to something else... you'd need to be able to calculate millions of calibrations in an instant."

Jeffrey and Liam turned to look at Nathan while he thought about this. "Well... if you program the right calculations into Oliver, I'm sure he can help me."

She shook her head at that. "It wouldn't work. You'd need to have perfect synchronicity with your computer. I know you're good, but that's nearly impossible."

"It would be, if it was any other computer that Oliver. But I made Oliver, his mind is a piece of my own, and I do have perfect synchronicity with him."

Jeffrey and Liam turned their attention back to Annie, who sighed irritably at them, but could apparently not think of what to say. She folded her arms, snorted in annoyance back at Nathan.

"It's too dangerous, Nathan. This isn't like anything you've ever done before. This energy's unstable, it could do all sorts of things to your body if you can't manage it. It could even kill you, like I said."

Nathan considered this a few moments, as much to gather his thoughts as his courage. "I'm not like other people. You should know that better than anyone. This is what you need me for. You never needed me for building a machine you know so well you can list all its parts, or to break into buildings you remember by heart. You need me to do this."

She stared at him with an expression he couldn't decipher, that looked like hesitation, hope, and fear all at the same time, but she didn't answer him. He looked at her very seriously and steeled his resolve.

"I want to do it, Annie. I don't regret going to the megaplex, and breaking in, and getting caught. I'd do it again if I had to. Well, I'd probably try better to avoid the getting caught part." Even as he said it, he realized that it was true. "Besides, I've gone so far already, I can't turn back now. I'm ready for this."

She looked at him for a short while, and sighed in resignation. "All right. Follow me."

She led him back inside the cabin, to the duffel bag she had been carrying when they came in. From it, she removed an intricate steel container which looked like one of the large coffee thermoses he'd seen people carry with them at the market. She sat with it on her lap, and looked up at Nathan. "Come closer."

She opened the container as he walked to stand right next to her. It held surprisingly little; the bulk of it seemed to be protective lining inside. While the container was almost taller than Nathan's head and nearly as wide as one of his thighs, its contents were a simple purple and white stone with jagged edges, which could easily fit in the palm of his hand. It seemed to glow, and he felt strangely drawn to it, like it wanted him to touch it. He was almost sure that if he did, he could do anything he wished.

"This is a piece of the meteor that Laura got me a few years after my... incident. I've been saving it."

Nathan frowned, momentarily distracted from the call of the stone. "Did you say Laura?"

Annie nodded. "We were friends when I was working there. She was the one I told you about, who kept leaking me information after I was gone, until she disappeared. I think you mentioned her before we left Three Walls; do you remember her well?"

Nathan nodded. "She was the only one who really ever talked to me. She wasn't supposed to, I think, and then at one point she stopped coming." Nathan looked back down at the meteorite. "She's the one who taught me what my name was."

Annie smiled. "I wondered about that. It does sound like her. She was a good person."

"Do you know what happened to her?"

"She disappeared. They must... have found out what she was doing."

Nathan nodded. He could imagine what had happened to her, if Annie's stories were true. His eyes kept being drawn back to the strange rock. He felt like he could see through its shell to the heart of it, and felt like it was pulsing, vibrating, irregularly, but with incredible strength. He didn't realized he had reached out to touch it before Annie stopped him, laying her hand on his wrist. He looked up at her then, and saw she was staring at him intently.

"What do you feel?"

He looked back down at the rock in her hand, and refrained from trying to touch it again, shoving his hands in his pockets.

"It's... hard to describe. But I think it's definitely something I can work with."

She smiled, and put it back in its protective container before he had time to try to lay his hand on it again. "Perfect. Well, Liam, I've got a new list for you."

CHAPTER 18

The list Annie gave Liam this time was considerably shorter and more manageable, and he left that evening with promises of coming back some time the next day with everything requested. Annie fed Nathan what remained of the burrito mixture, and insisted he get some sleep. Nathan protested that he was fine, and that he didn't need it at all since he had his stims, but when she made it clear that she wouldn't let him try the experiment until he slept, he reluctantly agreed.

He didn't ask her even if he wanted to, but she spent the night sitting on the bed next to him anyway, working on Oliver, while he slept with his forehead against her thigh. He didn't have any nightmares that night, and when he woke up, she was still there.

There wasn't much to do that day either. Annie was busy working on Oliver, entering all her calculations, and would not let Nathan help because she said it would be counter-productive. Jeffrey kept Nathan relatively entertained, at least for a little while, by showing him all the equipment in the recording studio that was behind the door that had been locked downstairs. It did keep Nathan busy for a few minutes, looking at all the buttons and switches, but when he interfaced with them, he found that their programming varied from basic to nonexistent, and he couldn't really talk to it, so he spent the afternoon in polite silence while Jeffrey went from explaining the various functions of the machinery to exposing his very firm opinions on the validity of his band's artistic expression, whatever that meant.

Nathan was immensely relieved when Liam finally came back, carrying a full bag and a large cage, in which were a half-dozen rats in varying proportions of black and white.

He expected Jeffrey and Liam to go and work on their music again while they left him alone with his thoughts, but they wanted to play with the rats as much as Nathan did. When Annie was finally done with her calculations, she had to look for them in the bathroom, where they had started to put together a maze in the tub for the rats to explore. She looked at them in puzzlement for what seemed like a long time before declaring that she was done, and that they should put the rats back in to their cage before coming upstairs to have their dinner. They reluctantly obeyed before going up to join her.

She was cooking meat again, this time it was white and had significantly less spices in it. When she was done making it, she tossed it on top of a bowl full of crispy green leaves, and tiny colored fruits and nuts. She covered the whole thing with some kind of sauce, then spent some time mixing it as Nathan watched from where he was seated with Liam and Jeffrey, at the island counter.

She served Liam and Nathan each a very generous serving of the mixture. It was light, refreshing, and deliciously crunchy, but even though Nathan ate a large quantity of it, he didn't find it terribly satisfying, and he missed the warmth in his chest that came from eating hot, spicy food. He said nothing except to tell Annie it was very good when she asked him expectantly how he felt about it. She seemed happy with his response.

"That's good. It's great for your health, you know'"

"It is?"

Nathan regarded the leafy green contents of his bowl dubiously. Then again, she was the doctor, so she probably knew better. She was looking at his left arm, though, as if evaluating something.

"What?"

"You're absolutely positive your arm is healed?"

He nodded uncomfortably, remembering for a brief instant Wilkerson's twitching, moaning shape. "I'm sure."

"Then I'll remove the cast after you've eaten."

She made marks on the hardened substance on his forearm as he finished eating, and when he was done, she used a minuscule electric saw to cut through the hard shell. Nathan remained perfectly still as she cut away the cast, terrified that she might accidentally cut his arm, though there was a green plastic guard on the saw that prevented it from going further than it needed to.

She removed the pieces gingerly and with the greatest care, making sure his arm remained still. When it was free, she examined the forearm with the same caution, first looking at it and then prodding it gently with her fingertips before picking it up with the lightest of touches to move it gently.

"Does this hurt?"

"No."

"Can you move it?"

Nathan twisted his wrist and elbow experimentally. It was as though nothing had ever happened; there was no pain at all. Annie watched him critically for a few moments before nodding, satisfied.

"Good! Looks like we can get to work."

She dug through the bag which Liam had brought back, and retrieved what looked like headphones, but turned out to be a very simple swimmer's headset, with two small electrodes that came to rest on the temples. She had three sets. She gave one to Nathan.

"Ever use one of these?"

He nodded, recalling the confrontation he'd had with the other technopath. This headset was much simpler, and more comfortable than the one he'd used, but the principle was the same. She started taking apart the two that remained in her hands.

"I need to make some instruments out of these. Can you link with Oliver and see if you understand the equations?"

There was no need for that, but Nathan did it just the same. As he suspected, Oliver understood the equations, which meant that Nathan didn't have to. Oliver did suggest testing the process before trying it on something potentially dangerous, so Nathan tried a few times to draw electricity and convert it to himself while Oliver calculated. By the third try, Oliver had all his calculations corrected, and he congratulated Nathan on the incredible sensory capabilities of his body.

Annie was done working on her equipment when Nathan walked back to her. She was sitting on one of the couches, making notes in her little pad. She looked up at him as he approached, smiling.

"Done?"

He nodded. The equipment she had been working on lay in a small heap next to her, and it was now in such a state that he wasn't sure if she was finished or not.

"What about you?"

"Yes, I'm done. The rest of my work will be done Oliver, depending on the results of this experiment."

She closed her notebook, leaving her index finger to mark the place she was at, and picked up her equipment, Oliver, and the metal case which contained the meteorite, motioning for Nathan to follow her downstairs. Jeffrey and Liam were there, watching television on the large screen, apparently finishing the movie they had started to watch with Nathan the day before. They turned to look at Annie and Nathan, Jeffrey leaning forward in his seat.

"Need anything?"

"Yes. I'd like to set up my lab in your recording studio."

"You what?"

Jeffrey raised an eyebrow, but Annie's face remained neutral. "Your recording studio. It's the perfect place to do our experiments."

199

Jeffrey seemed crestfallen. "It's soundproof, not radiation-proof!"

"Don't worry about your equipment. We won't do anything chemical."

"No, you're just going to irradiate some rats."

Annie raised an eyebrow and folded her arms on her chest. Jeffrey groaned and went to unlock the door to his studio. When he was done, she smiled at him brightly and thanked him, then went to get the rat cage from the bathroom before leading Nathan inside.

Once in, she put down the cage, and sat in front of it, retrieving a rat that was mostly black, with a white patch on his right ear, and began strapping one of the modified headsets on its head. "Bring me Oliver, please."

Nathan nodded, carrying Oliver to her, looking curiously at the rat. "What are you doing with Roger?"

She raised her eyes to blink at him, surprised. "You named it?"

Nathan sat cross-legged next to her, putting Oliver down on the floor. "Not just me. Jeffrey, Liam and me, we named two each."

"You named all of them?"

Nathan nodded, and pointed to the rats. "Those are Roger, and Rattigan. Jeffrey named them. Liam named George and Ringo, and I named Laura and 228B."

Annie frowned at him, this time more in puzzlement than shock. "228B?"

Nathan nodded. "I don't know a lot of names, so I wanted to name them for friends I had before. 228B was the name of the first lock I spoke to, the one that let me out of my cell the first time I escaped the lab."

Annie nodded, and looked down at Roger for a moment. "I don't know if that was a good idea."

"Jeffrey said you were supposed to name your pets."

"They're not pets. You don't usually name your test subjects."

Nathan's throat felt tight, but he kept his face and voice as inexpressive as he could manage. "Why not?"

"Because bad things might happen to them, and if you've named them, you usually get attached."

"Well, you should get attached. People should care if bad things happen to their test subjects!"

She looked up at Nathan then, and then her face changed, suddenly looking sad. "God, Nathan, I'm so sorry..."

She reached out to touch his hand but he stood abruptly. "I'm going to get Oliver's power cord," he said. "He hates it when he runs out of power."

He was out of the room before she could say anything else. If he had stayed, he didn't know what he would have done, but he was sure he would have regretted it. It took him some time to cool off, but when he made his way downstairs again, he noticed Jeffrey looking at him strangely.

Annie looked up from Oliver's screen when he walked back in the studio. "I'm sorry, Nathan. I should have thought..."

He raised a hand to stop her, feeling the anger rise up in him again. She didn't go on, though Nathan could see her need to do so painted all over her face. She motioned to Roger the rat, who was still wearing the contraption she had made out of the headset, and was currently connected to Oliver.

"I got Oliver to monitor Roger's brain function. Are you ready?"

Nathan nodded. The truth was, he felt tired, but he'd been waiting long enough, and he wanted to get started, so he took a stim and went to sit next to her while she retrieved the meteorite from its protective case. Nathan connected his own headset and put it on his head, linking with Oliver. He could instantly feel Roger's mind then, like he could reach out to it through Oliver, and he was able to tell that the little rat was hungry, and scared.

"I can feel him," he said. "Roger. I can tell how he feels."

She frowned at him. He thought she was seeing a problem, but it must not have been of great concern, because she didn't mention anything. She put the meteorite down next to him.

"All right. We're going to try and make Roger like me. Let Oliver do the calculations, and be very careful."

He nodded. Annie watched him fretfully as he concentrated and picked up Roger with his left hand, cradling him against his chest until he sensed the little rat was comfortable. Annie was picking up the cage with the other rats, and he let her step away from him before he touched the meteorite, though he could still feel her worried stare on him. When she was as far as she could be, he laid his hand on the stone.

It didn't feel at all like he had expected. With electricity, as soon as he touched it, it surged through him, and all he had to do was control its flow. This energy was different. It felt a lot like the life force had felt in Wilkerson, when he had drained him. It was there, at his fingertips, vibrant and tantalizing, but he had to reach for it, to stimulate it into coming to him, until it actually started pouring.

It rose in him in great waves, so different from anything he'd felt before that for a few terrifying moments, he didn't think he could control it. But then, he felt Oliver's presence, and surrendered his consciousness to him, letting him regulate the flow, and start the conversion.

Once converted, it was another difficult task to manage to pour the energy in Roger's body, instead of absorbing it into himself. He concentrated on Roger, squirming in his left hand, and on the feeling he had had when he had used his own life force to awaken Annie, that time he had rescued her from the warehouse. It seemed to work; he could feel the energy pouring out of him and into the little rat. He surrendered to Oliver again, letting him calculate what was needed according to Annie's formula.

Then, something happened. He could still feel Roger's mind on the edge of his own. But the fear that the little rat was experiencing was reaching its peak. There was pain, there, too, intense and raw, like the rat's body was about to explode. Nathan cried out, and wanted to let go of meteorite and rat, but Oliver's rational mind was still in control, and by the time Nathan was in charge again, there was no more fear, no more pain, and Roger the rat was hanging limp in his left hand.

"Roger?"

Annie was suddenly at his side, her arm around his shoulders. "Nathan, are you all right?"

He shook his head. Heavy tears were welling up in his eyes as he stared at the rat in his hands. She took Roger delicately from him as he watched, trying to regain control of his breathing. She listened to the rat's belly with her stethoscope, and as he saw it, Nathan suddenly felt it: Roger twitched. Annie's eyes widened slightly, staring at the rat expectantly. Nathan felt Roger's mind coming back, like a computer that was rebooting. The fear was back, but the pain had been replaced by confusion, and he knew before Annie spoke that it had worked. She put down the rat, which started to run in circles on the carpeted studio floor, held back by the device on his head, still plugged in Oliver. Annie was checking the screen, an excited look on her features that she was trying to control. Nathan guessed that if she needed to breathe, she would have been holding her breath.

He was done wiping his face dry when she turned to him, smiling happily.

"We did it, Nathan! Roger's brainwaves are the same as they were before. We did it! On the first try! I can't believe it! This is going much better than I thought!"

She leaned towards him to hug him tightly, but he couldn't share her excitement. The memory of Roger's fear, his pain, was still too vivid. She let go of him, frowning.

"What's the matter? We did it!"

203

"You didn't tell me it would hurt."

She looked confused for a second, then looked at Roger, understanding. "You felt his pain?"

Nathan nodded resentfully and Annie looked down. "I'm sorry. I didn't think that would happen. My experience with technopaths is somewhat limited, and you're something different and exceptional altogether."

Nathan removed the headset and put it down on Oliver's keyboard. "Am I going to have to do this with the others?"

Annie looked at the cage containing the rest of the rats, and then back at Nathan.

"It depends. If my formula is correct, then it'll work on Roger, and we won't have to. Otherwise, we might have to, yes."

Nathan nodded, staring at Roger. He felt too drained to do anything else that night, so he simply watched as Annie put Roger in a plastic box that had holes in it to keep him separate from the rats that were still alive. He barely protested when Annie insisted he get some rest, but only followed her to the bedroom, where she sat on the bed next to him as he fell asleep.

CHAPTER 19

The nightmares came back that night, though they were very different than the ones he was accustomed to. In these, he was the one doing the experiments, putting a human version of Roger through all the terrible tests he'd gone through when he was a child. Every time he awoke, though, Annie was there, and she managed to reassure him back to sleep.

He felt groggy and his head hurt when it was morning again, but he was finally starting to feel a bit rested, which was a feeling he didn't recall ever having had in his life. Annie brought him upstairs to serve him cereal, though when she did, she poured milk in it and put a spoon in the bowl. Nathan had never had milk in his cereal, in fact, he didn't think he'd ever had milk before, and was pleasantly surprised with the combination of tastes and textures.

They went back to work right after he had eaten. Roger the rat was circling his plastic cage, and Nathan could feel that he was still afraid when Annie linked him to Oliver. But Nathan breathed deep, convincing himself that this was going to work as he reached out to take the rat in his left hand, and lay his right hand on the meteorite. He reached for the energy, and let Oliver do the rest, while he monitored Roger's mind for reactions.

When he poured the energy into the rat, there was more fear, and more anxiety, and then it was as though there had been a short circuit and suddenly Roger's mind wasn't there. He looked down in his left hand as he felt Oliver stop the flow of energy. Distractedly, he let go of the meteor to stare at the dead rat in his hand, laying his right hand over him. He couldn't understand what had happened. He had been able to feel Roger's life force, his essence, when Oliver was pouring the energy into him, but somehow, what Oliver had sent far too little. He could see it, sense it, knew how to reach it; why hadn't Oliver been able to get there, with all his sophisticated calculations?

He started when he realized that Annie was sitting right next to him again, staring at him, her face full of concern. He had no idea how long she'd been there, but obviously, it was long enough for her to have realized that Roger was dead. Nathan returned her stare dully for a few seconds, then looked back down at Roger's lifeless form. He had felt such grief and distress when he'd hurt him the night before. Now, he felt nothing, like he was hollow, and he found himself wondering if that made him just as bad as Wilkerson.

Annie took Roger from his hands gently, as she had the night before. Nathan couldn't do anything else than stare at him. "What'll happen to him now?" he asked in a muted voice.

"What do you mean?"

She was looking at him with a little panic in her eyes, like he was asking her something difficult. "I mean, what are you going to do with him now?"

She looked slightly relieved as her eyes dropped to the tiny body for what seemed like a long time, and she had a small smile when she looked up at Nathan again.

"We'll have a funeral. What do you say?"

"What's a funeral?"

"It's what people do when someone dies, to show that they're sad."

Nathan thought about it for a few seconds, and felt it was appropriate, so he nodded.

Annie left him in the room while she went to arrange some things with Jeffrey. She took Roger with her, so that Nathan wouldn't have to think about him. He did anyway, of course. In fact, he couldn't stop thinking about Roger's lifeless body, cold and limp in his hand, and how he had been scared and in pain, how Nathan had caused that pain, how that fear had been the last thing Roger had felt before he had ceased to be.

It took a long time for Annie to come back, and she was quiet when she did, simply extending a hand to help Nathan up. He took it, and she kept hold of his hand as she led him outside to the beach. Liam and Jeffrey were just finishing up a small pile of wood and brambles, on top of which lay the inert form of Roger. Then Liam went to stand at Roger's head, and with a cigarette lighter, set fire to a tiny piece of cloth that was wrapped on top of a thin branch before handing it to Jeffrey. Jeffrey took it solemnly, and stood very still on the right side of the pyre, while Annie brought Nathan to stand on the left side. Then Liam cleared his throat to speak.

"Dear friends, we are gathered here to say goodbye to our new and dear friend Roger the rat, who gave his life so that Jeffrey and Annie may get theirs back."

Jeffrey stepped forward then, his dark face more serious than Nathan had believed he could see, and looked down at the little rat gravely.

"Roger, thank you for your sacrifice. It will not be in vain, and you will not be forgotten."

Then, he lowered the flame to the pile of branches, and left it there until the fire had caught.

They stayed there in silence while it burned, and Nathan finally felt his emotions returning to him, if not as intensely as last night. Still, he was glad when Annie pulled him to herself to hug him, and he felt an odd relief when they made their way back to the cabin.

Instead of getting to work right away like Nathan thought she might, when they were back inside, she went to the kitchen to start cooking. She mixed meats, sauce and large, flat noodles together in a pan, covered it with cheese and baked it until the smell was so mouthwatering Nathan couldn't think about anything else than the coming meal. He hung around the oven until she had to chase him away.

When it was finally in his mouth, he found it was the best thing he'd had yet. It was sweet and salty, heavy and wonderfully filling, making him feel comforted and warm.

He had two helpings, and didn't even feel bothered when she watched him wolf it down, though Liam felt intimidated and went to sit in the living room to avoid her scrutiny.

When he finally pushed his plate away from himself with a satisfied sigh, she smiled at him. "Feeling better?"

He nodded. He truly was. He hadn't thought food could make you feel better when you were sad and not just hungry. She smiled, nodded, and stood.

"Well, I've got a lot of work to do. Do you think you'll be all right for a while?"

He frowned. "What are you going to do?"

"Revise my calculations, try to figure out where I went wrong. I was sure I had it."

"I think you did. Well, almost, anyway."

"What do you mean?"

"Well, I felt it. I felt Roger's life force. It's like, Oliver almost had it, but then he didn't."

She had a sad little smile, and shrugged. "It's too bad you can't understand the equations. With an input like yours, it'd be solved in minutes."

"I don't think I need to."

She raised an eyebrow and waited for him to go on.

"Well, I think I can do it. I've got a feel for the energy, now, and I felt it, I felt Roger's life force, if I had just taken over, he would be alive right now."

She stared at him, shocked. "Are you sure?"

He nodded enthusiastically. "I'm sure enough to give it a try."

Nathan could see the happy excitement was back in her eyes even as she tried to hold back her smile. "Would you be ready to try it now?"

He sighed. "Sure, let me just take a stim."

Even that didn't seem to deflate her enthusiasm.

Turning Rattigan into an intelligent rat-ghoul was much easier than Roger had been. This time Nathan expected the pain and fear, and he could tell himself that it would be different, this time; that Rattigan would live, not only that, that he would permit Annie to live, too.

He felt tired as he watched her look at Oliver's readings for Rattigan the ghoul's brainwaves, but he said nothing, only took another stim to keep going, thinking gratefully of the meal in his belly. If not for that, he was sure he would have been falling over with exhaustion. But he wanted to try again right away, and he only nodded when Annie asked him if he was all right to go on. She accepted his answer with neither question nor protest, and handed him the ghoul Rattigan had become.

Nathan took him with his left hand. Instead of squirming like Roger had, Rattigan simply stared at him with his beady little eyes that were already starting to become white. Nathan shifted him until the dead rat was lying in his lap, but he kept his left hand on top of him. He eyed the meteorite nervously, and found that he was petting the cold little creature in his lap, trying to reassure both it and himself at the same time. He took a deep breath, and, with a decisive nod, grabbed the small piece of meteor with his right hand.

It was very different than when he had let Oliver calculate the flow, and at the same time, it wasn't. Instead of letting Oliver dictate how much energy he should send, this time, he went straight for Rattigan's own energy, feeling his way to the heart of it, faint but definitely there. With that in mind, he drew the energy from the meteor, slowly and carefully at first, then with more and more force and assurance. He could feel

Rattigan's energy pulsing to it, fluctuating, trying to draw it to itself, and, hesitantly, tentatively, he pushed.

At first, there was what felt not so much like a resistance, but more like an undertow in the flow of the energy. Then, it suddenly gave, and Nathan felt almost physically swept forward by the force of what he had to channel into Rattigan. But he had it, he knew he'd found the spark, and eventually the little rat twitched, squeaked, and Nathan knew he was done. He ended the flow of energy with a sigh, and then cried out in surprise and pain when Rattigan bit his hand to escape his lap. Cursing, he shook his injured hand in the air before sucking on the bleeding finger.

He glared at the treacherous rat as Annie sat next to him. Nathan inspected the finger that had been bitten, taking it out of his mouth. It was a very small mark, and it had already stopped bleeding, but it hurt like hell. He frowned when he noticed blood on his knuckles, though; that couldn't have come from the bite. He touched the skin over his lower lip, and he realized that his nose was bleeding. He heard Annie gasp then, and he looked up, wiping the blood under his nose with the back of his injured hand.

"Are you all right?"

Nathan nodded, and shrugged. 'It took a little more out of me than I expected, that's all.'

He turned to face her, and saw that it wasn't him she was looking at, but his right hand, still holding the meteorite. The rock was no longer translucent white and purple, but a large portion of it had turned gray and dull, and fell away when he removed his hand to look at it. His palm was red, and it felt a bit raw, like he'd burnt it. Annie took his hand in hers to inspect it.

"I'm fine, really," he said. He didn't have time to see if she acknowledged him before he felt an odd pressure on his foot, and turned to see Rattigan nibbling at the sole of his shoe.

"Hey! Leave me alone, you ungrateful little thing! I brought you back to life, you know!"

Annie looked down at Rattigan, picking him up. Nathan could read the anxiety plainly on her face when she leaned down to decipher the brainwave readings on Oliver's screen. "This..." she said. "This is... nothing like the calculations I put into Oliver. It's... Nathan, what did you do?"

"I'm not sure how to explain it. But... I could just... feel the right way to do it."

She didn't respond; her hands were trembling when she pulled out her stethoscope to listen to the rat's belly. She stared at Rattigan, her eyes wide, her mouth ajar, her expression somewhere between joyful and incredulous. She was holding the rat with both hands now, but Nathan could still see that she was shaking.

"Nathan!"

He looked at her, expecting her to continue, but her mouth was just wide open, as though she had no idea what to say. He frowned. "What?"

Her expression was hard to read. He thought she was happy and emotional, but her eyes looked like they should have had tears in them. He found himself wondering if she could cry.

"It... it worked! Rattigan is alive, and he has normal brain function!"

Rattigan squirmed out of her grasp, but she didn't seem to care, beaming at Nathan. She grasped his shoulders as soon as her hands were free, and squealed with joy.

"You did it! You did it! All these years, calculating, and you just... did it! You're a genius!"

She put her hands on his cheeks, and suddenly, her face was very close to his, her cold, dead lips pressed on his. Nathan felt an odd thrill at the sensation, like electricity coursing down his spine and building up in the pit of his stomach, laced with an oddly nauseating feeling, brought on by the slight, familiar smell of decay which emanated from her, and the coldness of her flesh. The contact only lasted a second, after which she withdrew awkwardly, but the memory of her lips lingered on his.

She seemed uncomfortable with what she just did, and Nathan was unsure of what to do about it. Fortunately, they were spared the unease of conversation by Jeffrey and Liam, who burst through the door. Rattigan took advantage of the commotion to slip outside and escape into the hall. Liam saw him and instantly started running after the rat. Jeffrey watched them, and turned his attention back towards Annie and Nathan.

"Hey! I thought I heard happy girl sounds."

She raised an eyebrow at him, smiling playfully. "And I thought you said this place was soundproof."

Jeffrey sighed. "Come on, have mercy, don't keep me waiting like that!"

"I thought you had a sense of humor."

"I'm dead! Give me a break!"

She had a giggle. "He did it. He's turned a rat into a ghoul, and then brought it back to life!"

Jeffrey grinned broadly at Nathan. "Yeah?"

Nathan nodded to confirm, and Jeffrey punched the air with his fist in a gesture of celebration.

"Yeah! I knew you could do it, little dude!"

He slapped Nathan's back in a friendly way which sent Nathan stumbling forward, then looked at Annie expectantly, rubbing his hands together.

"So when do we get to be turned back too?"

She looked down at the meteorite, or what remained of it. "Well... that might be another story entirely."

"Why? Did your hero dude burn out a brain fuse?"

"He didn't. But I'm afraid we'll need a significantly larger piece of the meteorite."

"That one's out of juice?"

Annie smiled. "As you put it. But most importantly, a large chunk was used up to revive this small rat. It'll take much larger amounts of it to do the same thing to creatures as large and complex as we are."

Jeffrey's eyebrows raised in an expression of worry. "You sure? You're not that large, and I'm not that complex."

She chuckled. "I'm sure. But don't worry, we'll get it. Nothing can stop me now that I know this can work."

"How much will you need?"

She shrugged. "Impossible to tell. Nathan managed this on instinct, and I don't know why my calculations were so off, so I can't safely estimate an equivalent for humans. But there's no cause for alarm. I've got a plan."

CHAPTER 20

By the time Liam had found Rattigan and brought him back Annie had already prepared a new list of things for him to go buy. He groaned and complained when he got it, but when Jeffrey suggested that maybe he wanted to come to the crater with them instead, he quieted down and left to go get the required supplies, if a bit sullenly.

Nathan was so exhausted after turning Rattigan back to normal that he felt dizzy every time he stood, and even the stims he took did not help at all. So Annie brought him to sleep in Jeffrey's bedroom, sitting, as always, on the bed next to him. This time, though, she didn't have Oliver to keep her distracted, so she ran her fingers through his hair as he drifted off.

The dreams he had that night were like none he'd had before. There was nothing painful or terrifying about them. In fact, it was quite the contrary. In one which he remembered vividly upon waking, it wasn't Rattigan he had brought back to life, but Annie. He remembered her cheeks, pink and flush with life, her eyes, bright and happy, and her smell, sweet and pleasant, without any hint of death and decay. The best part had been the moment when she had pressed her lips against his in celebration, like she had done in the studio. Only this time, she wasn't cold. Her lips were warm, and wet, and felt good on his.

He was strangely breathless when he awoke, and there was a strange sensation in his loins. She smiled down at him, still sitting next to him, and for some reason, he felt embarrassed at how close she had been.

Jeffrey and Annie were quiet most of the day as they waited for Liam to return. Nathan was too anxious himself to try and engage them in conversation, so he went downstairs to entertain himself with the rats. He found empty cardboard boxes in a closet in Jeffrey's room, and had built an elaborate, multi-level house for the rats by the time Annie came to find him. She looked at his handiwork with fond amusement, and informed him that they would be leaving shortly.

She gave Nathan a bag, which had in it a new pair of black pants and a long-sleeved shirt, equally black. She told him to put them on, and he saw that she was wearing much the same thing, so he changed quickly, leaving his other clothes in the middle of the bed so he'd find them again.

Upstairs, Jeffrey and Liam were arguing about Liam's car, which Jeffrey had intended to use to get to the crater. Jeffrey had changed into black clothes as well. In the end, Jeffrey won his point, stating that they had no other choice, and that the band was going to continue missing all its gigs as long as Jeffrey was still a ghoul.

Annie loaded the duffel bag into the trunk of the car. It seemed fuller and heavier than when they had come from the lab, and Nathan wondered what could be inside. They didn't say much to each other as they waited for the sky to be dark before leaving.

The drive was very long and uneventful. They had to find a road that wouldn't bring them too close to the lab, and the detour they had to make almost doubled the time it would take them to get there otherwise. Annie took the first half hour of the ride to explain what the plan was.

According to her, the crash site was the easiest place they could have picked to break into. Because long-term, repeated exposure to the concentrated radiation from the meteorite was known to be fatal to humans, there was no staff positioned there, be they scientists or security guards. All the obstacles they would encounter would be physical or electronic, although there were robots patrolling and mining the area. This aroused Nathan's interest.

"Robots?"

She nodded. "They have security bots patrolling the area, but in my day there was only a dozen of those, I can't see why there'd be much more now."

"Do they have really complex programming?"

"Well, not the most complex I've ever seen, but yes, I suppose it's at least as complex as a computer."

"Hmm."

Nathan frowned at the window thoughtfully. Reading his mind, Annie turned to look at him from the passenger seat.

"It wouldn't be a good idea to seek them out, Nathan. The best thing to do would really be to avoid every sort of electronic security. If we don't deactivate anything, they won't have any means of knowing anything is wrong."

Nathan nodded regretfully. He'd built robots in the past, but he'd rarely made one that could move around on its own, and never one he could speak to.

They were silent for the rest of the drive, each lost in their own thoughts. As Jeffrey turned the car away from the road to lead them into the forest, Nathan realized he was starting to fall asleep, and took a stim to wake himself up.

Progress was slow and difficult for Liam's small car when they had to leave the road and drive through the forest to get to the crater's edge. The trees that had fallen this close to the crater had been burnt almost to ashes, but some of the larger blackened trunks were still littering the undergrowth, barring their way at nearly every turn. They finally found a thicket of regrowth large enough and far enough from the main road that it could hide the car, and they walked the rest of the way.

Nathan felt the meteorite long before he saw the crater. Almost as soon as they started walking, he could feel its energy drawing him to it, warming his blood. It got so strong that Nathan wanted to break into a run to reach it faster. When

216

Annie stopped so they could get their bearings, he didn't even slow down as he told them to follow him, and led the way through the dark woods.

He was never unsure of the direction in which they should go, but he was still relieved when he started to discern the faint glow of electric light between the trees, about five minutes after the woods started to dwindle. The ground there was also rougher and harder than it had been before.

Annie made them stop before the trees were no longer large enough to hide them, and took a small pair of binoculars from her duffel bag to survey their surroundings. All Nathan could see was a stretch of black ground separating the trees from a chain link fence that must have been ten feet high at least, with coiled barbed wire on top, and signs plastered all over the links. Nathan couldn't read them, but he knew the large red letters could only warn of some kind of danger. There was light coming from the other side of the fence, below the ground. Nathan knew the meteorite was that way.

Annie finally put down her binoculars. "All right. I can see only two cameras from here, and they're pretty far. I think if we're discreet and quick enough in our movements, we can go unnoticed."

Nathan nodded resolutely. He had hardly any fear left in him, only the pull of the meteorite, powerful and unrelenting.

As they got closer, Nathan could see the fence was not on top of a hill as he had supposed, but on top of a cliff that was apparently part of the crater itself. He had heard about it before, but he never imagined it was this big. It was at least five or six miles across, and maybe one of two thousand feet down. He had thought it would be deeper than that, and smooth, like when you drop a ball in the sand and pick it up after, leaving behind a perfect half-sphere. This had an odd shape, though. Its edges descended in rough plateaus until the lowest level, then rose up to form a sort of mound in the middle. That was where the light he had seen through the fence came from: there were two buildings there, small and surrounded by huge spotlights that shone on most of the crater.

There was a road that led out from the buildings, and all the way to the rim of the crater, supported in its ascent by a colossal concrete structure. They were very far from the entrance of that road, almost on the direct opposite side. Nathan thought it would have taken them hours to walk around to the other side.

Annie took out a pair of huge wire cutters, much larger than the ones Nathan had carried around before his bag was taken, and gave them to Jeffrey. The three of them walked rapidly to the fence, crouched down so low they were almost crawling.

Nathan was so absorbed in his contemplation of the complex crater that he almost didn't feel it in time. Fortunately, he managed to seize Jeffrey's arm just before the cutter's blades touched the links on the fence.

"Wait!"

Jeffrey frowned at him, but Nathan's attention was entirely directed towards the fence. He reached out to touch it with his fingertips, lightly, and then turned to Jeffrey with a sigh.

"It's electrified. Don't touch it."

Jeffrey's eyes bulged, and he turned an indignant expression on Annie. "You didn't tell me that!"

"I didn't know. It didn't use to be. I guess they increased the security measures since I left."

Jeffrey glared accusingly at the fence. "They could at least put up a warning sign. All these say is to keep out."

Annie looked around nervously. "We need to move. We have to get out of here before we're spotted."

"I can deactivate it," suggested Nathan.

She didn't seem too pleased with the suggestion, but after a few seconds of consideration, she nodded. "Can you put it back online when you're done?"

"Shouldn't be a problem."

"Then hurry up!"

It was easier than he thought to push the electricity out of the fence. He had never really tried to control electricity other than to convert it for himself, but this proved to be no challenge at all. He held the energy back while Jeffrey and Annie cut their way through, and then simply let it flow again once he had gotten through the hole.

Annie looked at it, then at him, worriedly. "Did you feel an alarm on it? Do you think we triggered something?"

He shook his head. "Shouldn't be. I just held back the current, but I didn't deactivate anything, they'd have to be checking for exactly that to even notice."

When he reached his ghoul friends by the edge of the crater, Annie was pulling out a complex set of ropes and leather straps, and Jeffrey was hammering a metal spike into the hard ground. Nathan frowned at them suspiciously.

"What's all this?"

Annie smiled up at him. "We're going to be climbing down the cliff. Here, I brought this climbing gear for you."

He looked dubiously at the straps, and then stepped to the very edge of the cliff to look down. There were several plateaus on the way down, but the distance between each was nearly a hundred feet. He looked back at the rope and the straps that Annie and Jeffrey were fastening to themselves.

"You sure this is a good idea?"

She nodded; she did seem pretty convinced. "It's a much better idea than trying to go through the front door." She gestured to the road and its entrance through the fence, on the rim. "We wouldn't walk five minutes on there before being taken down by the guardian robots."

He let her strap him into a sort of harness made of leather, on which she hooked the rope. She hooked herself and Jeffrey as well. Nathan looked over the edge at the next plateau they would reach, and felt his knees weaken. He tried to concentrate on the comforting presence of the meteorite in his mind, just two or three miles away, but he couldn't go back to the confidence he had felt just before, so he took a stim before he started to climb down.

Jeffrey went down before him, and Annie after, so that he was between them. The first few minutes were difficult and terrifying, and then his foot slipped on a particularly slick piece of stone, and he fell.

It was only for an inch, though. When he realized he wasn't freefalling towards his death, he dared to look up and saw that Annie had caught him and was continuing her descent easily.

Nathan felt relief wash over him at that, and the rest of the way to the first plateau was easy. A small worry grew in his mind, though, nagging at him more and more. Annie and Jeffrey were much stronger than any human now, because of their condition. How were they going to climb back up this way when they were human again? How would Nathan manage it when his muscles turned to jelly from the exhaustion of the conversion, if he couldn't even climb down now?

When they reached the bottom of the crater, Nathan's hands felt cramped and sore from gripping the rope all this time, and the fear had weakened his knees to the point where he wasn't sure how he would walk all the way to the center. When he looked up to see how far they had come while Annie unfastened his harness, he couldn't believe they had made it down alive, and he didn't dare ask her about the way back.

They left the climbing gear there, and made their way towards the center. They were able to go at a brisk pace, because the light didn't reach this close to the rim, but as they got closer to the buildings, they had to slow down considerably, until Annie had them stop every time they encountered a boulder large enough to hide behind so that she could see whether or not robot guards were coming this way. Nathan spotted one from time to time, far enough that he couldn't see the way it was built.

He could see the buildings by then. They were smaller than they had looked from far away. Both had a single floor. One was obviously a hangar or warehouse of some kind, and the other was a smaller building that couldn't have a lot of rooms in it, looking more like a hi-tech shack of some sort. They stood on top of the mound that was in the middle of the crater. Nathan could feel the meteorite below his feet, in the ground. It wasn't in the buildings, and he wondered for a moment why they didn't simply stop here and dig. But although he could feel the energy very clearly, he had no idea how far down it was, and he had to have direct contact.

They continued making their way to the center with great care, until they reached the back of the smaller building, and pressed themselves against its wall. Nathan took advantage of the short pause to reach into his bag and take another stim while Annie peered around the corner at the second building. As he was swallowing the small pill, he noticed a green light beam sweeping his body.

He turned abruptly to see where it was coming from, and found himself staring at a squat, white robot. It was covered in black dust, but still looked sleeker and more sophisticated than the vast majority of the machines Nathan had encountered before. Its head was small, and in a shape that was exactly halfway between a sphere and a cube. It didn't have an actual face, just a computer screen, and it was very short, only half Nathan's height. Its two arms which ended in steel clamps, and it moved on a set of tracks that seemed able to cope with the rough terrain.

Nathan was thinking how much better his creations would have been if he'd only found a way to make tracks like that when the robot spoke in a toneless, computerized voice.

"Unauthorized personnel detected."

Nathan noticed that a door on the robot's belly was opening, and just as the thought was occurring to him that this would be the perfect place to store weapons, he heard Annie shout. He could not make out the words, though the tone was clear. He launched himself at the robot. There was a loud clack of, and he felt something pinch his leg, though he did not look down to see what it was, for fear of losing his momentum. He grinned as he reached the robot, feeling the familiar tingle of electricity coursing through his body. It was only a stun gun.

He slapped his hand on the face-screen. It was, as he had hoped, a touch-screen, and he was able to use it to link with the robot instantly, looking for its mind. It was almost as complex as Oliver's, and Nathan started by reassuring the guard robots that they were his friends, and that the robot wished them no harm. By the time he let go of the screen, he had managed to convince the robot of the simple fact that his orders had been changed from 'capture unauthorized personnel' to 'escort unauthorized personnel'.

Nathan turned to grin at Annie and Jeffrey when he was done, and saw that they were both staring at him, shocked and worried. Annie had something in her hand that Nathan hadn't seen before, though it looked a lot like the round metal balls she had used to blow up the trucks at the lab. He stepped protectively in front of his new robot friend, frowning at Annie.

"What's that?"

"An EMP grenade. What did you do?"

"I told him we were his friends. What's an EMP grenade?"

"It sends out an electro-magnetic pulse that turns off all the machines in the area."

Nathan opened his arms in a defensive gesture, shielding the small robot. "Well, put it away! G-11 is our friend, now."

She put the small object back in her bag reluctantly, a suspicious look painted on her face. "G-11?"

"That's his name. He'll respond to my voice. And he'll help us if we need him."

Annie shook her head in resigned disapproval, and leaned around the corner of the wall to peer at the other building, then turned back to Nathan, one of her eyebrows arched in that thoughtful expression she had so often.

"Can you get him to unlock and open the hangar door?"

"Sure! G-11, unlock and open the hangar door, please."

G-11 didn't hesitate, but simply crawled past Nathan, rounding the corner where Annie was to roll to the other side. Nathan joined Annie to watch what his new friend was doing. As he reached the keypad, G-11's belly opened again, and a small metal rod extended from it, plugging itself into a hole in the keypad. Seconds later, the large hangar door rolled open. Annie lifted her eyes, and Nathan followed her gaze to a small camera on top of the hangar, right under the peak of the roof, swiveling from left to right.

"Get ready to run to the door when we're in the camera's blind spot."

Jeffrey and Nathan watched attentively with her as the camera swung from one side to the other, but they still waited for Annie's shout to start running, all together, to and through the now open door. G-11 followed them inside without being asked.

The hangar was nearly empty. In a corner was a workbench with four robots lined up next to it, in various states of disrepair. Three of them were guard robots, but the fourth one was much larger, maybe three times the size of G-11. Its frame was relatively the same, a large belly with a door on it, but it had six arms, each of which ended in a wide, four-prong clamp. It didn't have a head, either. Nathan supposed the control screen must be in the back, because he couldn't see it.

The main feature in the room, however, was an industrial lift in the middle of the floor, large enough to comfortably fit at least twelve guardian robots. Annie looked around quickly to make sure there were no cameras inside, then made her way to the lift, followed by Nathan, Jeffrey, and G-11.

Nathan walked to the pad and lay his hand on it. There was only one way to go from there, and only one floor to select, so it was no trouble at all to get the elevator to take them down. As it lurched into motion, Annie dug three flashlights out of her bag, and handed one each to Jeffrey and Nathan. As she turned hers on, she looked sideways at Nathan, nervously.

"Do you still feel it?"

"The meteor? I've felt it since we got out of the car. Nothing's ever been clearer."

She nodded, apparently satisfied with his answer. They all stayed quiet as the lift descended further into darkness, with only their flashlights to show them the way.

CHAPTER 21

There was some light when they reached the bottom. The lift stopped inside a tunnel, crudely carved in the black stone, supported by steel beams. There were purple and white spots in very tiny specs all over the walls, which glowed faintly. Nathan could see pretty far, though the light was dim enough that he didn't turn off the flashlight in his hands.

He turned to Annie, waiting for her to lead the way, but found that she was looking at him. He must have looked confused enough, because she had that amused smile she always had when there was something obvious he didn't understand.

"It's been nearly twenty years since I left. There's been quite a lot of excavation since then, I'm sure. Why don't you take us to where you feel the strongest pull?"

Nathan nodded, turned around, and started walking right away. It was easy at first, because the tunnel took him directly where he wanted to go. Then, as they started winding away from his destination, his path became more unclear. The tunnels were many, though they always seemed to loop back upon themselves. At some point, Nathan became worried that they might not even be able to get back to the lift, but as he turned to share his concerns with Annie, his eyes fell upon G-11 and he came to a stop, frowning at the robot. Annie looked at him.

"What's wrong?"

He didn't answer her, still staring at his new electronic friend. "G-11, do you have a map of this place?"

"Please confirm: do you require a map of the mining tunnels?"

225

"That's right. I require a map of the mining tunnels. Do you have one?"

"Affirmative."

Nathan grinned, and laid his hands on the touch-screen face, linking with the robot. He associated for the map, and found it in instants. He had been going the wrong way entirely. There was a turn, close to the lift, that he hadn't taken because it seemed to be going away from the pull, which opened onto a network of tunnels that came back in the right direction. He released the screen, smiling triumphantly.

"G-11, take us to tunnel 13B!"

Without a sound, his new robot friend turned to guide them through the stony tunnel. Nathan grinned at Annie and Jeffrey as he skipped past them, following the robot.

"This way!"

They followed, and G-11 led all of them back where they came from, then swerved off before the lift into the tunnel Nathan had missed. The robot stayed in that shaft until he reached the end, then turned right into a shorter tunnel which was more brightly lit than the others. It ended abruptly, in a dead end, but Nathan knew they had found what they needed. There was a fissure in the rock, on the wall, through which he could see the bright purple light of a huge piece of meteorite, almost as tall as he was. Next to it, immobile, was a large, six-armed robot like the one he had seen in the hangar upstairs.

In a daze, he stepped towards the glowing rock, mesmerized, and touched it gingerly with his fingertips. He closed his eyes. He could feel the power coming from it, making his whole body vibrate. It had to be much larger than the portion he could see; it didn't even compare to the piece he had used to change Rattigan.

He turned to smile brightly at Annie and Jeffrey, and blinked at what he saw past them. Where there had been only been G-11, there were now three identical robots. He shook his head to make sure he wasn't seeing double, and Annie turned to see

226

what was happening. Then, four security guards turned into the hall towards them, followed by the small, balding shape of Doctor Wilkerson.

For a few seconds, Nathan was so convinced that it was a nightmare that he didn't even try to move. How could Wilkerson be there? And where had the guards come from? Things seemed to be going slowly, as if to give him the chance to better take in the desperate situation, but too fast for him to be able to do anything about it. There was shouting all around him, though his mind was incapable of discerning words.

He saw Wilkerson stop as the guards reached them, and suddenly the large robot next to Jeffrey moved one of its six arms to grab the tall ghoul by the waist, lifting him up in its huge clamp. Nathan had time to see another clamp reaching for his shoulders before he heard the telltale clack of a stun gun go off in front of him. He turned to see Annie falling to the ground, the receivers of the gun still stuck to her chest. Two of the guard robots had shot her.

Dazedly, Nathan ran to Jeffrey, who was struggling uselessly against the grasp of the strong robot which held his entire body in three clamps. He put his hands on the clamps and tried to link with the robot, but didn't have time to formulate a single thought before he heard Jeffrey shout his name. A cold, rough metal rope wrapped around his neck and pulled, yanking him off the machine and throwing him to the floor. He fell on his back, gasping, winded as much from the fall as the shock of his disconnection from the robot. He tried to look up, disoriented, and the rope around his neck tightened. The end of a metal stick, into which the rope was disappearing, pressed down on his windpipe, making him fight for every breath.

"I got him! I got him!"

"Nice work."

Wheezing and coughing, Nathan turned to glare at Wilkerson, who was approaching him while fiddling with a complex remote control pad. The doctor shot an angry glare at

Nathan as he lowered the pad, and Nathan felt the first pangs of fear pierce through the confusion. As Wilkerson got closer, though, the hate was still strong enough for Nathan to try and reach out a hand to grab him by the ankle, but the old man stepped out of his way, and barked at the guard who was holding the stick.

"Restrain him properly!"

The guard pushed harder on the stick, making Nathan choke and gasp.

"You little rat!" hissed Wilkerson. "You almost cost me my entire career! This is the second time you've run off, don't think there'll be a third!" Nathan turned back towards Wilkerson, who was shouting at him with such fervor that a little bit of spittle fell on his face. "I'll break you, you'll see! You'll be begging to cooperate by the time I'm through with you!"

Nathan looked back at Annie. She wasn't moving. His heart began to sink. Why wasn't she moving? What if she was dead? Could a stun gun do that to a ghoul? Wilkerson noticed him looking, and smirked.

"Don't count on Doctor White to help you, either. She's in no position."

The pressure on Nathan's throat was relieved at a gesture from Wilkerson, and the guard forced him to his feet by yanking up the stick. He stood, coughing, his throat throbbing dully, but the guard just pinned him against the wall, jabbing the stick in his throat again. He expected Wilkerson to tell the guard not to damage him, but no such thing happened. Panic was starting to make Nathan's mouth dry, and his eyes water. He heard Jeffrey shouting. "Leave the kid alone! He didn't do nothing to you!"

Wilkerson turned to give his control pad to one of the unoccupied guards. "Have the robots take the ghouls to the incinerator. And make sure they really burn, this time."

"No!"

228

The cold panic that had been gripping Nathan's heart was suddenly replaced by white hot rage and hatred. What happened to him didn't matter anymore; he had to do something to help Annie.

He grasped the metal pole with his hands, ready to use his adrenaline to wrest it out of the guard's hands, and then he felt it. It was faint, but as he focused on it, he could feel it better; the guard's life force tingled at his fingertips. He wasn't wearing gloves. Almost giddy with the realization, Nathan closed his eyes, and drew.

He knew from experience that even a partial drain was enough to leave a person helpless and barely conscious, so he was careful to take only a little, even less than what he needed to heal his bruised throat. The guard was on the ground and Nathan had the rope off his neck well before Wilkerson realized what was happening. Before the old man could do anything to defend himself, Nathan had seized him by the throat and began to drain him.

This one, he drained more than he had to. He drained him until his throat felt better, until he felt strong and awake, until the only reason for it was watching the old man twitch and whimper. Then he heard the sound of a stun gun being fired, and felt a familiar sting on his shoulder. He let Wilkerson flop to the ground unceremoniously, and grabbed the receivers just as the discharge was heard. He felt the electricity surge through him, and he sent it back, adding a little extra. The guard who was holding the transmitter fell, twitching, as the gun sparked. Nathan plucked the receivers from his shoulder, and turned to glare at the two remaining guards.

There was no fear left in him, only anger and hate. He could beat them. He'd taken down three of them easily. He planted his feet firmly on the ground and clenched his firsts, steeling himself for whatever it was they had to throw at him next.

One of the guards took a step back, then they looked at each other and, with an unspoken decision, turned and ran. Nathan blinked stupidly, stunned into immobility again. It was Jeffrey's voice which pulled him out of it.

"Little dude! Come give me a hand!"

He gave himself a shake, and hurried to Jeffrey, glancing at Annie on the way. She was still motionless on the floor, her eyes closed. For some reason, it made Nathan feel a bit better that they weren't open.

He put his hands down on the robot's metal clamp as soon as he reached the place where Jeffrey was held. It took him mere seconds to reach the robot's mind and convince him to gently put Jeffrey down and release him. Once he was free, Jeffrey stepped away from the robot, and stared at Nathan for a few seconds.

"You're pretty badass for such a small guy, you know?"

Nathan turned to Annie, and started to run to her, motioning for Jeffrey to come along. He kneeled next to her. He wanted to check if she was still alive, but of course, she wasn't, having been dead for twenty years. He could only think of one thing to do. He touched her neck lightly, and closed his eyes, searching for her mind, or life force, or whatever he could find. It was faint, and distant, but it was there. As soon as their minds touched, he could feel her want to pull at his life force, and he let go of her, opening his eyes. Jeffrey was crouching right next to him, looking at Annie with a worried expression.

"She okay?"

Nathan nodded, standing. "Can you bring her near the crack in the wall?"

Jeffrey picked her up and followed Nathan obediently to the fissure through which the meteorite glowed purple. Jeffrey stopped next to it and looked at Nathan, unsure. The guard that had held Nathan captive groaned and stirred, and Jeffrey gave him an anxious look.

"What now?"

"Sit down with her on the floor. Don't move.'

Jeffrey obeyed, keeping a nervous eye on the waking guard. The man didn't seem to move any further, though, and Nathan took Annie's hand in his own, laying his other on the warm, purple rock. He could feel her again, trying to draw from him instinctively, so he drew the energy from the meteorite and pushed it into her.

Nothing he had tried with the rats could have prepared him to the flow of energy he had to handle. He had thought that the amounts of meteorite needed would be the only thing to augment so dramatically, that he could control its flow without a problem. But the more he channeled, the more she seemed to need, and he drew and pushed and drew and pushed until he felt his whole body burn.

He glanced down at her, keeping the flow going. She wasn't awake, yet, but he thought her cheeks were pinker than they had been. The energy fluctuated while he was distracted, and he almost lost control of it. He had to close his eyes and grit his teeth to rein it back in. He realized at that moment what was wrong: the energy had found Jeffrey's body, who was still holding Annie, and was feeding him as well as her.

He didn't dare break off the flow now, to either of them, because he knew he risked killing them. So he pushed the energy to them, pushed until his blood felt like it was boiling, until he thought his bones would melt, until he felt like the energy was tearing pieces of his mind and taking them away with it, and his head would explode, but he managed to keep it up until he felt nothing at all.

CHAPTER 22

When Nathan awoke, he was lying on something soft and comfortable, and there was a warm weight across his chest. He had a moment of panic, but when he tried to sit up he found that his muscles would barely twitch. His head felt enormous, heavy, and hurt more than it ever had before. He felt the weight on his chest shift, and he saw that it was an arm. He turned his head slightly to see Annie lying next to him.

She appeared to be waking up, her face puffy and full of sleep, her loose, black hair a mess of curls around it. She was the most beautiful thing Nathan had ever seen. Her skin, having lost its pallor, was a rich, almost bronze color, and her lips were red and much fuller than he remembered, but the feature that captured his attention most was her eyes. They were a light hazel that was almost green, and they twinkled so brightly with her smile that it seemed to him that they shone. She caressed his cheek with her palm. Her touch was wonderfully soft, and warm, and sent a shiver of pleasure down his spine. It helped him wake a little further, and stirred a pleasant sensation in the pit of his stomach. He smiled at her, and found that it pulled at his dry lips painfully. It didn't matter, though. The pain was easy to ignore in front of her happiness.

"Nathan! You're awake! I was starting to worry about you."

His voice was a feeble croak when he tried to speak, and he had to clear his throat to be able to utter anything intelligible. "Annie! You're... alive!"

She smiled even brighter, though Nathan hadn't thought it possible. She put her second hand on his other cheek, bringing her face close to his. She smelled very different than she had when she was dead. Part of it, he recognized as the perfumes from the soaps he'd used to wash himself; she must have taken a bath. Another part, though, the part that was most pleasant to his nose, was the smell that was hers, the smell that was warmth, and sun, and comfort. He noticed how white her teeth were. Had they been this white before?

"I am," she said softly. Her voice was not exactly a whisper, more like a gentle caress in his ear. Her breath was deliciously warm as it tickled his nose. "You did it. You made me alive again. You saved us all, and then you brought us back to life. It's unbelievable."

Her eyes danced across his face, sparkling with mirth again. He couldn't think of what to answer, and he couldn't move a muscle, but it didn't matter; he felt perfectly content just looking up at her. She shifted her weight so that she was partially on top of him, her face an inch from his. He marveled at how warm her body was against his, and the feel of her, even through the clothes he was wearing, was filling his aching limbs with life, making his heart beat faster so that very soon, he could feel his own pulse in every inch of his skin.

She closed her eyes and brushed her lips lightly against his. The touch sent a rush of feeling throughout his whole body, not unlike electricity, but much more galvanizing. This time, there was no trace of nausea in the sensation, though the excitement was so intense that it did make his stomach flutter. The feeling seemed to pool in his pelvis, pulsating from there and slowly filling all of him, making his bones shiver and every hair he had stand up. He felt her pull away after this lightest of touches, and he found the strength to wrap his arms around her, pulling her back to him, unwilling to let her go, to let this feeling end. She didn't resist, but melted back onto him as soon as his hands were on her back. Her lips were hungry this time, and her tongue was soft, like velvet, and tasted sweet in a way that he couldn't even begin to compare to food.

They were both breathless when their mouths parted, and she lay on top of him for a while, her face buried in his neck, her wonderful warm breath somehow bringing goose bumps to his skin. He held her as tightly as his weak arms would allow, not wanting to let go, to stop touching her, wanting, needing to do so much more, but not really knowing what, exactly. Eventually her breathing returned to normal, and she lifted her head to smile at him, running a hand through his hair.

"How are you feeling?"

His head still felt heavy, and throbbed dully. The pain was also returning to most of his body, and his stiff muscles ached; his throat was so parched that he thought it might crack. Yet he felt better than ever before, and the only thing that he could seem to think about was how warm and soft her body was against his.

"I feel great. I'm a little thirsty."

"I'll go get you some water."

As much as he really did need the water, as soon as her warmth was gone, he regretted having said anything. He watched her step toward the door. She was wearing a black Zombies Eating Tomatoes t-shirt which he recognized as one of his, and an enormous pair of boxers that he had never seen before, but could only be Jeffrey's. She turned to smile at him before she walked out.

"Be right back!"

She closed the door as she exited. Nathan pushed himself up onto his elbows, in a semi-seated position. He was lying on the orange bed, in Jeffrey's room, still wearing the black clothes he had been when they left. He had no memory of anything past the point where he had tried to bring Annie and Jeffrey back to life. If this was not a dream, but really happening, as he was starting to suspect, then where was Jeffrey? Was he all right, too? Had Nathan succeeded?

With great difficulty, he managed to drag himself off the bed, and to the wall. It took him an eternity to reach the outlet, and by the time he got there, he was sweating, panting, and if it was true he hadn't been nauseous before, he now wished he'd thought of dragging the garbage bin with him, so sure was he that he was about to empty his stomach. He took a few deep breaths to calm himself down, and reached in his pocket for one of the paperclips he usually carried.

He cursed when he found none, and remembered he hadn't refilled on any of his usual supplies since he escaped the lab. He searched the floor around himself for anything made of metal, and his eyes fell on a set of keys. He reached for it gratefully and stuck it in the plug. He was finished and pulling it out, intensely refreshed, when the door opened to let in Annie and Jeffrey. The large man went to help Nathan up, grinning, and hugging him so tight that Nathan could hardly breathe. He released him after a few seconds, clapping him on the shoulders.

"You did it, big man!"

Nathan smiled up at him, taking a step backwards to avoid further physical demonstrations of Jeffrey's joy. Jeffrey's eyes had also returned to their original color, a dark brown that almost matched the rich, deep color of his skin, which had none of the sallow gray tint it had had when Nathan had met him. If possible, he looked even more vibrant and energetic than before.

Annie interrupted before Nathan had a chance to reply. "Don't be so rough with him, Jeffrey. He almost died."

She put the tray down on the bed. There was a sandwich, a glass of water and a cup of coffee on it. He sat next to the tray, picking up the glass of water and draining it before looking at Annie, concerned.

"I almost died?"

Annie nodded, brushing some of his hair away from his forehead as he picked up the sandwich. "You did. You weren't careful, Nathan. When I came to, you were having a seizure."

Jeffrey nodded gravely. "It was pretty gruesome, man. You were bleeding from your nose and ears."

Nathan touched his ear instinctively, but of course, there wasn't any blood there anymore. "Well... I feel all better now."

"It was close. You were unconscious for three days. I had to monitor your life signs using Oliver the first day, because you wouldn't stabilize. I... we were worried."

Nathan turned to the dresser next to the bed. Oliver was there, but he wasn't on right now. The swimmer's headset was lying across the keyboard.

"How did you get out? Did you have to climb the cliff again?"

He shuddered at the thought of dangling, unconscious and helpless, from that rope and that height. But from the amusement he saw on both Jeffrey and Annie's faces, he guessed he was wrong.

"What?"

Annie shrugged, smiling. "We drove out. We stole Wilkerson's car."

"You didn't bring it back here, did you?"

Nathan felt a twinge of fear. If Wilkerson had been obsessed enough to notice they had broken in to the crater, he would find the car they had stolen with no problem. But Annie only shook her head.

"We drove it back to Liam's car. We left it right there, by the rim."

He nodded, reassured, and looked down at the plate, which was now empty. Annie noticed his look, and smiled at him again. "Still hungry?"

He nodded. He was starving. He could have eaten six of these sandwiches. She picked up the cup of coffee and handed it to Nathan, then took the tray and stood, smiling at him.

"Come on. I'll make you another. Or more. As many as you like."

He followed her upstairs, sipping his coffee and walking alongside Jeffrey. Once there, Annie headed for the kitchen, putting the tray down on the counter and opening the fridge.

Nathan noticed two huge, elaborate gray suitcases sitting in the middle of the living room; they looked brand new, and very full. He frowned at them as he went to sit at the wooden island counter. "What are those?"

She turned around, knife in her hand, to see what he was looking at. "Oh, those? They're ours. A few things I had Liam pick up for us."

"Why do we need them?" He was starting to feel apprehensive. "We're not going to break into another place, are we?"

She laughed, putting the top slice of bread on the completed sandwich. There was something about her voice that seemed simultaneously fuller and lighter than before her transformation. She answered and brought him his full plate.

"Of course not. We're going to Thailand."

"What's that?"

He blinked at her. He never heard the word before. He wasn't sure if it meant something you did, or some place you went. She laughed again as he started eating.

"It's a country. It's very far. On the other side of the world. Jeffrey has a friend with a private plane. He's going to take us there as soon as you're up to it."

He nodded a bit as he chewed. She must have taken his silence for disapproval of some kind, because she leaned in to be closer to him, and sounded as though she was trying to convince him.

"You'll like Thailand a lot, Nathan. It has beaches, and a lot of sun. It's very warm, and I know how you like to be warm."

He smiled at her, and looked over his shoulder at the suitcases, wondering what could be in them.

"Of course I'll go."

She smiled happily, and this time, it was his turn to be amused at her. He did like to be warm, but at the same time, he almost didn't care at all whether it was hot or cold. Didn't she know yet, that it didn't matter where he went, as long she was with him?

ACKNOWLEDGEMENTS

I wrote this story long before I wrote any of the *Family by Choice* books, and, as such, it had a really long journey and passed through the hands of a lot of people before it got anywhere close to the way it is now.

As usual, I owe a huge debt of gratitude to my partner in all things, Joelle, but even more so for this book than the others. Originally, this story was a table-top role-playing game which we played together. I owe her the character of Annie, and a large part of the story.

A big thank you to my amazing editors Evelyn and Phil. Evelyn, your dedicated work is instrumental in making my books the best they can be, but for this story, your words helped me regain confidence. As for you, Phil, you were the first person to beta read this story, before being the last editor to work on it, and your comments were instrumental in changing not only the way I did this story, but the way I did *all* my stories, for the better.

To Annie, Felix-Antoine, and Frederic, thank you for being the models for the cover of this book. You had the patience to dress up, get dirty, and then sit or lie still in uncomfortable temperatures while some person took pictures of you. I am very grateful to you for indulging my whims.

To Mom and Manue, who took the time to read a very early version of this book, and give me their honest feedback, even when it wasn't easy to hear, thank you for your time and your honesty.

A very, *very* special thank you to Manon, Jessica, Muriel, Diane, Marie-Claude, Marjolaine. You were the original audience of this book, the people with whom I shared the very first version of it that I was happy enough with, and you listened to it patiently, week after week, when we held our critique group meetings. You have no idea how valuable this experience was to me, and to this story.

Finally, to everyone at Renaissance, a huge thank you for all the work, laughs, and family spirit. I owe you much more than I can say.

ABOUT THE AUTHOR

Caroline Fréchette is a sequential artist and author. She is the author of the *Family by Choice* series of novels, several short stories, both sequential and traditional, as well as two graphic novels. She is the founder, former editor and director for the French Canadian literary magazine *Histoires à boire debout,* works in a library, and has been teaching creative writing since 2005. For more information, you can visit her website at carolinefrechette.com.

If you enjoyed this book, you should check out these other titles by the same author!

Family by Choice series

An action-packed, fast-paced series about superpowers, crime, survival, and responsibility towards others.

Alex Winters is a young man involved in organized crime who also has the ability to manipulate fire. Through various confrontations which put him and his loved ones in danger, he learns that there is more to life than just survival.

Here's what people are saying about Family by Choice:

"I loved this. If you like dark fiction, supernatural, and a good dose of action, then try out this series. You will not be disappointed."
I Heart Reading book reviews

"Alex is a great character. He's complicated, and has many different layers. The story was good, and the writing was spot on the entire time. I was drawn into this book from the first page, and enjoyed it very much."
Forever Book Lover reviews

"Caroline Fréchette is one of my favourite fantasy writers in the National Capital Region. (...) The story has a great pace and the strong writing makes them an easy read."
Alejandro Bustos, *Apartment 613*

"While I find this series to be a quick read, it is also an incredibly good read."
Geeky Godmother reviews

http://renaissancebookpress.com/2014/09/03/family-by-choice-series/